THE LADY IN THE RED DRESS

Mackay Barr

ISBN:
ISBN-13:

Acknowledgements

To thank every person involved with helping me would be a nearly impossible task. However, a few people put in so much extra effort in beta reading, proof reading, and editing that their service to this book could not be understated.

My beautiful wife Amandalyn Barr for the

countless hours she spent editing and reading each draft as it came to fruition.

Carol Meyers for the hours she spent making my pages bleed with her red pen.

Rachael Barr for never being afraid to hurt my feelings when reviewing a book in a genre she hates.

David Gentry who provided some of the best editing and structural advice necessary to create the best story I could. Additionally, I would like to thank David for the exceptional cover art that he produced.

Joel Forsythe for helping to find plot holes and every tactical error imaginable.

Finally to my parents Deland and Salley Barr for always believing this was possible.

"…Across the darkened waves we found our way
Loves shining bright come night or day
From hidden coast to treasure's untold
Our heart's entwined the story goes."

- Pirate of love, Betrem

Prologue

He opened his eyes to see the familiar shapes of the building surrounding him. It was a room he had been in before, and instantly the layout felt familiar. His chest ached as blood bubbled from it with each breath. It was a tension pneumothorax, which might ultimately cause his heart to stop if the pressure of the air and the shifting of his lung pressed against the vital organ. The wound in his leg didn't seem to want to stop pulsing blood out of it. It wasn't an arterial bleed, but it was painful and caused significant blood loss, nonetheless.

The cold steel of the blade still rested against his fingers. 'I can cut the bindings,' he thought, feeling a flicker of relief at the prospect of at least having a way out. His biggest question was where to go after freeing himself. Looking at the skinned body hanging from the ceiling and the mystery man lying dead and propped against the wall, he felt an impending sense of doom—not for himself, but from the aching realization that he couldn't help someone who needed him now more than ever.

'Gone forever,' he thought, knowing this was the end. There was no conceivable scenario that would allow them to escape alive. He had failed miserably, underestimating his opponent and proving incapable of protecting the one person who seemed to matter.

'Fuck you,' he thought in frustration. I'm not going out like this… 'We' are not going out like this. This is not how the story

ends. 'Maybe I underestimated them, but they damn sure underestimated me.' Fumbling with the blade in his hand, he began sawing at the bindings until he felt the first zip tie break free. A breath of relief escaped his lungs as he furiously plunged the sharpened steel into the bindings around his knees and feet. One after another, the zip ties broke free, allowing him to move away from the pool of blood he was marinating in.

Scrambling to one knee, he collapsed again to the ground from the pain in his thigh. He landed mercilessly on the wound still throbbing in his hip. "Fucking pigs!" he yelled, thinking of the corrupt cops who had put him through this anguish. He was still confused because of the sedatives, but even with a sound mind, he had no idea who the dead man against the wall was or what he had to do with anything. There were enough problems without another body in the mix, which didn't make any sense.

'Get your ass up and get moving!' Determination and willpower were the only things propelling him forward, and he needed to move. The two of them would both be dead if he just lay there. He clambered to his feet once again, the pain shooting through his leg. 'Fight through it,' he thought, trying to ignore the agony in his leg. His breathing became labored as the wound to his chest continued to suck air in while blocking his lung from taking a full breath.

One foot in front of the other, he walked across the cold, hard floor, feeling each step as a jolt of electricity coursing through his body. The moment felt like an eternity, but he could feel it now: the sun was shining on his face. 'I'm coming…' he thought to himself. 'I'll find you.'

1

"Whoever sheds the blood of man, by man shall his blood be shed; for in the image of God made he."

–Genesis 9:6

Six Days Earlier

The man on top of her was several hundred pounds overweight. She could feel the hair on his back stand erect through her fingertips. His grunts and motions became louder and faster; with his size, it was impossible for him to roll his hips into her. Instead, he simply rocked back and forth.

She never felt like it was sex, anyway. He would give her $150 to leave the hotel room, but with someone of his size, it felt to her like being mauled or seized upon more than anything else. She moaned and spoke the phrases he wanted, mostly just things she had heard from the occasional porn flick: "Yes, *daddy, fuck me, slap my ass.*" It was all bullshit, and he knew it, but it worked.

Long before, Lacey had moved beyond being disgusted with herself for what she had become. None of it was truly her fault, but certainly, the decisions she had made led to that ultimate conclusion. *"Knock on the devil's door long enough, and someone will answer,"* her grandmother used to say. Her body never felt like her own, owned by one disgusting pig after another.

Tommy Johnson was a regular. He'd call her every few weeks when he passed through town to visit his brother at the penitentiary in Tennessee. Usually just 30 minutes, but occasionally he would book a full hour. She always dreaded it when he did that. It meant she would spend the first 20 minutes getting her head pushed down on his organ until she couldn't breathe. It turned him on to plug her nose as she squirmed and gagged. Starting innocently enough with just a simple blowjob, it eventually transformed into an hour-long violent conquest with her hands bound while she was abused.

Lying there thinking about a life in the mountains in her grandmother's log cabin, she found some semblance of pleasure. She loved going there as a little girl. The smell of the fresh mountain air and the intensity of the pine needles, as she trudged through the forest floor, filled her with nostalgia. A back country road led to the desolate location—a diamond in the rough, a unique few acres surrounded by National Forest. No neighbors for miles, and the Forest Service maintained the road for fire mitigation. Her grandmother would come to get her and her brother from their mom's trailer in an old Toyota Land Cruiser.

Lacey remembered the driveway out there. The Land Cruiser coasted along the roads flawlessly as she awkwardly shifted gears. Her grandmother's voice guided her on when to clutch and when to shift. The trees passed by in a green mist, and the tepid mountain air filled the cabin as her jet-black hair whipped behind her head. Few memories remained as enjoyable as those days at the cabin.

Tommy groaned on top of her, grunting heavily. Her daydream was interrupted by the pulsing and throbbing as he released himself into the condom. He rolled off her, leaving his penis hanging out while he caught his breath. The excess fat around his groin made all but the tip of his penis disappear into himself, as if it were a turtle protecting itself from a swooping hawk. He was still lying on top of the sheets, catching his breath, when a knock on the door came. It was Si, letting Tommy know his time was up.

The first time she had sex for money wasn't at the behest of her owner, nor at the threat of violence. Her deepest guilt lay in the knowledge that the first was her choice out of desperation—for a place to stay and a man to warm her, maybe even for some semblance of warmth, love, and affection. Si hadn't changed that, turning what was once a gift into something perverse. She had changed it herself first.

Tommy was grunting while he tried to dress. He always looked like such a fool—large and uncoordinated, with a flat-brim baseball cap, a 49ers jersey, and shorts that covered all the way to his ankles. His legs and buttocks were flat, with no visible muscle, and his body resembled a giant potato supported on toothpicks.

Lacey had just finished dressing and walked over to the dresser to grab her money, while Tommy lay fully clothed on the bed, watching sports. Tommy's time with her was done, but he would pay for the room for the night in case he decided to get another romp. She could feel him staring at her while she bent over to slip on her heels. She had a gifted figure that men would swoon over, so it was nothing unusual to feel their eyes on her.

Her addiction kept her thin, but she was naturally cut and, fortunately, genetically gifted enough that the drugs had not yet caused any permanent physical damage. Of course, she had never been a heavy user. Si didn't like his girls strung out; that created too many distractions, and distractions were bad for business. He wanted them to be dependent on him but not a problem, so he kept them in check with minimal amounts of product coming in.

Pulling the compact out of her purse, she gradually positioned a line of powder on the mirror and ingested it through her nose. She preferred cocaine to the uncomfortable effects of painkillers and opioids. Falling asleep in any of the precarious positions she found herself in was a level of control she was unwilling to submit to.

Tommy spoke to her in parting. He had a deep voice, and his size was evident in the way it sounded, as if the fat around his neck blocked the vocal vibrations. It boomed from his lungs like air escaping a baritone horn. "I'll be back in a couple of weeks. He gets released next month. You're going to need to make time for both of us when I do." Lacey didn't respond; she just nodded. She hated the thought of sleeping with his brother. He was in prison for rape, but everyone knew he had molested his stepsister. The thought of him touching her made her cringe.

Of all the 'Johns,' pedophiles were the worst. Knowing what they had done to a child disgusted her more than raping adult women, and the thought of them touching her made her skin crawl. Beyond being simply weird and socially awkward, they all forced some type of fantasy for her to act like a young girl.

Lacey left Tommy alone in the room to meet up with Si and give him his cut. Dawn was breaking, and she needed rest before her next shift. As she stepped outside onto a dimly lit mezzanine at the front of the motel, Si was already waiting. The sunlight was cresting over the horizon behind him, illuminating his silhouette.

The motel was a pay-by-the-hour kind of place, and the girls met many regulars there. It was right on the verge of a shady part of town, bordering a nicer area. Bessemer was a ghetto with some higher-end parts. A few miles away, Hoover was high-end real estate with affluent families to watch and marvel over.

Keeping them close to a life they would never have was a constant reminder of their bad decisions and the control their owners had over them. Like a prisoner watching their family on the other side of the glass box that entombed them, it was never made clear whether that was accidental or intentional on Si's part; nevertheless, the effects were the same.

She used to remember seeing all the real estate signs, thinking she could do that. She had dreams of being a millionaire and living a luxurious lifestyle—flashy cars, designer handbags, children, a husband—a dream that would never be. Hers was an existence to be endured rather than lived.

Si stood anxiously, waiting for his money. He never said much to them; there was little to talk about. He was their owner for all intents and purposes. They were beneath his social standing, like a gardener to an aristocrat. Holding a conversation or asking how they were doing—anything beyond getting his cash and ensuring they were unharmed—would have been considered offensive to his status. Seeing them unharmed was only in the sense that they were not permanently disfigured. After handing him the cash, Lacey's night had come to an end. She was tired, and it was time to go home.

Si was just under six feet tall and built solid, the kind of muscle one gets from lifting weights in a gym rather than throwing hay bales on a farm. His physique had a softness to it, as if it were built only for his personal vanity. A fake spray tan appeared comical, leaving an orange haze on a naturally dark-skinned man. With dark eyes and a short-trimmed beard, he was a nice-looking, albeit somewhat average man.

His vanity was his largest weakness; he dressed well and always seemed to know what to say. The local police knew what he was, but nothing much could be done. "It was a matter of resources," the police had told one of the girls.

In the traditional sense, Si was her pimp, but he was more than that. The girls fell in love with him one at a time until he got them hooked on one substance or another. Then it was only a matter of time before he owned them completely. He was their pimp, their lover, their father, their brother, their family—each girl intentionally picked, like a predator selecting its prey on the plains of Africa.

As if out of a profiler's report, he selected his women based on their poor family lives and the sense of abandonment the system had built around them. Lacey's story began when her grandmother passed, followed by her opioid-addicted mother two years later. Lacey was 15 when she entered foster care, substituting one broken home for another until she turned 18. Her brother was 17 at the time and had all but disappeared shortly after. It had been nearly ten years since she had seen him.

If there was ever such a thing as a true sociopath, it was Si. Shaking hands like a politician, grinning to his ears with charisma one moment and a volatile temper the next, he would have himself cutting one of the girls' faces before retiring her. He avoided killing the girls, not out of any desire in his soul, but to avoid police attention. Coincidentally, it was generally more profitable to sell them off to the South American slave trade when they were used up. If Dilaudid didn't cause the girls to overdose, he could sell even the most worn-out and scarred-up whore to the Colombians.

She always figured him for mixed Italian heritage, given his physical appearance, but he was fluent in Spanish and had a Puerto Rican accent. Some of the girls were foreign-born, and he had picked up bits and pieces of Russian and

French to communicate. Lacey learned years ago that speaking Spanish was a mode of survival for her because Si preferred to speak in his native tongue.

The girls didn't complain about him too much. He wasn't nice by any means, but he didn't hit them often, and he kept the contraband coming. Besides being reasonably adept at handling his business, he wasn't known for high intelligence. All they had to do was give him his cut and get on the rotation to satisfy his sexual urges, and life would be generally smooth. They knew what he had done in the past, and the pending fear was enough to keep the girls in line until they went home.

Home… that was a laugh, a studio apartment above an abandoned warehouse that was falling apart: A place so defiled that even rats wouldn't dare call it home. The water worked, but there was no power except for one outlet run from an extension cord pirated from the building next door, just enough to charge a phone so Si could reach them, and a mini fridge that had to be unplugged if she wanted coffee… *Home…* that was a laugh.

She could see her apartment from the hotel—a loft office above the old factory next door. The side entry didn't lock, and a loose steel panel in the back allowed stray dogs and raccoons to be a constant source of irritation for her. Her walk of shame across the street was similar to that of a college girl who had drunk too much and slept with the entire starting squad on the varsity team.

She strutted along the sidewalk between the two structures. Her figure moved with false bravado, supported by high heels as if they were lifting a damaged sense of self-worth along with her legs and butt. Dawn was breaking when she reached the side door, casting more light than it had previously. The hint of sun felt good on her face—a glimmer of sunshine in a bleak existence.

The cockroaches scurried into hiding the moment the squelch of the steel door echoed inside the open bay. Beneath the apartment were old offices that Si had originally intended to house more girls. In the end, nothing happened of those plans, and Lacey was there alone. During the daylight hours, she would make coffee, have a glass of wine, eat, and contemplate her life as she did every day.

Some days were successful in that she didn't try to commit suicide, and the thought didn't cross her mind. Other days, she had been able to at least draw blood down her wrists, but the majority of mornings entailed at least some fantasy of ending it all. She had been reasonably successful once and nearly accomplished it when a John walked in. He found her naked in a bathtub with her wrists cut and dialed anonymously for an ambulance before leaving her there.

Since then, she hadn't attempted it again and carried two jagged scars down her wrists as constant reminders that she lacked control over her own life. She felt like a prisoner inside her own body. When she came home from the hospital, Si had told her that if she attempted it again, he would kill Kelly—the only person remaining she could confidently call family.

Ultimately, Lacey wanted to escape that life, that pitiful existence of endurance rather than something worth enjoying. As she stood in her apartment, the smell of rotten steel and decayed concrete filled her senses. She couldn't tell if it was an actual smell or the overwhelming feeling of her home. She often thought of watching old black-and-white films with her grandmother; that's how her life felt to her—a colorless film.

Not today. She stared at her apartment in defiance, as if she were looking at her entire life. *I'm not losing today.* Reaching into the kitchenette drawer, she grabbed a sleeping pill and poured a glass of wine. She slipped off her dress and lay in bed naked, allowing sleep to overtake her. For the next few hours, she would dream and live in a world worth fighting for, worth existing in. T*here had to be something better than this…* she thought to herself before fading into a deep sleep.

Marion sat at his computer, staring out the window as he ran his hands through short sandy blonde hair. It was lakefront property on a private lake with only a dozen houses that made for a quiet community. He was the only full-time resident, having inherited the property when his father passed. Fortunately, his profession allowed him the luxury of working from home, and living only 30 minutes from the city was certainly no obstacle.

The water was smooth that day, clear as glass. Technically, you could drop a boat and ski on the lake, but it was small enough that most would consider it a pond, and the boat would have to circle the outer bank constantly to maintain speed. The majority of the residents simply enjoyed putting in a jet ski or small fishing boat on their weekends up there. The crowd was always late middle-aged families with young grandkids. The properties had high turnover; as the grandkids aged, their families sold the lots to new families, and the cycle continued.

The houses were all modern luxury homes, except for his and the one next door. Both were built by his grandfather in the 1950s and were the first houses on the lake. When the dilapidated house next door came up for sale, Marion bought it with the intention of restoring it and selling or renting it, but he had never found the time. All he had managed to accomplish was a new roof, paint, and the demolition before running out of funds. It was clean and safe for the time being.

Old oak trees engulfed the entire lake, reaching with their withered branches over the mirror-like surface of the water. Boughs of bark and fiber stretched toward the sky as their roots strained for nutrition from the gastrointestinal tract of the fish. Once a year, the residents would trim, prune, and remove trees around the pond's edge to keep the banks clear. In years past, it was a community event, but of late, most residents simply paid Marion to handle it, which entailed hiring arborist crews or doing it himself and keeping the money if business was slow.

His home still used an old wood stove in the center for heat, so his enthusiasm for the leftover firewood couldn't be understated. The chill of the fall air permeated the home as the wind blew over the open water. He tossed a log onto the coals in the stove and stood in front of it, enjoying the blast of heat for a moment.

He looked around the house, savoring the simplicity of his life. Though the house was old, it was renovated and appeared like something out of a magazine cover photo. The home had two bedrooms, and after the renovations, two bathrooms. It had a nice master suite and a jack-and-jill bathroom off the living room connecting to the bedroom. The kitchen was open, with a butcher block island facing into the vaulted living room.

The tongue-and-groove pine ceiling was left in its raw state, allowing every knot and imperfection to show through the stain. He had added a sunroom, which doubled as his office behind the carport and overlooked the water. An exterior entry was placed on the side after a new concrete parking pad was poured to accommodate clients without renting an office downtown.

In the driveway was parked an early 2000s extended cab black Toyota Tundra. It was meticulously maintained and in near showroom quality. The mileage was still under 100,000, and the interior was upholstered with black leather. Sitting in front of the stick shift was a ham radio that Marion occasionally used for security jobs. He wasn't an off-road enthusiast, and the majority of the vehicle was stock apart from the radio and a sound system that allowed him to have a GPS display. He had installed a mount to hold a tablet when he was following a GPS tracker, but it was usually removed and placed under the rear seat.

The day would be dreary and overcast, with a depressing aura. The sun, not yet ready to crest the horizon, left the lake engulfed in moonlight and darkness. It affected his general mood, but ultimately he was just bored being by himself with no new exciting cases. He had surveillance to run and needed to get eyes on a person of interest named Tommy Johnson.

Over the past few weeks, he had been staking out a hotel frequented by hookers because Tommy was known to be there when passing through. He currently had no address, and his mark was proving harder than expected to catch a glimpse of—not through any design of his own, but through sheer dumb luck of being a lowlife who avoided rent payments and spent his days couch-surfing through friends and family.

Tommy was known to transport drugs throughout the Southeast. He wasn't a kingpin or anyone of importance in the drug trade, and certainly not someone Marion needed to secure evidence against. But Tommy was a known associate in a case, providing Oxycontin to his client's spouse in a messy custody battle. All Marion really needed to do was get pictures of the delivery and payment to the spouse to collect a final paycheck.

Leaving his cottage required little more than grabbing his keys from the hanger over the kitchen counter and his day bag, which was full of private investigator gear he used regularly. His pistol was always on him, and though he cycled through several firearms to carry daily, he generally selected an old Ed Brown Commander 1911 his father had left him. Marion preferred a 9mm to .45 cal. He liked the magazine capacity of the Sig Sauer P365, Glocks, or M&Ps,

but ultimately he always ended up with that pistol in his appendix holster. Perhaps it was a bit of a nostalgic choice, but it just seemed to fit him well.

Marion grabbed his Emerson flipper knife and flashlight off the kitchen island to stow in his pocket. He had developed the habit of always keeping a flashlight on him in the military, and as a private investigator, he found it to be a more useful tool than even his knife. A spare magazine found its way to his belt especially when he carried a pistol with low capacity like the Ed Brown.

A black day bag sat on the island with his gear strewn about for the afternoon. He generally kept it packed and ready to go for work at a moment's notice. However, when time permitted, he liked to go through it before leaving for the day to ensure he had everything required. His meticulous nature had given him an edge in the industry and certainly was useful in keeping him alive in the Army.

Grabbing each item off the counter, he stowed his night vision goggles, camera, and a few spy cameras disguised as other items, a bug detector, spare magazines for his pistol, along with batteries and memory cards as needed. Lastly, he stowed the drone and drone case, which he had found useful on multiple occasions.

His pistol was checked every morning before putting it on. He always remembered an old lieutenant doing a press check before rolling outside the wire to ensure the chamber was loaded and the magazine was seated. It was a good habit, one ingrained deep in his mind. Removing the firearm from underneath his shirt, he clicked the safety off in the same draw stroke and pressed the slide back slightly to confirm the presence of a round. Satisfied with the bullet in the chamber, he dropped the magazine into his palm and counted eight rounds before reinserting it into the pistol.

Retrieving the loaded bag, he slung the weight over his

shoulders and made his way to the truck with keys in hand. In the rear passenger seat of the truck sat a small tub with typical office supplies—surveillance equipment, batteries, tripods, and a small medical kit. His vehicle was prepared for emergencies, but it always seemed excessive to carry another firearm in the truck; the only additional firepower was the spare magazine in his duffel bag and a box of NATO ammo in the tub. He never kept a rifle in the vehicle for fear that it would be broken into and stolen. Especially when he considered the crime ridden areas of town he frequented.

His truck fired reliably on the first crank, igniting the pistons into rotation. Pulling forward out of the drive, he continued down the circular path that passed his other property, along with a few vacant homes in the lot. The community was owned predominantly by absentee owners, who rented out vacation getaways during the summer. At that time of the year, there would be almost no one there until spring hit.

He came to a stop in front of the massive iron gate at the community entrance. It stood like a warning from Soviet Russia, only missing the hammer and sickle. The steel was cold and dark, with weathered brick pillars on either side. Decorative letters adorned each side of the swinging iron curtain, with the name 'Gamble' written on one side and 'Lake' on the other. His grandfather had built the gate when the house was put up, though at the time it was opened and closed manually. The electronic opener had been installed back in the 1980s as electricity and computer controls became more commonplace. It provided only a semblance of security as it was easy enough to walk or even drive around, though it did serve its purpose of keeping out unwanted solicitors.

Pulling through the gate felt like leaving a hidden oasis; a bland backcountry road entered the freeway as paradise was lost in his rearview mirror. The 30-minute commute to

Bessemer ended as uneventfully as it began. Country music played softly over the radio, occupying the foreground of his mind as he sat silently contemplating the events that would unfold that day.

Marion pulled his truck into a rundown parking lot across the street from the hotel Tommy was reported to visit. He intended to spend the day there, waiting for his target to appear. It would be dull billable hours while the hookers wrapped up their shifts for the night. He was hoping to catch Tommy driving toward Hoover after spending the night with one of the girls there. The theory was that Tommy would spend the night with a hooker, opting to meet his customer before heading to Tennessee… *Of course, it was just a theory,* Marion thought to himself.

The dawn was coming, and the light began to crest over the rear of the truck, glimmering off the front of the hotel. The building wasn't dilapidated like the one next door, but the paint was in better condition. Riddled with damaged lights and rust stains underneath the rain scuppers, the structure obviously needed exterior maintenance.

Every outward appearance of the building illustrated the intentions and occupants of the rooms. The terminal state of existence of the building, standing resilient against the occupants' repeated attempts to defile its soul, shed a sort of allegorical light on that of its inhabitants. *Who in the hell would ever stay here?*

Shortly after the sun broke its first rays across the black of the night, he noticed a hooker coming out of one of the rooms. *Damn, she's beautiful!* The woman wore a red dress with black heels, the slit of the dress coming all the way up to her armpit, exposing her tanned body on the side as if teasing him to pay for its full removal. Her hair was jet black and didn't appear to be dyed. It was short, only slightly too short for a ponytail. He was unsure of what products women used to give their hair that slightly damp and glistening look, but it was visible from across the lot, where he watched her strut toward the deplorable warehouse next door.

From that distance, he couldn't make out much else, other than her height being reasonably short—not tiny, but below average, maybe 5 foot 3, though the heels made her appear taller. He watched as she descended the stairs from the second-floor mezzanine. She didn't go far, just across the street before turning into the building. *Going to shoot up before bed,* he assumed.

Marion felt sorry for her, wondering what had caused a woman to end up like that from a little girl with dreams. She walked knowingly to the warehouse as if she had made the walk a thousand times. *Why was she going in there? Maybe to do drugs? Surely a John wouldn't be waiting in there. She wouldn't be living in something that foul. Why not shoot up in the hotel room?* The question of *'why'* perplexed him, but ultimately it was unimportant to his task of watching for Tommy.

He always wondered how someone like that could end up in such a desolate situation. The confines of their predicament didn't elude him, but how it first came to pass was the question he couldn't seem to answer. *At what point did this woman go from being a little girl to a drug-addicted hooker who couldn't see her self-worth? What decisions did she make? What decisions did others make that led to this life for her?*

The Johns made sense to him: he could understand why a man would pay for sex with someone, particularly if they all looked like her. But from the girls' perspective, he struggled to rationalize at what point would they submit to addiction or desperation to make ends meet and have sex with someone they ultimately found vile and disgusting.

Marion couldn't help but feel pity for them and anger at the pain they hid and harbored every day, knowing their lives would end either through disease, murder, or overdose.

There was no concept of a 401k or an IRA for them. Those were principles that would never matter to them, just as the concept of existential purpose doesn't enter a dog's thought process.

The woman disappeared from view, teasing his lustful urges with her curved figure imprinted on his mind. The day would be dull enough without occupying his mind with thoughts of the hooker. *Enough!* It was time to focus on the task at hand.

***

The trick to doing stakeouts has always been to stay comfortable, Marion thought to himself. You can't leave the truck running, so unless you're fortunate enough to have a hide site, you're stuck trying to run mini heaters and air-conditioning units that can generate their energy off a car battery without draining it.

In the summer, Marion had a small DC-powered air-conditioning unit that kept his truck reasonably cool—at least bearable—and could run on two spare batteries in the bed of his truck. For winter, his only real option was to dress for the weather. It was a cool, overcast day but fortunately, fall was reasonably nice in that part of Alabama, with nothing more than a light jacket.

There was little to see, but the motel was fully visible. All of the units faced him, so he didn't have to worry about which unit Tommy was in. Each end unit emptied into the exterior hallway rather than the front of the hotel. He assumed regular customers would be more inclined to use it for the psychological safety it provided by not walking out into the open.

Marion contemplated the situation from a 'Johns' perspective as he watched through a digital camera mounted on the dashboard. The camera was tethered to his tablet in the console, allowing him to lean the seat back so no one could see that anyone was inside the vehicle. He habitually checked his rearview mirrors and adjusted the center mirror to cover blind spots before leaning back. On more than one occasion, he was surprised by someone trying to open his doors, wanting to see if the vehicle was unlocked.

The last leaves fell from the only remaining tree in the concrete wasteland he occupied, carried away by a light wind. There was little traffic in that part of town, and only a few vehicles passed by on their way to work in the morning. Most were of a lower economic variety, with dents and scratches to match their current market value. His truck was old enough to blend in, but Marion's knack for meticulous maintenance made it stand out slightly among the sun-faded and wind-damaged cars that plagued the area.

The entire day ticked by with each stroke of his watch, failing to provide a glimpse of Tommy. Morning turned to afternoon, afternoon to evening, and evening to dusk. The patrons who visited the hotel during daylight were sparse—nothing more than a junkie or two, a low-level businessman and his secretary having an affair, and the occasional traveler who mistakenly purchased a room there. The working girls wouldn't return until nightfall, adding an aura of mystique to their profession.

At 6 o'clock that night, he saw Tommy emerge from the hallway the hooker had come from earlier that morning. *He must have been resting there the entire day since her departure*. The obese figure walked out to what could presumably be his car and retrieved a pack of cigarettes from the glove box. It was an old, red, 90s Honda Civic, a relatively low-profile vehicle for drug transportation. *It was actually a smart move,* he thought to himself.

Pulling up his phone, Marion checked the picture he had

from Tommy's Department of Motor Vehicle (DMV) records and compared it with the man he was spying on. The driver's license said 6'5" and 400 pounds. *It had to be him.* Tommy was so large that Marion wondered how the small Civic could hold him, as the man towered over it and appeared to be about half the vehicle's size.

He held a laser rangefinder to his eye and utilized the magnification to clearly view Tommy's face. He transitioned several times between the paper and the reticle and was finally satisfied that was his quarry. He dropped the rangefinder back into his duffel bag and monitored Tommy through the tablet screen.

Tommy stood outside, smoking his cigarette and making calls on his cell phone. It was late and getting increasingly unlikely that he would be driving anywhere at that time of night. Marion was able to make out the license plate: AFG787. As a PI, he had access to DMV records through third-party software, enabling him to search registrations from his home. That was one of the many times he wished he had a partner. Calling in the vehicle license plates in the lot would have been an easier way to determine whether Tommy was actually there. He could have placed the tracker and left for home that morning.

Marion grabbed the GPS device from the plastic tub in the back seat. In recent years, GPS trackers had fluctuated in legality; they first became legal with stipulations and were at that time virtually illegal. He maintained two of them mostly for protection details, where his clients signed an agreement to be tracked for safety purposes. However, as politics go, the bureaucrats making the decisions didn't have to do the work, and trackers were invaluable tools for single-member private investigation firms. Even with what he charged, most clients couldn't afford a three-man crew providing full-time surveillance, so that was the next best thing.

Tommy threw the cigarette to the ground before stomping it out with a size 15 shoe. He limped up the stairs with no ounce of athleticism, moving like a man with spine and back injuries. He wasn't injured; the limp was purely due to the excessive weight he was carrying. The trip looked like it winded him at the apex of the stairs, when he stalled for a brief moment to catch his breath. Continuing at a painful pace, Tommy finally found his way back into the room and closed the door behind him. Marion waited another 15 minutes to see if he would come back out or if he was suspicious enough to watch from the window. Not seeing any movement, Marion decided to place the tracker.

It would be too suspicious for Marion to walk across the lot with the GPS tracker in hand. Despite what the movies showed, a real tracker was much larger than the antacid tablet-sized ones the CIA used. It was approximately half the size of a standard car battery, with a large lithium battery that would last several weeks. There were smaller devices, but the GPS would struggle to always track and wouldn't provide minute-by-minute data. The smaller ones also had a tendency to lose charge, and certain models would alert any phone with Bluetooth that it was present. They simply weren't built for surveillance. Surveillance-specific models came in a package unit affixed with a magnet to be attached to the frame under the car.

The parking lot was relatively empty, but his truck could provide cover as he pulled it next to the Civic. Starting the truck again, he parked it next to the Civic's passenger door and pretended to drop something while exiting. Leaving the door open to shield him from onlookers in the hotel, Marion placed the tracker on Tommy's car. Needing a reason to be in the parking lot in case he was seen, he locked the door to his truck and casually walked to the main office to inquire about nightly rates before returning to his truck.

The clerk was changing shifts, and the night clerk was less than helpful, but Marion didn't really care about the rates, anyway. His ball cap hid his face from the security cameras in the building, and he was on his route home within ten minutes.

The GPS software would send him a text to let him know when the vehicle was on the move. He could monitor the situation from home, hoping to catch Tommy heading to the Birmingham area. He silently hoped that Tommy would stop for gas, allowing him to remove the tracker before the situation escalated. Crossing state lines could implicate him in even more felonies than the one he was committing by placing the tracker in the first place.

As he pulled out of the parking lot, he noted a Toyota Corolla parked beside the warehouse he had seen the hooker going into. He couldn't see the side of the building from the parking lot, so he wasn't sure when it had arrived; only that it hadn't been there when he initially pulled in. Maybe it was hers, but then it should have been there when he arrived. He assumed it belonged to another John. *Guess she wasn't off the clock yet.*

2

"Pain pays the income of each precious thing."

-William Shakespeare

Most people who knew Ewan Maddox recognized him as the city zoning official. He was pleasant, though not overly friendly. For all intents and purposes, he appeared to be an average citizen. He was neither short nor tall and did not stand out physically among any particular group. On the outside, his life resembled that of a weeknight sitcom and appeared on all fronts to be 'average.' Partly by fortune and partly by design, Ewan lived his life to avoid standing out… a nobody who would never be given a second thought.

The house he lived in was in a subdivision that was neither new nor old, with houses spaced far enough apart that you didn't know your neighbors. He spent years renovating a basement to suit his needs and was incredibly strict about allowing his wife into his space. Ewan's darkest secret, even more so than his desires, was his intelligence. With an IQ over 160, he found everyone around him to be inferior. Daily interactions at the gas station or grocery store left him irritated, like a teacher scolding a child for failing to comprehend a topic. The irony of his situation didn't escape him; he was regarded within his group of 'friends' as lacking intellect. Constantly, he took the blame for the stupid pitfalls of others, only to enjoy the lack of attention one receives for being two steps smarter than the village idiot.

Ewan didn't have friends so much as acquaintances for appearance's sake. Even his wife proved to be more of an annoyance than an aid. The thought of burying her in the backyard to never again hear the shrill sound of her voice and putting a bullet into every idiot he met was an increasingly overwhelming urge. However, maintaining pretenses and propriety allowed him to exist in the shadows. Acting on every impulse would reveal his existence to the world. Ultimately, he never cared for their opinion of him, but exposure would confine him to a jail cell and halt his extracurricular activities permanently.

He sat with a lit cigarette burning between his fingers at his kitchen table. Generally, he was an overly disciplined person but struggled to control himself in the face of his desires. He knew cigarettes would kill him, but the thought of it never seemed to matter or cause him any emotional discomfort. The concept of death or any afterlife was a distant thought, so far removed that it never registered in his conscious mind. Logically, he knew he would die, but there was no ability within him to register death on an emotional level.

The coffee in front of him was still steaming from being freshly poured a moment ago. He sipped it between drags of the cigarette, enjoying his morning paper. Ewan didn't like cellular phones or technology in general and belonged to the dwindling crowd of Americans who subscribed to a newspaper for current events, keeping only a flip phone in his car.

He cared little about political or social issues, so most of the paper was irrelevant. Overwhelming his thoughts and desires were the crime reports. Viewing weather as only a pragmatic obstacle in his life, he would gloss over it. What he cared most about were the missing persons' reports. He could never contain himself from cutting out snippets of his past prizes; those were the only trophies he ever took. Great care and detail went into disposing of the bodies, so there was never a press release to allow him a second moment with the girls. Taking trophies was far too risky, but a small snippet would only ever be circumstantial evidence at best.

Cops are stupid, he often thought to himself, barely a step above the teenager whose mind was only good enough for raking leaves in the fall. He felt seriously that 'the others,' like him were quite simply vacuous or at least reckless. *"The others"*—that's what he referred to anyone like him, anyone with the desires that preoccupied their every sense and presence. As it currently stood, the police didn't even know of a single victim, having only missing persons without a body or weapon to indicate a murder.

Failing out of college for lack of interest never afforded him the opportunity for law school, though he spent considerable spare time researching laws, evidence collection, and police procedures. The knowledge one could gain from the criminal justice section of a college textbook store would alarm the general public.

Obsessively reading the paper allowed him to relive his moments with past recipients. Her face was plastered on the third page with an article describing the incidents of when and how she went missing. Ewan scrolled the page repetitively while sipping his coffee and taking a long drag of his cigarette. He always enjoyed cigarettes with his victims, so the moment was an additional euphoric sentiment for him.

He had always been cautious, spending countless hours staking out places to take the girls. The sole reason for his employment at the zoning department was to have access to government documents, blueprints, and plot maps. He would research vacant, out-of-the-way buildings, break-in, and stage them for his pleasure.

Hearing Rebecca's footsteps in the stairwell above, he quickly grabbed his coffee and newspaper to avoid her in the basement. Lost in his focus on the newspaper, he hadn't noticed her moving around upstairs. Ewan couldn't stand to listen to her then, and that day being his day off, he wanted to make use of the time. He had found a location to stage for his next victim and wanted to conduct his initial reconnaissance. He would scout the area in his free afternoons to plot locations and routes home, away from surveillance cameras and police activity.

Being most vulnerable during the initial grab of the girls and again during transport to his house, he considered that step imperative, and it became a part of the ritual he rather enjoyed. There was virtually no forensic evidence to tie him to anything after the fact. Provided he didn't get pulled over for a busted taillight, he would be in the clear.

No one paid much attention to a city zoning official poking around abandoned buildings, so it was unlikely anyone would remember his appearance. Regardless, he knew his greatest attribute was his average appearance. Ewan didn't stand out anywhere he went. His skin was light Caucasian, giving him the appearance of European ancestry. In truth, he didn't even know, nor did he care. His hair was short and slightly balding on top. He always wore a ball cap that he would buy with cash from a local gas station on the way there and throw out on his way home.

There was little to identify him as anyone of significance anywhere he went. He wore navy blue slacks and a plain white shirt virtually everywhere, and other than a legal-length pocket knife, he carried nothing to draw attention to himself. With no body left behind, the police were looking for a missing person rather than a murderer. Any witness would only have a description of a Caucasian man wearing a then-discarded ball cap with slacks and a polo.

Before he could unlock the basement door, Rebecca was in the kitchen.

"Good morning," she said, still groggy.

It was still early in the morning, and it was a bit unusual for him to be required to interact with her. Rebecca was on every antidepressant he could remember and would usually spend the morning sleeping. Ultimately, she would wake up and bumble to the kitchen around noon in her faded blue bathrobe. People generally found her and her husband awkward to be around, so her group of friends was limited and shrinking. That generally meant she would remain in her bathrobe, watching television until just before dinner when she would shower, change, and prepare a meal. The only thing that annoyed him more than seeing her was hearing her voice.

He ached to kill her but was unable to draw that type of suspicion on himself. Eventually, he felt he might be able to engineer an accident, but he had yet to find an opportunity and lacked the imagination to create one. He had briefly considered taking her on vacation to the Grand Canyon so she could 'trip' off a cliff, but ultimately decided the travel time would be too much for him to handle with her by his side for 20 hours of driving. Listening to her excitement about the trip was enough to make him avoid it.

"I'm going down to get some work done for a bit, and then I'll be out running errands today." His voice was always matter-of-fact. There was no feeling, no empathy for a woman only seeking fulfillment—nothing. He was empty.

"I thought maybe we could do something fun today… Maybe dinner and a movie tonight."

"I'm busy; maybe next weekend," he snapped, shutting the door behind him.

She never let him hear it, but he knew she was in tears. He didn't care. *The bitch should mind her business,* he thought to himself.

He descended the old wooden stairs to the unfinished basement. The room opened to cinderblock walls. A steel exterior door replaced the original wood door, with two locking deadbolts, one of which was lockable only from inside the home. He flipped on the lights to illuminate a room meticulously cleaned and sanitized, providing even the best hospitals with staunch competition. The floor was polished concrete, and the ceilings were spray-foamed to provide sound deadening. LED lights hung like stalactites from the ceiling, shedding light in every nook and cranny so that no area was without illumination.

The basement appeared like a craftsman's shop with no identifiable characteristics of his true self. He had built a forge to incinerate the bodies and even had the tools. Each crime was conducted with various found objects that he would bring home and smelt down into unrecognizable trash. The bodies would then be taken in, piece by piece, to be similarly incinerated.

His workbench was secured against the wall, with tools of his trade hanging perfectly in order, with drawn outlines on the pegboard behind it. In the center of the room stood the gas forge large enough to fit a German Shepherd. The inside of the forge was lined with fire bricks that he intended to replace periodically to dispose of trace evidence.

In truth, he had little interest in blacksmithing, but in order to keep up appearances, an anvil stood beside the forge with an assortment of forging tools and books on a shelf behind it. He had learned the hobby out of necessity but found some use for the tools and techniques in disposing of collectibles from his kill sites. Even when he didn't want to take trophies, sometimes the urge was more overpowering than his self-control.

Part of his thrill was in inflicting pain with what he could salvage. Studying the work of 'the others,' he found it boring that they insisted on killing the same way every time. There was no gift or talent to them, no strategy or intuition. Ewan insisted on devising a creative plan for killing each of his girls. The specific method employed would be determined when he secured his location. But more importantly, they would tell him... Their eyes would tell him how they wished to be killed and in what manner he was to deliver them.

Each location and gift, as he referred to the women, was unique, as if his mission were ordained by something outside of that world. He would show them the instruments of their demise and tell them the story of their death. Then they would expose to him how they wished to die. Their faces and eyes would speak to him as if it was spewing forth from their lips.

For him, the peak of sexual gratification came after their death, while their lifeless bodies lay dormant for his desires to be carried out. He had spent years in his adolescence studying sexual fascinations and their relation to death. The *Eros* and *Thanatos* of his life perplexed him, not knowing why a deceased body aroused him. He knew only that necrophilia was an impossible urge for him to resist.

'The others' were beneath his level. They lacked skill and the ability to evade detection or the courage to carry their desires to fulfillment. Many were caught because they were missing the intentional fortitude in their constitution to kill the antagonist of their fantasies. They fulfilled themselves only with surrogates—men and women who looked like the targets of their hate. Ewan was different... a better, more refined type of 'other'—one lacking weakness.

His victims were all different—black, white, short, chubby; it didn't matter. He lacked preference and was almost gynephilic, being attracted to feminine characteristics. Nor was erotic climax attained in the manner of death, provided the pain was sufficient to relive the moment, while fixating his sexual hunger on their deceased corpses. Any buffoon could hit someone with a hammer. It took talent, creativity, intellect, and dedication to inflict pain with what he could scavenge from the site in the weeks preceding. To exhaust that level of pain and keep his victims alive was an even greater thrill yet. The greatest climax was achieved only if they died during copulation rather than before.

It had only happened to a few of the girls. The torture was so severe and the blood loss so great that he felt their life exit their bodies as he entered them—or even before. In that moment, he felt their energy and force pass through him, as if his body asked them permission to die.

If the moment passed too quickly, if he was too eager to harm them, his moment of ecstasy would never come, leaving only frustration and torment for his next prize. The second, having built desires from the first, would be the greatest release of all but ultimately the hardest and most difficult to control.

Though the killing floor was his ultimate moment of power and release, he received almost as much joy from stalking and hunting. Deciding the selective nature of how they would be harmed and the location of the affair would ultimately prove a minor moment of satisfaction that built upon the eventual climax. His erection swelled as he held the newspaper picture of Logan Ferris under his arm.

That day, he would drive to the next location. He had found an abandoned warehouse in the property tax records, out of earshot of the hotel next door. Nothing close, but a pay-by-the-hour hotel filled with hookers and tweakers. They wouldn't care about a distant scream from an undisclosed location. It was in an old, rundown industrial area. The hotel originally maintained occupancy with transient workers from the factories, but most of the factories were then closed, and the hotel's lifeblood came from being a dry room and hot shower for society's parasites.

His hunt would soon begin, but that day he would prepare the field. That day, he would find the routes in and out of the area; he would find the weapons to use and the victim... *I'll find her soon.*

A loud bang woke Lacey from a deep slumber. She was accustomed to weird noises in the building—*rats or raccoons, more than likely*. She rolled over and tried to go back to sleep, but there it was again. That time, it was inside the building. *Someone was here.* She knew it instinctively and without question. The hairs on her neck stood on end as the fear of the unknown shifted down her spine.

She bolted up out of bed and cautiously walked across the open room, grabbing a knife from the kitchen drawer. The apartment was a depressing squalor, void of any sense of decency or pride. Previously, it had been an office with an overview of the factory floor. Recently, it had been converted to an apartment for Si's girls, but she had no idea whether it was rented or owned, or whether she was squatting. *Maybe the owners,* she thought. Her instincts told her that whoever it was had more nefarious intentions than she would have liked.

Her cell phone screen shone brightly on the counter next to the drawer, showing that it was 6:16 PM. *Maybe the owners...* she hoped again. The window overlooking the shop floor had accumulated so much dust and grime that looking through it was like trying to see through a bottle of whiskey. The half-missing pane in the lower right corner provided a limited view of some of thc factory floor.

Keeping her body hidden behind the wall and attempting not to cast a shadow, she peered through the broken slit. A man in business slacks and a button-down shirt was walking and pacing as if contemplating something. His face was hidden by a University of Alabama hat with "Roll Tide" written across the front. It was illegible at that distance, but the logo was familiar to anyone in the area and could be determined through context. He looked remarkably like an accountant from a movie, and it seemed impossible to make out any distinguishing characteristics.

He gave no reason for her to be afraid or for her sixth sense to ping in the back of her mind, but still, something nagged at her to stay hidden. Lacey always trusted her gut, even when the evidence seemed to suggest otherwise. Like an antelope on the plains of Africa, she knew when she was being hunted. That man frightened her; it was as if she could sense death when he walked in. Lacey didn't scare easily, but she was frozen in place. Her eyes darted side to side as she tried to find a place to run. *I could scream... but no one would hear me.* His movements mesmerized her as he paced in a manner that spoke as loudly as words. He was angry and excited simultaneously. The mystery guest searched around the building, finding bits of rubble, broken glass, scrap metal, wire, and a long piece of cable. Most of it he tossed aside, but a few pieces, including the 30-foot length of cable, he set on an old steel bench bolted to the outside wall.

H*e knows I'm here*. Something in the way he moved and the change in his gait for just an instant sent her more primal instincts into overdrive, screaming at her body: *Hide!* She could feel it telling her. Lacey slowly slipped back from the opening to avoid confirming his suspicion with a sudden movement. There was no escaping the small loft without walking directly in front of him. Her primal mind took over as if she were watching herself from above.

On more than one occasion, she had needed a place to hide from drug addicts and teenagers needing a place to fornicate or shoot up. The loft had an open top, and the leaks in the roof had deteriorated the drywall years before, leaving a small opening to slip through. Lacey climbed on the counter, peering at the mechanical platform the heating and air system had been supported on. The components had been ransacked for their contents long before, but the platform had been left intact.

Slowly climbing, watching each precious step to avoid making a sound, she slid the knife up and quietly pulled her naked body up. The location was familiar and smelled of mold and decaying plaster. In the past, she had contemplated keeping a change of clothes up there and was kicking herself for not following through with the plan as she lay naked and chilled from the frost in the air.

Damn, she thought to herself, lying in the dark. More importantly than forgetting clothes, she had left her cell phone on the counter. If he saw the phone, it would be a dead giveaway that someone was there. With only a few hiding places in the tiny apartment, anyone would find her if they knew someone was present. Lacey clasped the knife firmly in her left hand and kept it steadily aimed at the small opening, praying no one would follow her through. She waited, thinking the office door would open, but it never did. *Maybe he hadn't seen her.*

She heard the loud bang again as the strange man exited the building through the broken panel in the wall. Si wouldn't be expecting her for a few more hours, so then was her only opportunity to get more sleep before going to work. *Work,* she thought, as if she were a high-powered attorney from a billboard, as if she had a career or a meeting to attend. Lacey knew what she was... There was no job interview in her future... No corporate meetings... There was no future in her future... Only a meeting with a man named John.

Ewan had already driven the route a few times, but he couldn't stop thinking about the girl. The dark-haired one in the red dress. He had spotted her on his first pass by the building as she walked in. *She must be squatting in the loft,* he thought, imagining why anyone would be living in a building so foul. The building stood in a manner that was disgusting to the point that even the rodents avoided it.

Satisfied with his route, he had pulled in behind the building, where he noted a broken panel that would allow him access. He could just use the front door as the hooker had, but then he could be seen from the street. *The broken panel was better and less risky.*

As he pried it from the wall, the rusted rivet broke loose, and the panel crashed to the ground. *Shit.* He climbed through the opening, and another small crash occurred as the adjacent panel snagged his shirt and slammed back into position.

The room opened into a steel-walled warehouse bay with holes in the ceiling and stained concrete under his feet. The floor was littered with rusted metal and broken beer bottles from teenagers and vagrants. Though the steel beams overhead were still present, the hoists used to lift heavy objects that would carousel from one to another were long gone.

He felt more energy than he knew what to do with and couldn't contain himself from pacing frantically back and forth. His excitement about what he was finding was beyond his control. An erection began to swell and tighten the front of his pants as he laid eyes on the rusty screwdriver and scrap aluminum.

But then he saw his holy grail: a steel cable coiled and

banded nicely under a pile of rubble and scrap debris. He could string her up and hang her from the steel beams while he filleted her skin. The dirty rags lying around would be used to gag her screams while he showed her the pieces of skin he removed from her body.

Slicing would be disciplined and methodical, with small sections of flesh being removed over the course of several hours. Scattering kitty litter underneath her would absorb any blood, and he could simply dump it in a river on his way to dispose of the body.

He was scraping together supplies on the table when he saw the movement from the loft window. She was watching him… His excitement grew, knowing that she could see him. She would remember that moment as her chance to get away, but she wouldn't. She had already given herself to him. She would hide and forget him. Once he was gone, she wouldn't remember his presence. But he would make her remember… she would always remember him, and he would always remember her. The power he would feel over her, the release he would get before exsanguination, and the memory of owning her body going forward with him.

How wretched her body would look after he removed her lips, trimmed her ears, and filleted her skin piece by piece. The blood would cover her body, and her muffled screams would exist for an eternity in his mind. He would take from her every ounce of beauty bestowed upon her. She would be his… *for eternity.*

***

He had spent most of the day and a half tank of gas driving back and forth from his neighborhood to the property, planning different routes, checking traffic camera locations, and avoiding commercial property security cameras until finally landing on a route that took about 45 minutes to get there. He even found a few parking decks and one burned-down mechanic shop that he could either use as his next location or as a safe spot in the event he noted police activity on his route home.

Ewan avoided speed traps, large shopping centers with lots of high-end security cameras, traffic lights, and anything that would be a potential hiding spot for the police. In the modern world, it was effectively impossible to avoid camera detection, but he made every attempt to mitigate it. Over the next few weeks, he would travel the route to look for police hiding locations while searching for a victim. That was the initial plan, but as luck would have it, it seemed he had already found his next gift: the lady in the red dress.

I can see it in her eyes. She wanted it. She wanted me. The passing glance she gave him as he drove by said everything about her. The way she watched him pace and move inside was as if she were erotically charged by his strength and power. She wanted to be released from her turmoil and existence. She gifted herself to him as if she were a parent on Christmas morning handing out presents. It wasn't a subtle cue she gave him but a direct plea for him to take her—to send her away, to be absorbed into him.

He thought to himself, smiling inwardly at the fortune of his prize being already at the location. Whether by fate or happenstance was an irrelevant query in his mind. Being there told him from a source outside of himself that she was intended to be his. He wouldn't even have to go through the risk of transporting her. He would simply wait for her to get off shift and grab her there.

Ewan drove the rest of the way home in silence, his mind deep in thought while staying observant enough to avoid traffic violations or the slightest sideways glance of detection. In his mind, it was impossible for people not to see him for who he was. Each bank teller or parking attendant he crossed paths with, Ewan thought they would see through him. They could see the anger and rage beneath his eyes as if they could look into the past to see what he was underneath, to really see him beneath the surface, and to see the depth of the ghoul that took up residence in his body.

He clocked himself in the rearview mirror, looking for the sign in his eyes that they should see. Staring back at him was something dark—a blackness that maybe they simply didn't recognize. He had occasionally run across some of 'the others' in life, and each of them was able to see who he was just as he had seen through them. They wore a mask that only people like him could see, a perfect facsimile of their face over the carcass of something from the darkness. If he peeled their skin back off their face, he would see the creature that lived beneath.

His was the face of the monster lurking under the bed or hiding in the closet, the thing that reached its hand up in the night to pull you into its lair. It was the face of despair, desperation, anger, fear, and loathing... But he saw none of that staring back at him. All he could see were the eyes of an empty man lacking a soul, no red glow or blackened sclera... only the hazel brown eyes of a middle-aged man driving home. In those moments, he knew that was what everyone else saw as well.

Hookers in that area didn't walk the street corners like Hollywood workers; if men wanted time with them, they just called Si, who would text the girls a room number and time. They could charge whatever they wanted, but Johns wouldn't pay much for it. Si even had a business license to run an escort service, allowing him to feign ignorance when the cops rolled up on any of his girls. He charged the girls for a constant stream of clients, protection, and locations. It was a flat rate regardless of what they charged the clients.

On that particular night, Si had given her the hotel room to meet the next John on her list. It was just a quick 30-minute blow-and-go. He would pay $60, and she would work his member in her mouth, trying to get him off as quickly as possible for a maximum of 30 minutes. Surprisingly, she didn't get many of these, as most customers wanted to take it all the way. Even if that's what they scheduled with Si, they would often change their minds halfway through and demand full penetration. The girls would raise their rates, and some even did it intentionally, ensuring the customer didn't finish within the 30-minute time frame so they could charge $150 for a full hour.

Lacey made her way up the stairwell, a dimly lit concrete fortress in the middle of a row of detached rooms. Ten rooms on the right, another ten on the left, with the one she had been in earlier with Tommy in the center just off the hallway. He was supposed to be in the last one on the left. It felt eerie that the lights were off on the catwalk, not just the room lights, which was normal. It didn't matter… it wasn't like she could call Si and tell him she was scared of the dark.

As the door opened, she saw his shadowed figure propped upright on the bed. "Hi," Lacey said, with a large smile; her teeth were so white they could have glowed in the moonlight streaming through the curtains.

"Don't waste time talking, just get started," he said coldly.

Lacey did as she was told. Guys like that were a dime a dozen; they had no control at home with their wives and kids, so they got a little rough with the hood rats. She already knew she was going to get slapped around a bit. It usually wasn't too bad; sometimes a bit of choking got out of hand, but nothing she wasn't capable of handling.

This time, things were different. Every instinct told her something was wrong, this was a situation to run from. She had no idea why, but the feeling was the same as she had experienced in her apartment earlier that afternoon. Something was telling her that night would be worse than normal. *Danger, Will Robinson!* Her mind screamed, flashing back to childhood memories of Lost in Space.

In no position to leave, she was forced to do his bidding. She may have been in danger then, but she would absolutely be in danger if she left and told Si to get another girl for that particular John. She wasn't certain what Si would do with her, but in reality, it would be worse than what that particular client would do.

Her situation went from bad to worse as each moment passed, escalating into a blend of shock and panic. She was holding him between her lips, sliding her head up and down, when he started forcing her head down longer and longer. He would wait for her to gag and retch when she couldn't breathe, then let her up to catch a breath before forcing her back down again. If she tried to pull her head off, he thrust his hips up harder.

It wasn't long before he said he would pay the full fee. When he said it, it wasn't a question but a statement of what she was going to do. He stood her up and aggressively ripped her clothes off. With another client, she would have told him to stop ruining her clothes. Instinctively, she knew he wouldn't allow her to take charge of the situation. *Submit, Lacey… it'll be over soon.* She stood there for a moment, unsure of what he was doing behind her. She figured he was waiting to get himself hard again, assuming he had gone slightly soft while getting her clothes off. It was a constant problem with some middle-aged men, but even more common with those who needed to hurt a hooker to maintain an erection. Then he grabbed her hand and slipped a handcuff on one side. "Wait, stop!" she almost shouted. "I don't do that… it's too dangerous!" she screamed, but the screams never escaped her lips, being buried inside her mind.

He pushed her over onto the bed. Her cute tanned bottom was sticking straight up in the air while he held one hand on her head, pinning her face down. Then he slid himself into her and began thrusting his hips forward. She could feel him for a while, but then he started going limp, and he started choking her. The choking helped for a few minutes but didn't seem to make much difference; his penis was flaccid again.

Before she could protest or fight back, he had a ball gag shoved in her mouth and tightened it around the back of her head. Lacey scratched and clawed at his hands and face, but the mystery man was too strong. It took him no more than 30 seconds to get the gag on, and then he had her non-handcuffed arm tucked behind her, pushing it up toward her shoulder. He didn't stop for her muffled screams; it just seemed to make him tug harder until she could hear the pop of her shoulder exiting its socket.

The pain was so severe she could feel the darkness creeping in. *Don't pass out,* she told herself. If he was going to do that, she was going to be strong enough to take it. He lifted her other arm high above her head and secured it to the sprinkler pipe with the handcuff. He gave no warning before swinging the dislocated arm down and then up to secure it to the other side of the handcuff. She could feel it grinding out of its socket against her bone; the blackness was creeping in again, but she forced herself to stay awake. *Don't pass out Lacey… you can take it!*

She could feel him getting harder again as her pain intensified. He had one hand around her throat, choking her, while the other guided himself again into her. That time, the thrusting resumed much faster and more aggressively, and the choking didn't let up. The lack of oxygen started sending her in and out of consciousness. Each time his grip loosened, her brain received a little more oxygenated blood, craving it.

Stay awake Lacey!

Her mind raced, screaming to be strong and fight him. Not wanting to give him the satisfaction of winning, she fought with everything she had to keep her eyes open. Her attempts to fight were futile. The world spun into a blur and then darkness. Lacey wasn't sure how long she had been unconscious, but when she awoke, the mystery guest was gone.

As she lay on the bed, still naked, her left arm throbbed and tingled from the interrupted blood flow. The room was dark, but she could sense that he was gone. Her eyes had adjusted to the lack of light, and she could see her clothes strewn about the room, torn from being ripped off. In the dim light of the television's LED indicator light, she could tell they were soiled with mud and debris from his boots.

Grabbing her clothes, Lacey attempted to dress herself with her one good arm. It proved surprisingly difficult and was made even harder by the torn buttons and ripped fabric that no longer clung together as they should have. Forced onto the bed from the exhaustion of dressing herself, Lacey knew she needed a hospital. Her arm would have to be put back in its socket for her to do anything beyond lying there, trying not to pass out.

Si would be annoyed at the situation but would ultimately realize that a beat-up whore couldn't produce. Beyond that, he would be left holding the bag for the rest of her appointments for the evening, and if it was a busy night, he would have to turn people down. She almost laughed at the thought… *Motherfucker could blow them himself!*

Wincing as she reached for her phone, Lacey sent Si a text to come to her. It wasn't often that they summoned him, so he would know there was a problem the moment he received it. The pain shot down her arm like a lightning bolt toward her fingertips. *Fuck this hurts! she groaned,* holding her dangling appendage. She reached into her purse, grabbing a small canister of pills. Defeating the child lock on them proved even more difficult with one hand, but eventually, the canister split open, spilling most of them onto the ground.

She downed one of the two remaining pills, trying to force them down her throat without water. She laid back on the bed, waiting for Si to arrive or for the drugs to start numbing the pain. Time moved slowly as the seconds ticked down on the cheap analog clock above the TV. The pain relief began to seep into her system, and the aching in her shoulder grew to a more bearable dullness. Her eyes began to feel heavy, as if she couldn't control her lids to stay open. It cast over her like a cloud crawling across a beach on a sunny day.

What the fuck... The thought was nearly incomplete in her mind. It was as if her brain could think it but not complete the phrase. She hadn't realized her eyes were then closed beyond any voluntary control of her body. Her strength wasn't enough to open them as they struggled to stay closed, fighting off her brain's signal to open them and stand up. The sleep was welcoming, the slumber of a child after a long day of play. She couldn't resist it, nor did she want to. *Go to sleep now, Lacey,* her grandmother's voice echoed, hovering over her as it bid her off into the comfort of the darkness.

3

"The life of the creature is in the blood."
–Leviticus 17:11

Si stood outside Tommy's room, pounding on the door. He had seen the red Honda Civic in the parking lot and knew Tommy hadn't left yet. Si knew his clients, and Tommy was probably intent on ordering up another girl the next day. The door slammed open as Tommy stood there without a shirt, wearing only a pair of sagging sweatpants.

He was a tall man, big beyond just being obese. His hair was normally covered with a ball cap, but without it, his balding head was more apparent. The hair lacking on his head was replaced by hair covering his chest and back. The massive volume of his stomach concealed the upper half of the sweatpants, hiding the drawstring. The backlights of the room cast a shadow over his pectorals, which jutted out like flabby slabs where his chest should have been.

"What the fuck do you want?" Tommy demanded.

"Let me in; we need to talk," Si said, as he entered without an invitation.

The room was the same as when Lacey left that morning but with the addition of snack food bags littering the floor and empty beer bottles on the nightstand. The college football game played in the background was turned down low but audible enough that Si walked over and shut off the TV while Tommy closed the door. "What do you want? I paid the bitch."

"That's not what I'm here for! The girl, Lacey, the one you like…"

"Yeah?"

"She O.D.'d; the bitch is dead on the floor five rooms over."

"Sounds like you've got a problem," Tommy said, somewhat uninterested. He had always liked Lacey but knew she could be replaced by any one of the dozen girls Si had.

"Nah, papi, WE have a problem," Si snorted back.

"How's that?" Tommy was slightly more interested in what Si had to say but hadn't quite realized how that reverted to him.

"Whose DNA do you think the cops are gonna find on the dead whore? Yours, compadre."

Tommy didn't respond. The realization of his situation began to dawn on him. Lacey was dead, and he had committed a felony before her death. Though buying a hooker was a somewhat victimless crime in his eyes, Tommy was a multiple offender, and DNA on a dead body meant no one would believe he hadn't forced drugs into her. Beyond that, he would be arrested and charged with soliciting a prostitute.

Si could see recognition flash across Tommy's face. His car would be searched, and they would ultimately find more drugs. A death occurring during the commission of a felony would result in a manslaughter charge. Past criminal records would be taken into account during sentencing. Ultimately, Tommy's phone would show him as the last person to contact her, and a body showing up would elicit an investigation.

"Look, man, I don't have time to get rid of her, and I can't leave while I've got girls working. Take her up North toward Nashville and dump her in the woods. Bury the body, and I'll give you a girl on me when you get back."

"What the fuck is this? Coupon night! No. I hide the body; I don't pay for bitches ever again. I come through. I get to run through whoever the fuck I want."

"Fine," Si snapped. He wasn't worried about negotiating with that buffoon. Tommy could have disappeared without anyone noticing, but he didn't have time to deal with it then. The Mexicans were meeting him with a shipment, and they wouldn't take kindly to rescheduling.

"Take her, but make sure she's gone. She has to be buried deep enough that the dogs don't dig her up. The last thing I need is some hunter stumbling across a body that could be linked back to me… She's in room 5; here's the key." Si passed the metallic device with the oval room number insignia attached.

"No one else is here but my girls, and they won't talk. I'll call you from the street corner to make sure it's clear to move the body to your trunk. Don't fuck this up."

Si didn't wait for acknowledgment; he just turned and left, slamming the door behind him. Tommy grabbed a T-shirt and started putting on his shoes. His stomach was so big it blocked him from tying his laces without contorting himself into various Yoga positions. His breathing was labored from the fat pressing on his lunges. *What the fuck did I get myself into?* he thought, panting to himself.

He finished dressing and walked the concrete mezzanine toward the room number Si had told him. The number was stamped on the tag, leaving no guesses as to which room she was in. Tommy opened the door slowly, as if he expected the dead body to jump out and attack him from beyond the grave. Even without the lights, he could see Lacey's lifeless body lying on the bed.

She was motionless and sprawled on the bed, looking peaceful and docile. Opioid overdoses usually made people froth white spittle from their mouths, but she appeared to just be resting. Tommy poked her a few times to see if she responded but got no movement. She didn't look dead, but then again, he wasn't an expert and couldn't see her chest rising and falling. There was no dog-like panting that seemed to happen right before someone stopped breathing.

On turning on the lamp beside the bed, her body remained motionless, and he could then see the white substance dried to her face, which had gurgled out. *Shit,* he thought, not caring about the girl or the issue at hand. His mind was riddled only with thoughts of his time with her. He enjoyed screwing her and only thought it a shame that she was gone. She was by far the prettiest girl Si had, and it just felt like a waste that she was gone.

Waste of a good whore, he thought to himself as he wrapped her in the rough cotton sheets of the hotel bed. Tommy rolled her up like a burrito to hide her from view if anyone were to see. The moment he finished wrapping her body, his phone rang with a text from Si. It was simple and direct, telling him the coast was clear and to move the body then. *Fucking spic… I'll move her when I'm ready.*

Hoisting her onto his shoulder, Tommy peered out of the cracked doorway to check for himself. He would be the one to pay the price if they were seen, not Si, and he didn't want to give anyone something to remember. Even wrapped in a sheet, a dead body looked suspiciously like a dead body, and Tommy's size would be easy to articulate in a police report.

He could see from the doorway that Si had blocked the view from the road with his red Camaro. Presumably, the girls in the rooms were all occupied, or at least he hoped they were. With Lacey over his shoulder in a fireman carry, Tommy clumsily carried her to the trunk of his car where Si was waiting.

"Take her North a few hours and bury her. Don't let her body get found."

"I won't. I'll be back in a few hours. When I come back, I want Kelly, so have her ready for me."

"Fine. Hurry the fuck up," Si said coldly, annoyed at Tommy's demanding tone.

Without another word, Tommy clambered into the car, which seemed several sizes too small for him. Si wondered quietly how someone that big could comfortably drive a car like that, but he truthfully didn't care. A moment later, Tommy pulled out and was out of sight. Si stood watching the night sky, wondering how that would end. *Stupid bitch… cost me a ton of money.*

It was around 2 a.m. when Marion's phone vibrated with three short dings. Wiping the grogginess and sleep from his eyes, he rolled in bed to see that Tommy was on the move. The app alerted him almost immediately, indicating that Tommy had left the hotel only a minute or two before the text came in.

Marion watched the screen, deciding whether he needed to address the issue and follow or go back to bed. He wasn't sure whether it was the sleep inertia and his mind not operating at full capacity, but something didn't sit right with him. Tommy was traveling on I-65 Northbound, leaving the city and heading away from where his client would have wanted to meet. The movement seemed unrelated and somewhat erratic. *Shit!*

He knew Tommy had a brother in Tennessee, and he might be heading there. That created a substantial problem for him, as he had a GPS tracker on the car going over state lines. Marion needed to retrieve the GPS before Tommy crossed the imaginary divide because the tracker was not only illegal in

Tennessee, but he also wasn't licensed to work there. Thinking that through, Marion regretted the decision to ever use the GPS tracker. *I should throw the damn thing out.*

The decision to follow Tommy, at least to the edge of the greater Birmingham area, seemed prudent, albeit unnecessary. Marion decided to intersect Tommy on I-65 and ensure his client's husband hadn't decided to meet outside the city. During custody battles and divorces, lawyers will tell their clients to be aware of PIs. If his client's former spouse had been tipped off, it might have caused him to change tactics. Regardless, he needed to get the tracker back before it was too late.

The travel distance to the interstate for Marion and the travel distance for Tommy to reach a point where catching up would be nearly impossible was approaching. Not wanting to lose time, he hurried with his clothes and nearly forgot his pistol as he headed out the door. Marion grabbed a small snub-nose revolver he kept in the kitchen cabinet next to the keys. He wasn't a fan of snub-nose revolvers; they were difficult to shoot well and nearly worthless at distances beyond 10 yards. A 50-yard shot was within his capabilities on a static range, but with moving targets, panic, adrenaline, and weather, it became less likely to hit the intended target. They had their place, and in that instance, grabbing it meant leaving armed, even if minimally, and it was unlikely he would need it.

The Tundra in the driveway was gloss black but still managed to blend in well at night. If he turned off the lights, it was nearly impossible to see. The entire vehicle had a rewired lighting system to aid in surveillance. All the vehicle's lights, including the cab lights, running lights, and license plate lights, were routed through a secondary circuit panel with a switch just below the radio to shut them all off without affecting the rest of the vehicle.

This was a trick he had picked up from a Kansas City police detective who taught criminology classes at the university, and it was one he used regularly when conducting surveillance. It wasn't exactly legal if you were on a public road, but it wasn't illegal to use when the vehicle was parked. Occasionally, he had used night vision goggles to navigate backcountry roads while tailing someone if the moonlight wasn't enough to drive unassisted.

Once on the road, it took Marion little time to catch up after merging onto the main highway. Heading North toward Nashville, Tommy was driving five miles per hour under the speed limit. That struck him as unusual; Tommy wouldn't typically drive under the speed limit unless he was actively transporting drugs. He hadn't figured him for the type to be overly cautious and honestly expected him to be speeding, if anything. It took some discipline to drive slowly, especially on open roads at night. Tommy had been moving 'product' for a long time, and most people tended to get complacent. That was particularly true when performing the same task repetitively.

The roads were quiet that night, and aside from the highway lights, there was little ambient light and less traffic. They seemed to be the only two vehicles on the street. Going slightly over the speed limit allowed Marion to close the gap, and with the tracker in place, he was able to maintain a healthy distance between them. Forcing himself to keep his spacing so as not to get burned, Marion cursed the fact that no one else was on the highway to buffer the zone between them. Even hanging back with the tracker, he had to drive excessively slow to stay behind and was constantly getting within visual distance of Tommy.

They had been driving for nearly 20 minutes when he saw the dim flash of a blinker to exit the interstate. They were near the Cullman exit, heading out into the countryside toward farmland. The property surrounding them was littered with trees and open fields needing to be plowed and fertilized for next year's crops.

Why would he exit here? There was no gas station or public parking anywhere in sight. No mutual meeting ground, just ranching and farmland for miles, the kind of area you would have to know as a local to avoid getting turned around in. The endless fields seemed to absorb the blackness of the evening as if clawing their way toward an infinite point on a chart.

Periodically, Tommy would turn onto a gravel road to shortcut between two main highways, but Marion continued past the roads and would parallel Tommy on a different road, watching the GPS. He used the main light control switch to kill the lights when the distance between them was less than half a mile. That went on for over an hour before the GPS tracker pulled off onto a gravel road and stopped in what looked like an open field on the GPS screen.

Both vehicles sat on a gravel county road off of several other county roads. There were no houses or cars, nor anything in the vicinity to mark the area as owned by anyone. It was void of any semblance of life apart from recently logged land and fencing for cattle that were nowhere in sight. The eerie presence of the night sent a chill down his spine, along with the urge to unholster and press-check his pistol to ensure it was loaded and ready. Marion grabbed the pistol and cursed again, forgetting he had grabbed the snub-nose revolver rather than his 1911.

They were less than a mile from one another, but he would have to backtrack on the road or walk through the woods. Unsure of what he would find in the woods, and with his night vision goggles resting in his reconnaissance bag at the house, he might get detected if he was seen pulling down the highway with the lights on.

Ultimately, he decided his best approach was to move on foot through the forests, hoping to reach Tommy before they left. The frost had killed back some of the vegetation, and though difficult, it wouldn't be impossible to traverse like it would have been in the spring or summer. He could have jogged the distance in well under ten minutes on open ground, but pushing through trees and brush, he figured it would take him closer to half an hour. His only prayer lay in Tommy wanting to talk with his client more than usual to prolong the meeting.

Still, he faced the issue of how to get the tracker off the car. He couldn't exactly walk up to them and ask if he could have it back. The first option that came to mind was to get photos of the deal and hold Tommy at gunpoint while he grabbed it. Once the customer was gone, it would hardly matter if Tommy saw him, and there would be no way for Tommy to prove any of it, even if he wanted to complain. *Drug dealers can't go to the cops…*

As he opened the door to his truck, the chill of the night air hit hard, sapping the oxygen from his lungs as he stepped out of the vehicle and buttoned his jacket. The coolness felt like a sledgehammer striking his chest, and it took several moments to collect himself. He lifted the collar on his black denim jacket to protect his neck and turned the light button off before locking the pickup. If he was coming back to it in a hurry, he didn't want the lights to give away his location.

He was thankful that the jacket had a flannel liner, but the frost was peeking through and chilling his body. Moving through the woods would warm him, but he silently prayed he wouldn't have to sit and hide watching for very long to determine what was going on with Tommy. His main goal was to get the tracker back before he was found.

Maybe this was a mistake? Should I have stayed at home? Something is wrong here. This isn't a drug deal. He's not meeting my Mr. Hager. I should leave. But he didn't leave. He trudged forward through the underbrush. His feet rustled with the dried leaves on the forest floor, as the pine needles scraped his face. Every footfall on the dried forest debris echoed through the still night, sounding like tiny gunshots. He cursed each one silently, wondering which would give him away and spook the two men before he could reach them. *Slow is smooth, smooth is fast Marion.* He told himself, trying to slow his pace and walk cautiously through the woods.

Tommy pulled the car into the clearing. The ground would be frozen, and he didn't want to fight the tree roots as well. It was going to be a long night digging into the frozen ground. After leaving the hotel, he stopped briefly and purchased a shovel, axe, and pickaxe from the garden section at a 24-hour store known for selling a little bit of everything. *Nothing illegal about a man planning a garden.* He rehearsed his answer to the police. *In the middle of the night…* He wanted to slap his forehead at the last notion crossing his brain.

The car rocked back and forth as he exited, like a canoe shifting on water. He pulled the tools from the back seat, along with a 6-pack of beer. Setting the beer on the bumper, he grabbed the pick, not bothering to determine which area would be the easiest to dig through. His first swing with the pick barely broke the ground and seemed to disappear into the brow-matted vegetation. He swung again with more force, but the frozen clay soil was like digging through a rock. Swing after swing after swing, he tried to breach the surface to the looser soil underneath. Swing after swing, his attempts failed.

Dirt particles flew and clung to the perspiration on his shirt and face. The cold air felt like a release of menthol as it wicked the heat from his skin. *Should have brought some food.* He had been digging for nearly 30 minutes when he had moved enough ground to bury a small dog. *Motherfucker,* he kept thinking to himself, *I should never have agreed to this.*

Laying the pick and shovel on the ground, he decided to take a look at the girl once more and satisfy his curiosity. Truthfully, he needed to catch his breath, and a beer sounded good at the moment. Popping the tab on the can, he opened the trunk and peered in at Lacey's figure. Part of her leg and buttocks had rolled out of the cloth sheet she was wrapped in, exposing her tanned skin to the frosty weather.

He salivated looking at her, wiping excess beer from his lips and chin. He contemplated the idea of taking a break and having another go at her. He wasn't into necrophilia by any means, but her curves were hard to resist. *Never done it with a corpse before,* he thought, thinking it was worth trying. He spent a few minutes staring at the body, justifying the action to himself. *She doesn't look dead...* he kept repeating in his mind. *She won't care. Not even sure why this is illegal.*

He rubbed a hand over her thigh, feeling the skin again as if they were back in the room. His giant palm looked like a catcher's mitt against her petite frame. Tommy was unsure about the rules of rigor mortis and when bodies were supposed to become stiff, but she was still loose and pliable, lying in the back of the trunk. He reached his other hand out to touch her exposed breasts. The warmth startled him at first, and he jumped back. *Aren't they supposed to be cold?*

Lacey's body was still warm to the touch. Not hot like a regular body would be, but Tommy expected it to be cold and stiff by that time. He was never one to enjoy reading but had seen enough crime shows to reasonably believe that the body had to be cool to the touch and at least starting to get stiff. She wasn't the first person he had disposed of, but he never paid much attention to the bodies of the others, mostly because they were men and wrapped in cloth or bags.

He just dumped them in the hole and left them. He wasn't

clear on the timelines and tried to think back to what the other bodies felt like. *How long before they got cold? How long until they were stiff? Did they stay stiff?* He realized there was a lot he never knew about a dead body. He thought to himself that they must have all been like that; he just hadn't noticed.

Taking another sip of his beer, he wished he had time to go at her again, but it would be dawn in a few hours, and digging in daylight would not be advisable. He threw his empty can in the backseat and grabbed the shovel and pick again, sauntering toward the hole. The digging was taking longer than he expected, but the soil was beginning to loosen. The shovel was making quicker work, but the clay soil was still so hard that he simply had to keep moving if he was going to finish before light. Pick, then shovel; then pick, then shovel… It seemed like an eternity, but the hole was getting deeper and wider at a faster pace.

Two hours went by, then the third. The beer was gone, and bottles littered the back seat. *Once the bitch was in the hole, it wouldn't matter as much if he got pulled over.* He thought to himself, trying to invigorate himself with false motivation. He drove under the speed limit the entire way there to avoid suspicion, but his nerves had been on fire during the drive, silently praying he wouldn't get stopped. His mind started relaxing, realizing it was almost over once the hole was finally deep enough that he struggled to climb out of it. It was deep enough and still dark out. The feeling of accomplishment engulfed his body, filling him with the same endorphins as if he'd run a marathon.

Tommy collapsed on the ground as he clambered out of the hole for the last time. Lying on the matted grass beside the grave, he panted with his arms outstretched beside him, his large belly bouncing up and down with each breath. His shirt was soaked in sweat, and his arms were shaking from not being fueled by anything more than his considerable fat deposits.

Dragging himself up the side of the car, he stared intently at Lacey. Lacking any feeling toward the girl, he knew he would still miss her figure. She was by far his favorite. He ignored any sense of appreciation for her and reached under her arms to yank her from the trunk and let her body collapse on the ground.

Despite his size, Tommy lacked any substantial muscle capacity and struggled to drag her to the hole. Panting beside her, he was interrupted in his quest to drop her in. *She fucking moved*. He wasn't positive, but he knew he saw her twitch. He watched for a moment. It was a moment that seemed to drag on and felt like an hour. He watched until he saw her eyelid twitch and her finger move again.

Fuck! She's alive. He reached for his cell phone to call Si, but it was no use. He had been out of service for more than an hour. It was one of the reasons he picked that location; he knew the cell towers couldn't pinpoint his position out there even if the body was found. Close to it maybe, but they couldn't get him to within an hour's drive of the body. Besides, that lot was privately owned and sat in the middle of farmland. The nearest house was a mile in any direction. She could wake up screaming, and no one would hear her.

Fuck! He screamed to himself, debating about what to do with her lying beside the hole. A blow to the head with the shovel would be quick and not considerably messy, as opposed to sticking the pick in her face. A part of him wanted to try and get her to a hospital. After all, if she lived, he'd still get to fuck her when he came through town. But he knew instantly that it would never work. Dragging a drugged-out whore to the hospital would garner way too many questions that he couldn't answer, and if she died, they'd then have a body tying him to the murder. Ultimately, he chose the only option available to him.

Tommy grabbed the wooden handle of the dirt-stained shovel and held it like a baseball bat winding up for the swing. *Sorry Lacey…* He thought to himself as he swung down with all his force to cave her skull. *Sorry, it came to this…*

Ewan couldn't sleep. His mind was occupied with images of the dead whore, her face disfigured and covered in blood, her lifeless body hanging above him in the warehouse and the juice of her life pouring out over him. His erection at the thought of it was on the verge of exploding. He sat with his pants off, letting the cold plastic of the bar stool chill his hamstrings. He held his member in his hand, afraid to touch it more than just a little to prolong his moment.

A mirror sat across from him so that he could see himself in these moments of relief. There was a certain voyeuristic aspect to viewing himself with no one else watching that excited him further. The slight pain of his engorged testicles reminded him of the feeling of pre-climax just before his prize would pass into death.

He squeezed his scrotum to the point of causing pain so he could stop the erection from releasing for the next few moments. Observing himself in the mirror, he was absorbed and fascinated by his own body. He was muscular, with a layer of softness over it from a sedentary job. His pectoral muscles were still well–defined, and he was fortunate to not look soft as his fat tended to store dispersed over his body, rather than collecting at his stomach.

The receding hairline was more prominent then, showing his dark brown hair without a hint of gray to it at present. He was slightly shorter than average and was unable to place his feet on the ground while sitting on the stool. His toes rested on the chair supports as he watched his erection throb.

Finally ready to release, he continued to squeeze his penis, thinking about how contorted she would look and what her body would look like suspended by its feet as he inserted his penis into her lifeless, lipless mouth. He was so grateful to have the shower there. This time, he could make as much of a mess as his heart desired.

He would enter from behind as he choked her and strangled the last bit of life while he released into her. He'd spend some time just resting and marveling at her lifeless body before lowering her figure and raising it upside down by her feet.

Years ago, he had killed a girl while she was tied to a bed frame upside down. It turned out to be a huge mistake because she kept passing out from the blood rushing to her head. He had learned from her to only invert them after they were dead, which provided a satisfaction similar to that of a second copulation with them.

Feeling their lifeblood flowing through him, their energy erecting his body, making him stronger and more powerful, he thought of the other girls in the past, the memories fading of each moment of conquest as a drug addict's high is never as good as the first one. She would be different… His lady in red was exquisite and would give him the same feeling as his first gift had.

In the past, he hadn't been as selective about his targets, but from then on, he would only choose specimens that were even more flattering to his taste and appealed to him as much, or more than the last one. The other girls seemed ugly in comparison to the girl in the red dress. She would be his ultimate prize, even better than his first one all those years ago.

His penis began to go flaccid, trying to pull up older memories. She would be his; she belonged to him. He would always remember her, having forgotten all but a few of the girls. That prize was special and would be one to carry with him. Only with the special ones could he draw any meaningful recollection. But there she was again… the girl in red flashing across his mind.

Her imaginary screams imprinted on his mind soon faded, and he couldn't hold the memory that hadn't yet happened. *She's mine. My property. My pleasure. She belongs to me.* The moment had passed without a climax. His penis was flaccid again, leaving him frustrated and demoralized. *She's mine!* His mind was screaming in frustration at losing his erection. "Fuck you," he said, looking down at his dwindling penis.

Tommy's room was disgusting. The hotel wasn't known for its clean rooms, as was typical for that kind of low-rent hotel, but Tommy was a slob. He had been there less than a day and beer cans, wrappers, and trash littered the room. Si felt like he needed a shower from sitting on the bed.

What a pig. He thought to himself, as he looked around the room, waiting for Tommy. It was nearing half past 5 in the morning, and his car wasn't in the lot yet. Si worried that Tommy had got picked up by cops already, or some other issue had arisen. Tommy was notoriously a bit of an idiot, and the idea that he was drinking a beer and speeding with a dead hooker in his trunk hadn't occurred to Si until after his car had pulled out.

Tommy would cut a deal in a heartbeat, telling them he was forced to do it out of fear. If he got pulled over for a broken taillight, he would cut a deal… *But wouldn't they be here already? What the hell happened? Why isn't he back? Maybe, he's gone further up North or is struggling to dig in the frozen ground. Calm down, Si. There's a logical explanation for this.*

He wasn't sure whether he would kill Tommy or not yet. Disposing of a body that big could prove to be more hassle than it was worth, and the DNA evidence on the body would lead to Tommy anyway, so there was little risk to Si leaving him alive. He could just as easily play stupid with the detectives. As far as they were concerned, Si was an employer with a legitimate escort business, and one of his girls disappeared. It's not uncommon in that industry, and there's no law saying an employer has to file a missing person report if someone doesn't show up for work.

It was a bit of a Hobson's choice. Take it or leave it/kill him or leave him. No matter the decision he made, nothing could be done without Tommy returning to the hotel. He sat in patient silence, waiting for the car to pull back into the lot. He watched intently through the grime-covered window. *Where are you, you fat fuck?*

Sitting patiently, he decided Tommy wasn't worth killing, but he absolutely could not honor the deal he had made. A free girl, whenever he wanted, was simply far too much to ask for. He would give him a few free nights and then deal with him like any of the pathetic Johns who didn't pay their bill.

Si was anxious, and the feeling was hard to shrug off. In the morning, he would go to the gym and burn off the nervous energy, but right then, he needed something to occupy his mind. He wasn't a smoker but decided to bum a cigarette from the nightstand. He lit it up and enjoyed the moment as the smoke filled his lungs.

Cigarette smoke had a fullness to it that cigars and pipes lacked. The smoke filled your body as if it were an empty vessel begging to be topped off. No sooner was it to arrive, then it left again, leaving the recipient feeling empty until that next drag filled their life again. The smoke consumed his lungs and engorged his body with its luscious aroma. The enjoyment was in the ritual of the process. The smoke filling his lungs and watching it being exhaled, the lighting of the cigarette, and even opening the pack was part of the fun. The cigarette calmed his nerves slightly as the ember glowed brighter with each drag.

Pacing the room, he watched, intentionally looking out the window, waiting for the Honda to pull back in. The lot was empty, and no lights could be seen on the horizon at the end of the road. *Where are you, you fat fuck?*

4

"Getting away with murder is easy… Just don't tell anyone."
–Dr. Spencer Reed

A pain pierced Tommy's leg, and warm blood oozed down his thigh. "FUCK!" he screamed in horror, holding his leg. "What the fuck was that!" he shouted as his body collapsed to the ground, dropping the shovel mid-swing. It was agonizing; the wound was warm, as if something was smoldering inside the cavity. *I'VE BEEN SHOT!* The screaming in his head dulled the sound of anything around him.

Before he could move again, he heard a voice from behind him.

"Don't move."

"Who the hell are you?" Tommy asked, unable to contort his body around to see his shooter.

"Shut up!" Marion snapped.

His attacker was standing over the body of the girl. Marion instantly recognized her lifeless body and instinctively bent down and checked the pulse in her neck. It was weak, but he could feel it. *Shit.* He thought, kicking himself for not intervening earlier. Assuming Tommy was burying a body, he stayed back to snap pictures for the police. He was too far away to see any movement from Lacey, but seeing Tommy with the shovel told him that the girl was alive. He had waited until he was certain that she was going to be bludgeoned to death with the shovel before firing.

Seeing Tommy raise the shovel over his head, he knew the girl was alive and was forced to draw his pistol and fire. It was a hard shot to make with a snub-nose .38 special from half a football field away, and it had to be quick. He was lucky he even got the leg at that distance, quietly cursing himself again for not grabbing a larger pistol. The snub-nose pistol had however done its job and stopped her murder. *At least for now…*

Now he had a series of issues to deal with; taking the girl to the hospital meant getting the police involved always looked bad for PIs, especially ones using GPS trackers illegally. She could die in his care if he took her home, which would be worse. And he certainly couldn't let Tommy go in any situation because the girl wouldn't be safe.

He pondered the scene for a moment, trying to determine what he was going to do, while he wrapped the girl in his coat. She wouldn't last long out there without a jacket as bitterly cold as it was, and he needed to get her warm. Barely conscious, she needed the Naloxone that he kept in his trauma kit at the truck.

Not wasting time, Marion scooped the girl in his arms, deciding at a minimum that he had to get her to the truck. She was petite and lightweight despite her curvy figure. Marion supported her head with his chest. Carrying her through the woods might kill her just through the sheer shock, trauma, cold, and time it took to carry her the mile back to his truck, including the physical exertion the toll would take on his body with outstretched arms carrying dead weight for the distance.

He laid her delicately in the back seat of Tommy's car. "Keys," he snapped at Tommy.

"Fuck you! Get me a doctor!" Tommy screamed, agonizing on the ground.

Marion pressed his heel into the wound on Tommy's leg. "KEYS!" he screamed, watching Tommy writhe in pain. A part of him had hoped Tommy would refuse and allow him to continue hurting the pathetic excuse of a man on the ground in front of him. He wanted him to pay for the things Tommy had done, pay for harming the girl, selling drugs, and being related to his pedophile brother. To a certain extent, Marion wanted Tommy to pay the price for his own sins as if he could place his own guilt and turmoil on Tommy.

The pain in his leg was excruciating even without a heel digging into it. The bullet wound felt as if a hot piece of iron was sizzling inside of him and pulsing repeatedly atop the nerve endings. "Ok!" he shouted, yanking the keys from his pocket and tossing them toward the car.

Marion released the pressure before kicking Tommy in his stomach to satisfy some of his own moral compass. He ran to the keys and scooped them up before climbing hastily into the driver's seat. As he inserted the keys, the car cranked over allowing him to blast the heat on the girl.

"I'm getting her to a hospital. When I come back, you'll still be here… Tommy." He added the name at the end to be sure Tommy knew.

"How do you know…?" Tommy asked as Marion got in the car, but he didn't hear the end of the sentence. No service on his phone meant Marion couldn't navigate with that.

The roads looked identical to one another, and he was somewhat worried that he wouldn't be able to make it back to Tommy's body. It took 15 minutes for him to see the glow of the rear reflectors when he pulled in behind his Tundra. Sprinting in a panic, he started the ignition to get it warm and grabbed the Naloxone nasal injector from his trauma kit.

The Fentanyl crisis in the South East forced the Governor to offer free doses to the general public. Keeping them in your bag in that profession just seemed prudent, and it wasn't the first occasion he had needed it. Climbing into the back seat with the girl, he squirted the dose in her nose. The response was nearly instantaneous, taking less than a minute for the effects to hit her.

She didn't bolt upright in the seat, but her eyes opened slowly, and she was alert. Putting a flashlight to her eyes, he could see her pupils responding. "What's your name?" he asked her several times before she answered. He could barely understand as it passed over her lips in a weak breath.

"Lacey."

"Ok, Lacey. You're safe now. I'm going to pick you up and move you to another vehicle. I have to leave you for a minute in there. Lock the doors, and I'll be back as soon as I can."

She didn't answer but nodded her head; he knew she understood. She was light and easy to maneuver out of the vehicle and into the front seat. He leaned the seat back, grabbed his old Army wool blanket from under the rear seat, and wrapped her in it. "I'll be back," he said, and without waiting for acknowledgment, he closed the door.

The overdose had slowed her breathing to the point that they assumed she was dead. In the trunk of the car, Lacey was becoming hypothermic from the cold environment, causing her body to slow even more. A physician in one of his trauma classes in the Army told them all, "They're not dead until they're warm and dead."

The Naloxone would only last for about an hour in her system, and she would need to be on an IV drip if she was dosed with fentanyl. He hoped silently to himself that she had just overdosed on milder pain meds and that the effects of the dosage would wear off around the same time as the

Naloxone.

The drive back to Tommy's location was faster without having to think about the roads. He wasn't sure what he was going to do with Tommy. The thought of just killing Tommy had been cruising through his mind the entire drive there. Marion had killed men in the war, and he could stomach the decision, but he still didn't like the idea of killing him in cold blood. It was prudent, practical, and preemptive, but it didn't feel right. *Then again,* he thought to himself, *son-of-a-bitch deserves worse.* He knew he would have to ditch the pistol and dispose of the evidence so the slug couldn't be traced back to him, but that was a minor issue at that point in time, luck beings somewhat on his side because the 1911 would have forced him to dispose of a gun he loved and find the empty casing in the wood line.

Pulling the vehicle into the field where Tommy's body lay, he found that it seemed lifeless, as if the blood had been drained. He placed the car in park, still unclear of what his options were, but he double-checked his pistol. Marion kept thinking to himself that he couldn't be dead but must have just passed out. He'd shot people in the chest, who had lived, and it seemed surreal that Tommy could have died from a leg wound.

As he hopped out of the car, the cool air hit his skin the moment the door opened, and Tommy didn't move or make a sound. Before addressing Tommy, he decided to grab the tracker so that he didn't forget about it. Marion kept one eye on Tommy while reaching blindly underneath the car until his fingers grasped the familiar feel of the device.

He was staring at Tommy when he noticed the blood pooling around the body. Tommy was sitting in a puddle of it, not moving. *Too much blood,* he thought to himself. The scene looked like someone had poured gallons of red syrup on the ground underneath the body. The realization occurred to him but took a moment to process. He had hit the femoral artery. It was a small nick, which is why he hadn't noticed the spurting, but it was enough to cause Tommy to die of blood loss in the 30 minutes it took for him to return.

Marion stared at the body, somewhat irritated with himself for not putting a tourniquet on the wound before he left. Had he subconsciously wanted to kill him… or maybe it was conscious. He knew he was hoping that Tommy would die but logically didn't think it was likely. Tommy's death may be more convenient, not having to send him to a hospital and having a slug removed that matched his gun.

Uncertain if he was going to kill Tommy anyway, he had the time on the drive back to construe a plan in the event he had decided to end his existence. No one would be looking for Tommy, and certainly not out there. The vehicle was truthfully more of an issue than the body. Fortunately, the hole was already dug, but he would need to hurry; dawn was coming and fast. He was already sensing the creeping of the light beyond the horizon, and within 30 minutes, he would be working without the cover of any darkness to shadow his movements.

Marion pushed both arms underneath Tommy's torso and started rolling the body into the hole. *Son-of-a-bitch, he's heavy,* but the hole was only 2 feet from where Tommy had died. Still, it took considerable effort to roll the substantial massive-of-a-normal body that was literally dead weight. In this case, his knees and feet kept sliding on the patches of dried grass beneath him, stopping any forward momentum. Rolling over the edge of the grave, the body hit the dirt bottom with a dull thud as if it were a sack of wheat slamming to the ground. Filling it in took less than 10 minutes, with Marion sprinting with the shovel and perspiring from the effort. *Literally dug your own grave.*

Being an investigator had its advantages. Over the years,

the state homicide department contracted with him on multiple occasions to do grunt work on murder investigations. This experience had taught him that satellites were used to find grave sites and fresh dirt being moved in a way that would suggest a body was there. He also knew he had likely left trace evidence in the car. Smart criminals buried their victims in a hole that was deep and narrow to place the body upright rather than long and narrow to where the satellite artificial intelligence (AI) could determine that it was a possible gravesite. In that case, he was using what he had, and he and the girl simply didn't have the time for another grave to be dug.

Once the hole was filled, Marion parked the car directly over the top of the grave to block the satellite imagery. The first rain would wash away the blood; he just had to hope that no one noticed it before then. It was cold, but fall was still the second rainy season for that area, so it would be less than a week to ten days before a storm would come through.

The biggest risk was the fire, but it would be absolutely necessary. He climbed under the car, pulled out his pocketknife, and began cutting the gas line while filling each of the beer bottles he found. He used some of them to spray down the inside of the car and seats with gasoline. Grabbing one final bottle, he opened the hood and sprayed it over the entire block. A wire from the harness gave him the chance to spark it across the battery terminals a few times until it ignited the fumes in a small explosion, driving him back from the vehicle.

Marion watched from a distance as the flames consumed the engine compartment and then the rest of the vehicle. It would burn for hours as fire department protocols generally stated to let the vehicles burn. There was little reason to waste resources on extinguishing it, and they were difficult fires to put out. It was a typical policy to contain the fire. In that case, he doubted anyone would notice the flame, especially with the sun beginning to crest the horizon. Hopefully, the smoke wouldn't attract any attention. In all likelihood, the car wouldn't be found by the property owner until they moved the cows to that position in the spring.

The ground underneath would be scorched from the inferno and as long as no one paid attention, the disturbed dirt would be blackened and not raise suspicion of the body directly underneath. The heat of the fire would cook the blood making it nearly unrecognizable until the rain washed it away. If he could make it to spring, any chance of trace evidence would be washed away, and no one would ever find Tommy's body.

Eventually, a farmer or rancher would see the abandoned car and have it towed to a scrap yard and the grass would cover the spot. Tommy's body would be dissolved by the worms and beetles. Every trace of his existence would disappear with only bones and a single .38 slug remaining behind to tell the tale. He kicked himself silently for not retrieving the slug, but the gun would be disposed of anyway, so it was an irrelevant point.

No one would ever be hurt by Tommy Johnson again: no hookers taken advantage of, or overdose victims from poorly cut products. Tommy's lifeless body had been laid to rest with all his sins carried with him. *Some justice…* he thought to himself. Marion didn't stand by to contemplate the issue any further. He sprinted off into the woods and was gone as quickly as he had arrived.

Ewan knew that driving across town that soon after visiting the warehouse was a risk, but he had to get his eyes on the girl again. She occupied his thoughts and consumed his mind, and he had to see her again. Being able to fantasize about it was every bit as much of his ritual as the killing and the preparation. Usually, he would have taken a picture, but that scenario presented itself differently with her living at the crime scene. Originally, he thought it would take weeks to find a suitable subject, but fortune smiled on him.

Having been left sexually frustrated and unable to reach a climax presented its own obstacle in this case. Ewan was frustrated and anxious, lacking any semblance of release. His mind was becoming increasingly infatuated with thoughts of the woman in red. No substitute would do; it needed to be her. She would have to agonize over him the same way he did for her. She needed him… needed to be his gift… needed to be freed from his mind.

Ultimately, in the background of his mind, he had very little consideration for society, but the end result of his prizes was always a benefit to the community. Thinking of them disgusted him. They weren't women but filthy whores. He didn't always target professional prostitutes, but all the women were whores in his mind, opening themselves to anyone that met their fancy. *They should thank me.* Disposing of their body had become as much a part of good counter-forensics as it was in riding himself of their filth. He hated his desire for them as much as he despised them in that moment.

Her being a whore was simply pragmatic and coincidental in that no one would report her missing. A streak of panic shot through his body when he realized for the first time that there would be no missing persons report in the newspaper for her. No second coming for his fantasies. No trophy to collect. He would have to take something, maybe a locket of her hair or a piece of jewelry.

Trophies were risky and never a part of his *modus operandi* for fear of getting caught with them. But that one would require an exception; she would require him to keep something to remember the moment—to immortalize his prize for his mantel. He had never thought of trophies much before and allowed himself to keep only small newspaper clips. Either the obituary or a missing persons report would suffice.

There was some allure to the obituary over the missing reports as it gave him the satisfaction of knowing the wound he had inflicted on others. The psychological trauma and carnage he brought to their families and loved ones was sometimes worth the body being found. The idea of sending a loving parent recordings of his actions as they screamed and cried out for them was enticing and one he considered in the past. Ultimately, the thought of getting caught prohibited the action. He knew he had to control himself to keep from spiraling into an infinite rage.

It was still dark outside when he backed into the lot across the street. He needed to wait for the girl to come out, needed to see her again. He felt like a teenager waiting for his crush to appear at the lot behind the schoolyard. She never showed. Hour after hour ate through the clock on his dashboard. Dawn broke, and the first business cars began passing by. It wasn't a busy street and only provided easement for a few local companies. He waited patiently for her to show; his irritation and anger fumed within him. *Where is she? She should be heading home by now!* His head was screaming.

Expecting to see her at any moment, he couldn't contain his anxiety. Sweating and panting, Ewan drove across the street and parked his car behind the warehouse, at the opening in the wall. His adrenaline was running as he exited the vehicle and pushed through the hole. Panicked uncontrolled motions made more noise than he would have generally allowed. His body was sprinting, and his heart was pounding out of his chest.

Where was she!? His mind screamed and rattled inside his head. She wasn't here. He couldn't feel her watching him and didn't sense her presence. She wasn't there, and he knew he hadn't missed her. There were no eyes on him. He was alone. His senses were good; he knew when he was being watched, and no one was looking at him right then.

Panic flowed through his veins like steroids through a racehorse. First, anxiety and then anger suffocated him from the inside, making his skin ache. The anger replaced any emotion within him like a rabid animal drooling on itself. The energy coursed from his mouth as he salivated in fury. Sweat beaded down his face with each drop striking the floor where her blood should be.

"FUCK! SHIT! MOTHER FUCKER!" he screamed, furious at letting her go. He couldn't contain his rage. If she were there then, his control would be gone, the sexual gratification no longer existing within him, and she would pay the price as he beat her to death. He could imagine his fist punching through her face, smashing it and hitting the concrete behind her, crushing her skull with each contortion of his arm into her body.

"WHERE ARE YOU BITCH?!" His frustration stirred between tears and a burning hate seated deeply in his soul. He couldn't control his emotions any longer and collapsed to the floor in a blubbering heap. Curling his knees into his chest, he assumed the fetal position while his body convulsed in anguish. Unable to stand until his anger and his tantrum subsided, he was on the ground like a small child being denied candy at the grocery store.

His tears leaped between frustration, panic, fear, and failure. Each emotion came over like a dark wave crashing into the coast, one right after another, striking the surface of a rocky beach. There was anger for her not being where she was supposed to be, as well as panic and fear that he might not find her again. *No…* That wasn't an option. He had to find her. The lady in red was his prize; she belonged to him.

He sat on the floor for nearly an hour—afraid to move for

fear of collapsing again and afraid to stand and leave, fearing she would arrive after his departure. He was stuck in a Morton's Fork, unable to decide knowing the outcome was the same... she wasn't going to be there. The waves of emotion began to settle, and he was able to clamber to his feet. Ewan decided his only option was to come back the next morning and try again. Maybe, she was off... *Do whores get a day off?* He didn't know the protocols. Maybe, she was with someone, and it was taking longer than expected. Regardless, he would keep trying until he found her.

Walking across the concrete floor toward the opening, he noticed the beauty of the place he was in, the metal rusting and fading with scrap materials strewn about. The roof had leaked in several areas, and birds nested in the steel rafters. It would be a depressing location for anyone else, but for him, it was the essence of his life, a standing building broken, torn, deteriorated, and defiled beyond use or recognition. It only remained to serve his dark purpose then.

As he pulled back the metal panel at the entry, the sun hit his face as a blow landed on the left side of his jaw, and another struck the center of his chest, pushing him back into the building and knocking him to the ground. He gasped for breath, peering at the haloed silhouette in front of him. Si pushed through the opening and kicked Ewan again in the stomach, causing him to vomit on the floor.

Ewan's fascination with pain was limited to his distinct taste and satisfaction at seeing it in others. He didn't care for it. There wasn't a fiber within him that was masochistic or even that maintained a sense of pride to try and fight back. He only attempted to submit to his attackers in whatever manner provided the best chance of remaining in existence after that moment.

"Who the fuck are you?" Si commanded. "Where's the girl?" His voice was firm but not a yell, like a man speaking to a small child. He kicked again in the stomach. "Where is she?"

Ewan spit blood as he tried to answer and scrambled to his knees. "I don't know."

"Then, why are you here?" Si asked, punching into Ewan's ribs and knocking him to the ground again.

"I was looking for her," he shouted back, holding his hands in a surrender position, so as to not be struck again.

"Why? You needed a piece of ass? A little of that cake?"

"Yes."

"How'd you know she lived here?"

"I followed her home!"

Not satisfied with the answer, Si punched again, striking him in the face with his right hand. He reached into Ewan's pocket and grabbed his driver's license.

"Come back here again… Ewan Maddox," he said, reading from the license, "and I'll kill you."

Si emptied the cash from the wallet, stuffing it into his front pocket, and threw the billfold at Ewan.

"I'll keep this," he said, holding the license in his hand as he walked back through the opening in the wall, leaving Ewan writhing again in pain. *Stupid fuck!* Ewan's mind screamed at him. *You'll see me again.*

When Si reached his long-term rented hotel room, he wasn't sure of his emotions. Fear, anger, and confusion swirled in his mind. *Where the hell is Tommy?* He paced angrily in his room and texted Kelly to join him. Kelly was one of his girls, like the others, but she happened to be close with Lacey.

He wanted to call and text Tommy again. He typed the words on his phone: WHERE ARE YOU? *You fat fuck!* He added in his head before closing the phone and setting it on the end table. Calling Tommy too many times would raise suspicion if anyone looked at the phone records. As it stood, he was just a client, and some communication could be justified.

Still pacing anxiously across the room, he heard Kelly knock on the door, opening it without waiting for his answer. Si didn't acknowledge her presence; he didn't have to. The girls knew why they were summoned. Lacey had been a favorite among his clients, but he had always preferred Kelly.

She was a tall woman, nearly Si's height, but slender with small breasts and a round backside, the only girl to wear low heels to avoid towering over the Johns or her pimp, fearing she might emasculate men with sensitive egos. She had pale skin, though not sickly, and long, curly blonde hair. She was from somewhere in Eastern Europe and had a thick accent. Si thought maybe she was from the Czech Republic, but he couldn't be certain. Scandinavian heritage was evident in her striking looks. Kelly Slecha was not as popular as Lacey but was still a favorite among many of his regular customers.

Si needed his release at the moment and cared little for the Johns' opinions on which girl they wanted. A mixture of frustration and anxiety boiled within him. "Shut the door," he said firmly, not waiting for a response from her as he unzipped his jeans and dropped them to his ankles.

Kelley didn't need to be told what to do. "Where's Lacey?" she asked him, before getting on her knees.

"Bitch is dead. Unless you want to join her, I don't have time for questions." He was always stern with the girls and didn't like being questioned, particularly when things were not going his way. Answering a direct question would give her a moment of dominance over him, one he absolutely couldn't allow.

Kelly didn't need to be told twice, having been down that road in the past. She loved Lacey. They weren't blood-related, but they looked out for each other as sisters do. Kelly stifled her tears and thoughts, knowing she would have to grieve on her own time. A girl missing only had one answer: she had been either sold or killed. *I'm sorry, Lacey…* She thought to herself. She would always miss her, but she was happy that Lacey was finally free.

Si thought to himself as he enjoyed her talents. *I'll call Steve and see if Tommy was arrested.* He needed to understand what happened. At the very least, if Tommy was arrested, he would know within an hour. Beyond that, he would have to pay Steve and the detective to find out what happened because nothing else made sense. There was no scenario he could envision that accounted for a missing 300-pound drug dealer and a dead whore. DO YOU HAVE TOMMY JOHNSON IN CUSTODY? he typed out on his phone before pressing send and laying back on the bed to absorb a moment of pleasure in what had become a terrible day.

Marion sat with Lacey; she was asleep on his guest bed, covered with blankets and breathing steadily. He had given her another dose of Naloxone when they arrived at the house, but it was probably unnecessary. Her breathing seemed normal, and she was in and out of sleep, remaining conscious. Whatever was in her system was fast-acting and passing through. *Thank God it wasn't Fentanyl.*

"I don't know if you can hear me, but you're safe here. I'll be in the other room if you need me, and then I have to go out for a bit."

Marion stood and watched over her for a brief moment. Lacey's hair was as jet black as he had observed from across the street and didn't appear to be dyed. She had a light olive tan encapsulating her entire body. He felt somewhat ashamed as he placed her naked body under the sheets and had to force himself not to look at her. Her features were nearly perfect, but he couldn't help but pity her as she lay helpless in the bed.

Her shoulder had been dislocated for an unknown reason, and it took some force to set it back in place while she was passed out. He had never performed the procedure on someone else but had had his own come out of joint once while boxing and knew the procedure for getting it back in place. Closing the door, Marion left her to rest and deal with the fallout from the evening.

Destroying the pistol was his priority. Silently, he was grateful again for not having to use his favorite 1911 and dispose of it. The .38 special was cheap in comparison and replaceable. He went to his office desk and prepared some tools for the job. He pulled the pistol from his appendix holster and laid it in front of him before retrieving his tools from a shelf in the carport.

The gun held five bullets, with only one being expended. Marion's experience working alongside various police departments on many homicide investigations gave him a solid foundation in forensics. The gun could be traced back to the firearm if the body was discovered and the slug was removed. However, there was no database of fired bullets, so it was a simple process of disposing of the casing and making the gun untraceable.

He pulled an electric rotary tool and a rat-tail file out of his toolbox and then unloaded the pistol. The four unfired bullets couldn't be used against him, and he had another gun that used them, so owning the ammunition wouldn't be probable cause that could be used against him. Shoving them into his desk drawer, he ground the base of the shell casing off so it couldn't be matched to the firing pin and separated the primer from the casing with a punch. Grabbing a steel paperweight, he smashed the casing flat, ensuring he split the brass and set it aside.

Various acids and electronics could be used to re-image a ground-out serial number, so he used the rotary tool to completely grind away the spot that held the serial number. A small flathead screwdriver removed the cover, and he was able to file the firing pin into an unrecognizable chunk. Finally, he used the rat-tail file, ramming it down the barrel so the rifling couldn't be used to match it to the slug. Working the file, he ground so much of the barrel that the grooves were almost completely gone.

He placed all the parts and bullet casing into a plastic sandwich bag and wiped them down to avoid fingerprints. Collecting the pieces, Marion threw them under the seat of his truck and drove out to the county, searching for ponds, streams, and a small lake to dispose of each item individually. He spent the next hour discarding each piece into a separate water source miles away from his home. Every component found its way further from his house until only the frame and barrel were left. That was the most damning piece of evidence. Current science wouldn't trace it back, but who knew how forensics would develop in the future? He didn't want to take any chances.

He began the long trek to Smith Lake, which was roughly an hour in the opposite direction. The water would corrode even stainless steel over time and the gun was nearly unrecognizable as a firearm, being disassembled and destroyed as it was.

Stopping and walking out on a dock would only draw attention, but Smith Lake had a large bridge where he could toss it from the window without anyone being the wiser. In a few months, he would report the gun as missing, and the water and nitrogen-rich soil at the bottom of the lake would finish the rest.

His thoughts about everything that had happened consumed him during the steady motion of the vehicle's tires thumping against the asphalt. Maybe, he was better off calling the police and dealing with the fallout. He could have placed the GPS in his trunk and told them he just stored it there for his job… It was a reasonable explanation. In the end, a death while committing a felony would be charged as a minimum of manslaughter, and he would likely serve prison time, lose his life savings, and have his home repossessed.

Ultimately, he wasn't sure why he decided to conceal it. Maybe his instincts to protect the girl were stronger, or maybe he wanted to protect himself. One thing was for certain: neither of their lives was worth risking for someone of Tommy's caliber. Marion knew what she was. But he wasn't disgusted with her, nor did he blame her for her circumstances. *Surely she hadn't chosen this life; surely this wasn't the life she dreamed of as a little girl.* Ultimately, whatever led her there was beyond his understanding. Maybe that was God's way of giving him purpose again after leaving the Army. *God…* he thought to himself.

It was a subject he hadn't considered in a long time. He had grown up as a strict Catholic but began questioning his beliefs after witnessing some of the atrocities soldiers often witnessed. Certainly, if God existed, then that was more than coincidental and was coming together for a purpose. However, if his agnostic proclivities were correct, then he may have royally fucked himself.

***

Disposing of the firearm proved uneventful, and Marion was soon home, drinking coffee and watching the morning sun from his office couch. He was exhausted, having been awake for most of the night, and would need to sleep soon or risk crashing. Lacey had slept solidly through the night. He had made it a point to check on her periodically; she was breathing steadily and moving in her sleep. Rest and time to recover would heal her. If she was addicted to opioids, the next few days of withdrawal would be rough on her.

The drive had given him ample time to debate what to tell her. Covering a homicide was one thing; admitting it to a girl he didn't know was another entirely. He hadn't fully decided on what excuse he would give her for being at his house and how he happened across her. If she ever decided to dig into Tommy, she could potentially find out the truth. *Maybe, she's not that clever.*

He pondered the options until he heard a noise from her room just after 10:00 am. He wasn't sure what it was, but she must be awake; the thump sounded like someone trying to leave the bed but unable to fully control their movement. His house still had the old-style brass doorknobs, and it made a high-pitched scraping noise when he cracked the door.

She was sitting upright, with the pillow holding her head up and resting her back against the headboard. The water glass he left for her had been knocked to the floor, indicating to him the source of the noise. Her eyes were a beautiful green color and seemed to be caught somewhere between curiosity, uncertainty, and fear. Even under the covers, her figure showed through, teasing Marion's imagination.

"You don't need to be afraid. You're safe here," he reassured her.

"I heard you say that last night." He heard her voice truly for the first time. It was beautiful, though not of a distinguishable singing quality, and had a slight raspiness to it, like a smoker's voice. Only, that was natural and not artificially made through years of abusing her body.

"Oh… I wasn't sure if you'd remember. Or even if you'd heard me." He was surprised, thinking she had been sleeping.

"Who are you? Why am I here?" She was still somewhat groggy but becoming more alert by the second.

"My name is Marion Gamble; most people call me

Mary…"

"Mary?" she interrupted.

"Yeah. When you get a name like Marion, it's easier as a child to lean into it rather than fight it. Everyone's always just called me Mary."

"I think I'll stick with Marion if you don't mind."

"Suit yourself."

"Why am I here?"

"What do you remember about last night?" he asked, hesitating to answer the question. He needed to know what she knew so he could come up with an appropriate response.

She thought back to the man in her room, remembering her shoulder. She reached up and grabbed it, noticing the soreness then. The arm was comfortably back in its socket. The joint was swollen but usable.

"I put it back in its socket while you were passed out. I was afraid it would lose circulation if I didn't… and it didn't look like either of us could deal well with a trip to the hospital."

"Us? Why does it matter to you?"

He thought about what he was going to tell her. Unable to divulge everything, she would need some answers.

"I'm a private investigator. I happened to be tailing the man who was intent on burying you. He noticed you moving before burying you, and I stopped him before he could finish."

"Who was taking me?"

"A guy named Tommy Johnson."

"Tommy," she said, surprised. "Why him?"

"I have no idea, but I stopped him, gave you some meds to counteract the opioids you had taken, and your breathing returned to normal. You rested here for the night, and now this is where we are."

"How did you know I had taken anything?"

"I didn't, but unresponsive people will respond to

naloxone if you have opioids in your system. If you don't, nothing happens, so it's a clear indicator. There was no risk in giving it to you, and had you not responded, it would have indicated a more severe injury. If that had been the case, we would have had no option but to go to the hospital. If that had happened, you would be answering questions to a district attorney about your… profession." He paused, unsure of how to continue.

"It's okay. I'm well aware of what I am," she said, emotionless and almost stern.

Marion took a seat in the wooden rocking chair in the corner. It was a family heirloom that had been passed down, one that he had been personally cared for in as an infant.

"Maybe… what you are is not the same thing as what you do." He wasn't sure if it was a line to feed someone in a vulnerable state or if he truly meant it. Up until that moment, he hadn't considered her as anything more than what her profession advertised. "Either way, you would be discussing drug use, where you got them, who your pimp is, and any manner of other crimes they could throw at you to get you to talk."

"That doesn't answer why YOU didn't want to go to the hospital," she said, not relenting on the subject. Her voice was soft but skeptical. Obviously, she was used to working with people who had an angle for intervening. *Did she think I wanted a free go at her or something… As if sex was the currency she had to offer.*

"I was using a GPS tracker on Tommy's car. They aren't legal anymore for PIs to use. Having been found out, I would have lost my license and possibly served some jail time." It wasn't a complete lie, but he was able to leave out the part about Tommy. A dead man with a hooker knowing the truth at a minimum gave her a bargaining chip with a DA if she was picked up in the future.

"Wherc's Tommy now?"

"No idea," he lied. I left him out there when I brought you home.

"Shit!" It came out of her mouth in a forceful whisper. She tried to stand but couldn't support herself yet and was unsteady on her feet. Marion bolted forward to catch her.

"It's okay. I've got you," he said softly, easing her back into bed while holding the nape of her neck.

"I have to go. People will be looking for me! If they find me here, they'll kill us both! Thank you for everything, but I have to leave right now." Her voice was panicky. Her calmness in being somewhere strange had given him the impression she didn't scare easily, but she was terrified of something.

"It's okay," he reassured her. "No one will find you here. You're not a prisoner; you can leave anytime you want."

"No. Si will be furious, and I'll owe him money, but he won't kill me."

Marion couldn't tell her about Tommy, but if she returned, he knew she would be killed. She was a liability at best and easily replaceable. Equally important, she would be forced to tell them about him and this place, and he wouldn't be safe there.

"You'll be killed one way or the other, Lacey." He had given more away in that one sentence and couldn't hide the gravity in his voice. He hurried, trying to change the subject, hoping she wouldn't notice his slip-up.

"I'll run to town and get you some clothes today. No one will find you here. For the time being, you're safe with a roof over your head and food to eat. Be happy with that for a moment and heal for a few days here."

She pondered the idea for a minute. The room was nice. He had military paraphernalia hung on the wall, and the lake was visible out of the large picture window. It was a beautiful sight; the pine trees kept the forest looking green even with the oak trees losing their leaves. The cool air created a mist that sat on top of the water as though a cloud had descended on it.

It had been years since she felt safe, dry, warm, and fed. She was comfortable there, and it wasn't a feeling she was used to having. The bed was warm and clean, the kind of cozy feeling that made it hard to get out of bed on cool winter mornings. The down blanket engulfed her body, begging her to stay put.

"Okay… I'll stay."

"Good. I'll get you some things today. I have a few errands to take care of in town." *I need to figure out if Tommy's body was reported,* he thought without stating it. As he stood to leave, Lacey stopped him.

"Can I ask you for something?" She was smiling then, the flirtatious smile of a child wanting an extra cookie after dinner.

He smiled back at her. "You can ask." His voice lacked the same playful tone she had. He hated feeling manipulated, and he wasn't clear if she was doing it intentionally or accidentally, like a stripper telling every guy in the club they're the best-looking one there. After a time, it becomes so ingrained in them that they struggle not to do it.

"I have things at my apartment. I don't care about my clothes or anything there… Under the sink in the old workers' bathroom is a black lockbox. It's hidden behind the cleaning supplies. Would there be any way to get it?"

"I'll try. I'm not sure. How important is the box?"

"To me… it's very important. It wouldn't mean much to anyone else, and it'll just be thrown out when someone else moves in there…" She trailed off at the realization that another girl would just take her place.

He stared silently at her, thinking and realizing if he looked too long, she would either get the wrong idea or be able to read his mind. If he told her it was too risky, she would ask why, and then he would have to tell her he had killed Tommy. But another solution occurred to him at that moment.

"It's too risky. Your pim… employer will probably be looking for you. If he sees me there, it could lead him back to you or me."

It was quick thinking but not good enough. Her face scrunched in dismissal of the idea.

"No. That shouldn't be a problem. Si tends to sleep most of the day. He's usually up all night with the girls. Please, Marion, it's important to me, and it won't take even five minutes. It's really the only thing I want back."

He stared back again, thinking if there was any way he could avoid it. In her eyes, he was just passing a sleeping pimp who wouldn't even know he was there. In reality, he knew that with a missing hooker and a John who might be the supplier, Si would be on high alert and watching the apartment. He wasn't sure why the words came out of his mouth. He wanted to shout "NO!" at her and tell her how foolish it was.

Maybe, it was her beauty or destroyed innocence that made him want to protect her and help fix the situation. Maybe, it was his protective nature that always turned him into a sheepdog. It was stupid to deny that her beauty played a part in the decision. Ultimately, he couldn't come up with another excuse in the brief seconds he discussed the decision with his inner being and nodded his head to her.

"I'll get it." He didn't say anything else. He just walked out of the room and grabbed his truck keys off the hook on the wall. With errands to run, a murder to check on, and a box filled with unimportant personal items to collect, his plate was admittedly full. *What the fuck are you doing, Mary?* But his body ignored the warning klaxon from his alter ego. It defied his mind with each step, as he walked briskly toward the truck and the road disappeared under his tires. *What the fuck are you doing?*

5

"Hunting is not a blood sport; it is a sport that's in my blood."

–Anonymous

The drive home was littered with traffic violations and errors. His demeanor was void of his usual disciplined actions. Being beaten by Si had caused Ewan to lose even a semblance of control. He felt like a butterfly being forcefully shoved back into its cocoon, fighting against an attacker who controlled every fiber of his existence. More than anything, he was aching to hunt and kill him. It conflicted with his desires for the girl, which were becoming secondary to his need to hurt Si. Finding a way to kill the man would be easy, and there was little sport in that. Men like him were always easy; they never saw themselves as victims. A lion doesn't glance over his shoulder while hunting a gazelle. He looks at his prey with such intense focus that they can no longer see the threats to themselves.

Ewan wasn't an alpha male, and he wasn't threatening in demeanor. An average man wearing business casual wasn't even worth noting. The kind of man anyone would forget five minutes after he left. But he was a dangerous man, one not to be trifled with. In nearly every room Ewan entered throughout his life, he was the most dangerous person present. It took every ounce of his conceivable energy to control the deep-seated desires in the back of his mind… *who to kill first?*

Pulling into the garage, he noticed his house represented him well. It was an outward expression of himself, telling the community that walked by who he was. On the surface, everything looked tame and akin to every other house in the subdivision. Each home had an identical layout to the house three blocks down. All of them painted an HOA-approved base color with accents to make it 'unique' to the owner. Nothing about his life stood out, and his home was no exception. Everything was in its place, carefully selected to appear as 'normal' and as sane as possible. Much like himself, the house held a dark secret locked away in the dungeon that no one else knew of.

A dungeon… It was his preferred way of looking at his basement, a cavern built solely for one purpose on which his castle rested. Stone walls were replaced by concrete and iron doors with steel ones. The thought often arose in his mind that he might one day build a house in the country. It was his only reason for saving for a traditional retirement. In his mind, he imagined a place where his victims could be taken in solitude, allowing his lair to be used to its full potential.

Fantasies of H.H. Holmes' murder house had filled his dreams for years. He was infinitely jealous of the unlimited resources Holmes had available to him. A murder house combined with some intelligence and forensics of the late 1800s were wasted on a man lacking the intellect to properly utilize the systems appropriately.

His dark desires and fantasies were never shared with anyone. Even finding one of 'the others' held no interest for him. The extracurricular activities of his life belonged to him alone. Though he would not have been able to deny a partnership with some of the more prolific 'others'—Dahmer, Bundy, Holmes—all intrigued him to the point of wishing he had one opportunity to work with any of them, but Holmes most of all.

Contrary to pop culture, Ewan had emotions. They were just dulled, as was his desire for companionship, but there was a small desire. Emotions outside of anger seemed to affect him less than an ordinary person. His rage and anger were more pronounced and harder to control than someone devoid of his condition. Worry, love, and affection held only the smallest importance in his mind and occupied none of his conscious thought process. Recognizing the feelings but not succumbing to them was a more accurate description, as they existed only in the farthest reaches of his mind.

He found the concept of being in love as foreign to him as astrophysics. If he were to ever love anyone, he wasn't sure who it would be. Ewan had no knowledge of immediate family and truly had no one worth caring about. *Being in love… I could be in hate of someone. Falling in hate… in anger.* That was an emotion he was far more comfortable with and found useful. He fantasized momentarily about the pimp, drawing his desires into the foreground as one would a memory from the past.

Not yet… Knowing he would need illicit help to find the girl, the pimp was too useful at the moment. Even if that help did not come willingly, it would be a requirement before killing him. That particular hunting trip had gone from an easy scouting trip to chaotic turmoil in the span of a few hours. Like a big game hunter missing the shot on a prized elk, the second shot to come days later would be even more gratifying.

He needed the girl… His mind was aching with each thought of her. It was as if his memory was bleeding into his brain. The pain in his head was going beyond figurative and becoming literal. A pulsing sensation arose behind his eyes as though the frontal lobe was swelling and pushing his eyes out of their sockets. *I need to find her... I need to find new hunting grounds... I need to kill...*

"Jesus... what happened to your face?" His wife asked in an irritable yet earnest manner that was both loving and annoyed. It interrupted his thought process, and he had to replay his lie back to himself before speaking.

"Nothing; I was mugged at a gas station."

"Mugged?! Did you call the police?"

"No. There wasn't any need. I was able to get away with my wallet, and the gas station was a low-end hole in the wall with no security cameras. I just need to ice it and get some bandages."

"Okay. But I really think you should tell the police. It's not right that they should get away with it. What gas station was it?"

"Some mom-and-pop shop in Bessemer. Nothing to be concerned with, and I don't have time to deal with a police report that will go nowhere." His voice was cordial but firm.

"What were you doing in that part of town?" A slight hint of suspicion was in her voice.

"Checking out some property that is getting re-zoned. I couldn't find anything on the computer system for it, so I decided to drive over and take a look." *She should buy this... This was plausible.* Incidents happened in that part of town with some regularity, and it wasn't unusual for him to go look at a property in person.

"But it's your day off? Why were you working, anyway?"

"It was something I needed to do, and I decided I would take care of it while I had some time. I'm really tired, and my ego is shattered more than anything, so if you don't mind, I'd like to just read the paper and relax for a bit."

"Ok," she said in a huff, clearly not satisfied with his answers but knowing when to push the subject with him.

Ewan propped his feet on the ottoman in the sunroom while taking a seat with his newspaper. His secret life consumed his every thought, and he found himself staring at the same article about the missing girl he had disposed of. Feeling his mind slowly losing control over his second life, Ewan felt like he was devolving into something unrecognizable. The monster beneath the surface was clawing its way from the pit and attempting to break free of its bonds.

Today was different… Ewan threw the old paper to the side and reached for that day's news. Furiously checking the missing persons and obituaries, he was concerned only with finding his woman in red. She wasn't likely to be someone reported missing, but it was worth checking. Women like that never had anyone to actually report them, and the police wouldn't spend a dime chasing them even if they did. *I wonder if anyone will report the pimp missing?* Killing the pimp would break his rules and draw some attention, but it was becoming a moot point. He had already stipulated the risk in his mind and decided it was worth the trouble.

His mind wandering slightly, he thought of the pimp's body being mutilated. He would be the first male victim, and Ewan wondered if it would provide any sexual satisfaction. The thought of it gave him no satisfaction in the moment. There was no rush of blood and hormones to his lower extremities. No urge to defile the body. There was no sexual satisfaction in the notion of it, only the simultaneous release that killing anyone would give him. It was a nicotine patch to lessen the craving for a cigarette.

The notion hit him and called for a cigarette to stifle the nerves. Ewan broke open the pack from his pocket and hit the striker on his lighter. The first plume of smoke filled his lungs, leaving him to contemplate again on his prized trophy. The pimp was just a bur in his side. Something to be removed that was in the path of progress. Ultimately, he would spill everything to receive an ounce of mercy from his tormentor. He would give everything for one more breath, one more moment of painlessness that would never arrive.

"Look man, I told you! There's no Tommy Johnson in a hospital or in any lockup that I can find. I don't have a fucking clue where he is, but he ain't in the hospital, jail, or the morgue!"

"Then find him! What the hell am I paying you for?!" Si demanded in frustration as spittle flew from his mouth.

"You pay me so I can run these favors for you from time to time. Not so I can issue a statewide manhunt for a piece-of-shit dealer." Officer Steve Jacobson was firm but not angry when answering back.

"Fuck you, puta!" Si said, before slamming the phone down. *Where the fuck are they?*

He thought through every possible scenario. Tommy having a heart attack, getting in a car accident, or getting stopped by the police—nothing fit. Every scenario meant that he would either be jailed, injured, or dead. It wasn't exactly easy for someone of Tommy's stature to disappear. He certainly lacked the skill necessary to disappear intentionally.

Si sat in the shabby hotel room he kept rented as a long-term unit. Technically, he had an apartment somewhere across town. In reality, he simply paid a landlord a quarter of the month's normal rent to put him down as a tenant and never actually lived there. It was a good deal for the owner of the property, who collected extra cash and rented the unit to a family of illegal migrant workers. The only warrants that could be served on Si were served there, a place he never visited.

He stared at the eggshell-colored walls of his room, trying to will an answer that would tell him where they had gone. Every scenario he thought of hadn't worked out. Lacey was dead; he was sure of it. Even if she hadn't been, Lacey would immediately try to get back to Si. The morgues and hospitals had no record of Tommy, and Steve was unable to find a traffic accident matching his car.

He ran through the limited scenarios he could determine over and over again until his head was spinning. The whore was dead. He was sure of it, but time and time again, he came back to the only answer that fit. Lacey was alive. She was alive and Tommy had taken her. Otherwise, he knew she would have come back to him for fear of his retribution. She wouldn't try to hide, and certainly not with a disgusting pig like Tommy.

If Lacey hadn't been dead, maybe Tommy would have taken her somewhere to have another go at her. He might still kill her and dispose of the body, but there was no way Tommy would let her go or befriend her. It wasn't in his nature, nor did he have the moral capacity to care for another person beyond his brother. *Was it possible he had brought her back to the apartment? Maybe she left something there? Something to tell me where she would go if she were ever free?*

He thought again of the situations that could have arisen. If she had still been alive and Tommy brought her back, maybe she thought that was a gift or a way for her to escape the clutches of that life. If she were alive, she would try to go back to her apartment. People were creatures of habit, and sooner or later, she would end up back there.

***

It was noon when Si finally gave up inside Lacey's apartment. He had turned everything over, tearing it apart.

The room looked ransacked, as if burglars were searching for a cocaine stash. The mattress was cut open, its stuffing removed; the few pieces of furniture were destroyed as he ripped them apart, looking for a hollowed-out chair leg or an envelope taped to the back of a drawer. He opened the kitchen cabinets and scattered their contents across the apartment. He even checked her hiding spot in the ceiling. There was nothing worth coming back for, and nothing appeared out of place.

He recognized the clothes in the dresser, knowing full well he had seen them all and nothing stood out as missing. There was no stash with a hidden passport or cash taped to the back of the toilet.

The apartment lay in ruins, dried food from a pantry cupboard littering the floor, along with every conceivable item she had owned. Cotton stuffing littered the floors and filled the air, making him choke and cough with each breath. Lacey was neat and organized, managing to turn even the most foul location into something worth coming home to. Sitting on the bed, he noted that the room was ransacked to the point that it mirrored the squalor of the facility where he had kept her.

His frustration oozed from his pores as he sat panting and perspiring on the ruined mattress, unsure of what to do next. *Back to square one…* No one had been there, or at least nothing had been disturbed, and there was no sign that Lacey had been home. With her clothes present and her toothbrush still on the kitchen sink, he knew she hadn't packed a bag. *She hadn't taken any cash…*

That was the clue he had been looking for. There was no cash. Every hooker kept a stash box of cash in case they ever had to leave. Each time he sold a girl to the Colombians, he found a small cash stash when their rooms were cleaned out. *Lacey was smart.* She would have a stash hidden somewhere, though it seemed to be out of his grasp to find it.

If she hadn't been there yet, his opportunity to find the girl might still be intact. His girls left when he gave them permission, not when they desired to. She was his, and he hadn't sold her. If she were alive, then she still belonged to him, and she would return to get the cash.

The hotel was visible from the window, and he could see his own rented room. The entry and the bedroom would be visible from his hotel room. He could watch the apartment from a distance and enjoy the air conditioning and television of the room while he waited. If anyone came, he would be able to see and tail them. *Did she have a friend to send? Someone she met… maybe a John who took pity on her.* Perhaps, she had found a safe place to live, a place outside of that world. Underground railroads still existed, trafficking hookers back into a normal life.

It wasn't inconceivable that if Lacey were alive, she could have found help through any number of victim-advocacy organizations. It didn't answer the question of what happened to Tommy, but he couldn't imagine any scenario where he was missing and she wasn't alive. At least for a time, he prayed silently that he simply fucked her and then killed her before heading to Tennessee, and would text him when it was convenient. He knew instinctively to his core that wasn't the truth. He felt like the captain of the football team, hoping the head cheerleader would text him back, knowing she would have done so by then if she were interested. In his bones, he knew the truth… Tommy had to be dead. Somehow, she had killed him and gotten away from him.

Si would have to kill her, if for no other reason than to make an example of the other girls. If she came back… When she came back to him, he would kill her as painfully as he could while the other girls watched. *This is what happens when you run.* That was the message he needed to send to the other girls. *I won't kill her…* he smiled somewhat at the satisfaction it would bring him. *I'll cut her feet off and sell her to the Colombians.* They'd use her up, and all of his girls would know that was what happened when they ran.

It would be a scarlet letter branded in their minds. Run from Si, and he takes your feet. These were his girls, and the image of her tortured body would be branded on their psyche. He'd explain to them all that if she had come back, she would still be alive. They were his property, and they would leave only with his permission. Permission he didn't give.

Lacey had told him how to get into the apartment, about the opening in the back wall, but the front door was never locked and had deteriorated to the point it couldn't be secured. Marion drove around the block several times, looking around to see if anyone was watching. For a brief moment, he thought he saw movement in the hotel room overlooking the warehouse, but the curtains were drawn, and he never saw the motion again.

Pulling the truck into the alley behind the building, he entered through the hole in the back, as she had instructed. He decided caution was the better part of valor and snuck into the building through the broken panel at the rear to avoid being seen. It was lit inside by the many holes and remaining skylights, though the light was muted compared to the exterior sun. It took a moment for his eyes to adjust and for the warehouse floor to come into focus. Marion pulled out his flashlight to illuminate the corners and to use as a striking weapon if he encountered anyone. Mostly, he was worried about vagrants and junkies, but the thought of the pimp sneaking up on him was prevalent in his mind.

The area was about half the size of a football field, with

remnants of factory parts and debris littering everywhere. The mezzanine to the office was on the right side of the building, with a steel catwalk across the front of the upper office floor. Rain dripped through the holes in the ceiling, saturating the debris and causing it to mold and deteriorate. His eyes puffed and itched as the mildew worked its way into his sinuses.

A worker's bathroom was below the office, but only the framing and a few bits of drywall remained after the copper had been stripped years ago. His heart sank at the sight. He grieved silently at the thought of Lacey living there… at anyone living there. *No one deserved this.* Without her baggage, Lacey appeared to be at least a warm person. *Places like this should be reserved for the worst of men, not women with nowhere else to go.*

Before looking for the box, he wanted to ensure he was alone in that condemned building. He moved to the base of the stairs and tested the weathered components before committing his full body weight to them. The metal was rusted on the catwalks from years of a leaking roof, but still solid enough to support his movement. He took the steps slowly to avoid falling through a busted tread or deteriorated rivet. The hard rubber soles of his boots clicked on each rung as he climbed, echoing through the entire building.

Her bedroom door leading into the loft was open, and the inside of the apartment was visible from the top step. Something was off. The room didn't look like that of someone living like a slob but rather like someone had torn it apart to find something. *Drugs, maybe,* he thought, wondering if her dealers had come looking for leftover products. He paused for a moment until the realization hit him: *she was the product… they were looking for her.*

The apartment was large, and the entirety of its contents wasn't visible from his location. Originally, it had been designed as several offices and maybe a conference room or break room, but the interior walls had been knocked out to create living space. It gave an eerie vibe, making the hair on his neck stand up.

Marion pulled his 1911 from the plastic Kydex holster carried in front of his waist and positioned the light on the side by weaving his left hand underneath. He peered around the corners to expose as much of the room as possible while giving himself protection from the door frame. Entering the room with the gun tucked tight into his body, he aimed at the ground to fire from retention if needed. The light was turned off as it wasn't needed with the ambient rays of sunshine funneling into the room. He wanted to be sure he could blind someone if necessary, and keeping it off would help conceal his location from a potential attacker hiding after hearing him enter.

Though the room was large for a studio apartment, it was relatively simple and would have been easy to search thoroughly. Marion re-holstered his pistol after clearing the area sufficiently. There was almost nowhere in such a small space for someone to hide. There was nothing to be gained from spending time in her apartment beyond sympathy for Lacey. Marion walked back down the mezzanine stairs to search the bathroom. He opened the cabinet under the sink to see a large brown cockroach staring back at him before scuttling away. Pushing the cleaning products to the side, he spotted the black box.

It was slightly smaller than a shoebox and had a metal handle on the side. The contents were protected by a combination lock on the side, which she hadn't given him. It was made of thin metal and wouldn't have been difficult to pry open even with a pocket knife if someone wanted its contents.

Regardless, he wasn't there to open it, and he certainly

didn't enjoy being in that place any longer than necessary. Carrying the box with his left hand, he moved intentionally but cautiously from the bathroom, through the warehouse, and back outside to his truck. He threw the box on the passenger seat next to the clothes and shoes he had bought her that morning.

His drive to the freeway seemed uneventful, apart from the growing sensation that someone was following him. Checking the rearview mirror, he saw no obvious tails, but he trusted his instincts, knowing his mind processed far more information than he could consciously think about in a moment. Cautiously, he watched at each turn in his mirror, slowing down his rate of travel to cause any surveillance vehicles to expose themselves. He was on the verge of running a surveillance detection route when he noticed the red Camaro.

Marion had spent a lot of time training in surveillance and counter-surveillance. This wasn't his first time being tailed. The red Camaro had been parked at the hotel the day before when he placed the tracker on Tommy's car. *Two times is a coincidence; three is confirmation, he thought, recalling* his counter-surveillance training.

He pulled his pickup into a drive-through coffee shop to confirm his suspicion. As he waited in line, the Camaro pulled into the parking lot across the street. Usually, his next stop would have been to run through a bank ATM or a fast-food burger joint, but he had the confirmation he needed. The Camaro was following him. Not the most inconspicuous vehicle someone could use for surveillance, which told him more than his stalker would have wanted.

It wasn't the police. They would never have been foolish enough to use a red Camaro, nor would any PI. They always drive muted vehicles of common varieties such as Honda Civics, Toyota Corollas, and small SUVs. That was a dealer in some capacity, connected to Lacey either through drugs or selling her. Whoever it was already had his license plate number. Without a front license plate being required in Alabama, he couldn't identify his stalker. For a moment, Marion debated how to get behind them to obtain the plate number, but it truly didn't matter. He wasn't going to go after them, and Lacey would probably know who it was, anyway.

More importantly, he needed to lose them and get back to her without them knowing it. If they were tailing him out of suspicion, then trying to lose them would confirm their suspicions. Traveling from Bessemer back to Springville, he could run through downtown Birmingham, which had a plethora of one-way roads and stoplights. It would be the easiest spot to ditch them.

Driving cautiously to keep his movement consistent, they traveled together toward downtown Birmingham. The Camaro followed him in a convoy, being led effortlessly into a trap. Marion kept his speed constant and easy to follow. Once at the traffic lights, he tried several times to lose the car at stale green lights or by accelerating through yellow ones, but the Camaro stayed on him. The speed and acceleration difference between the Camaro and his 25-year-old truck gave all the advantage to his follower. It was a 15-minute drive to University Blvd. Traffic was medium, with no serious breaks, and any light attempts to lose them proved fruitless.

The 4th Avenue hospital parking lot would be the easiest place to ditch them, but he would have to move fast, getting through the ticket line. The turn onto 4th Avenue was blocked by delivery trucks and large older brick buildings. Once he made the turn, the Camaro would lose sight of him for a minute or two until they could make the turn safely. With any luck, he would have a red light, providing an even greater absence of visual confirmation. Pulling into the hospital would also give them the impression that Lacey was there rather than at his house.

Just before pulling up to the 4th Avenue turn, he pressed the gas to get a truck between him and the Camaro. Marion changed lanes abruptly in front of a large Veterans Administration transport van that laid on the horn as he merged in, cutting them off. He pulled up to the stoplight on 4th Avenue, as pedestrians and hospital staff waited for the crosswalk sign. The truck crept forward, as he watched the red tail-vehicle fight traffic to merge into the turn lane. The light was red, and Marion rudely pushed through a break in the pedestrians crossing, eliciting a few angry faces and a universal sign language signal from a middle-aged woman. There was no gap for the tail car to push through, and he was able to round the corner into the parking deck.

The hospital parking was on the right, and pulling in provided another barrier between him and the Camaro. As fast as he could, he rushed past the ticket counter and out of view of the street, accelerating to the second deck where the Sky Lounge was located. At the Sky Lounge, there was a bridge across the road that would give him a clear line of sight to the follower.

He sprinted from his truck, barely shutting it off, and made his way as quickly as possible to the bridge. The glass was tinted and wouldn't allow them to see him but gave a clear view of the road traffic passing underneath. The Camaro made several passes around before pulling into a pay-by-the-hour lot behind one of the older buildings. The original intention to disappear without incident was fleeting from his mind. They were waiting to see if they could find him again and must have suspected the hospital as the likely culprit for his disappearance. *Maybe a warning would be beneficial.* Marion pulled out his pocketknife, leaving the blade closed, and swapped it to his left hand.

It took less than a minute to follow the hospital stairwell

down and out an exit-only door leading to a back alley, putting him directly in line behind the Camaro. It took all of his self-control not to run toward the car to avoid suspicion. Marion knew people noticed rapid movement out of the corner of their eyes, and he needed the element of surprise. He moved at a brisk pace to close the distance between himself and the red car. Target-focused with tunnel vision, he was only a few feet from the driver's side window. Marion clasped the knife firmly between his knuckles, leaving the handle exposed like a punch extending from between his middle and ring fingers.

Crash! With one strike, the glass shattered, startling the dark-skinned man in the driver's seat. Marion didn't wait for a response before pushing his other hand through, grabbing the nape of his neck. With a flick of his thumb, the blade extended. Slowly, he placed the blade below Si's left eye, pressing it into the skin. He tilted the blade to ensure the man could see the shine of the crucible steel.

"Why are you following me?" His voice had an eerie calmness to it. This wasn't the first time he had been tailed, and his follower knew instantly he had made a mistake.

"I'm not following you, puta!" Si yelled back, fear gripping his voice.

"The girl's gone. You won't see her again. You won't come for her."

"Fuck you! I wasn't follo—" Marion gripped his neck tighter, shoving the knife in, causing it to pierce the skin.

"Fuck! Puta! Okay, the girl's gone! I got it!"

Marion pulled the blade back before releasing Si's neck. "Don't follow me again." The words were cold and calculated, exaggerated by the blade still dancing in front of Si's eye. There was no quiver of emotion in Marion's speech. He forced himself not to look behind himself as he walked away. A part of him wondered if the man would shoot him, but his instincts told him he wouldn't risk it in such a public place. Walking the same path he had arrived through, Marion stuck the knife tip into Si's rear tire before disappearing into the alley behind the hospital.

The warning wouldn't work. He wasn't sure how he knew it, but he knew that his follower would take that as a challenge. There was nothing he could do at the moment. The Camaro already had his license plate number. They would have his home address within the hour. Any PI or cop on a dealer's payroll could dig up the information in ten minutes. Marion turned back only once to check the license plate before the car was out of view. The black letters spelled it out to him: J97QRF. *I'll know where to find you, too.*

By the time Marion had walked back to the bridge that crossed from the hospital to the parking deck the Camaro was gone. It was only a few minutes to reach his truck and he climbed into the driver seat thinking through the events that had transpired. He needed to get home to Lacey. His instincts were telling him the man in the Camaro would be heading there as soon as he found the address and she wasn't in any condition to handle him.

Plugging his keys into the ignition Marion cranked the starter to the failing sound of a dead battery. *Shit.* He turned it over again to the same sound. His maintenance was always meticulous, and Marion changed batteries long before they were due. This one was only a few months old and it was already struggling to hold a charge. Either a bad battery or faulty wiring somewhere that had drained it was now leaving him stranded in the damn parking garage with the Camaro on its way to his house. *Fuck.*

The pain in her shoulder was excruciating, and the swelling made the use of her arm almost impossible. It hurt so much to lift it for anything, and she had little strength to get out of bed. Knowing her only way toward recovery was to get up and get moving, Lacey forced herself to her feet. She stumbled as gracefully as she could, using the nightstand to support her weary movements.

Everything annoyed her… she was suffering through the withdrawals of not having any cocaine for a day. *This was going to be rough,* she thought to herself, but that was the first time she could remember wanting to actually quit. Everything in her life had changed, and she was safe, comforted, ironically shacking up with a guy who seemed to genuinely care about her well-being and not want to sleep with her.

A few hours before, she was nothing more than a strung-out hooker. But the taste of freedom was at her fingertips, like an inmate getting set free at the gates of their last mile. She wasn't sure if she was the prisoner going to the execution chamber or the one at the doorway to freedom, but either option felt liberating at the moment. It seemed to hinge on that mysterious man who had rescued her from Tommy's grasp and was wrenching Si's hands off of her.

He's cute too. The thought left her mind as quickly as it had arrived. He would never want her, anyway; he seemed like a good man with his life together. She seriously doubted he would ever be interested in a worn-out whore like her. But it didn't stop her from thinking about him or what he represented to her: a normal life… It was a life she hadn't considered for herself in years but suddenly felt to be within her grasp.

This wasn't love by any means. That was something that was earned over time and dedication. But she was in love with the idea of him, not just as a man to share her life with, but as a life worth living. More than anything, he represented the possibilities of a different life from what she had.

Thinking of his light sandy-colored hair with hints of gray

scattered throughout, she pictured it in her mind not curly but not straight, with the sides trimmed and the top longer, almost slicked back. He had broad shoulders and a good physique—not that of someone who spent every day at the gym, but how one would envision a blacksmith from the 1800s, a hard physique. Everything about him seemed strong and capable.

He was tall, around six feet or maybe more, and obviously Caucasian, but with a hint of something else to his skin tone, just slightly darker. His eyes were blue, looking like an explosion of color against the darker background. She wasn't sure what his tattoos depicted, but his right arm had a quarter sleeve extending just below a T-shirt, while his left arm had a bracelet of some sort of Celtic knot.

Her daydream came to an abrupt end as the pulsating detox headache and throbbing shoulder struck her while walking out of the bedroom. Her shoulder was so swollen that she thought it might pop like a water balloon if poked. She grabbed a bathrobe he had presumably left for her and bundled her naked body in it. With no clothes, money, or even an ID, she was virtually at his mercy to help retrieve her belongings.

Making her way to the kitchen, she felt a degree of guilt as she rifled through his cabinets. Not intending to be nosy, she was hoping to find some tea. *There you are.* In the very back of the cabinet above the coffee, she was able to find a herbal mix that sounded good from the lemons and flowers on the packet. Having not eaten anything since the day before, she suddenly realized the full effects of starvation as she listened to her stomach growl.

It didn't take long to prepare some eggs and toast to enjoy with her afternoon cup of tea. She needed to hurry and clean the mess before he got home. It just seemed rude to leave his kitchen messy. His house was meticulously put together.

Every single item had a place, lacking only a drawn silhouette to show where it should go. The plates in the cabinet had a colored pattern, neatly aligned with the plate below them, forming a line down the front showing their place. The mugs in the cabinet were all the same color, with handles facing 45 degrees to the right and a perfect two-finger spacing between them.

Unsure of where to eat, she sat on the couch in his office. Silently, she sipped on the tea, admiring the view. *Beautiful.* Everything was as it would be in a fairy tale. That small cottage overlooking the water was perfectly clear, begging to be drunk straight from the source. Across the lake, she could see a small stream feeding into it. The overflow must be around the bend from his home and out of view.

From the office, there was a clear line of sight down the road leading to his home, with the only other home being the one next door sitting on top of a rocky alcove. The gate for the entire lake wasn't visible, but the road leading to the ring around the lake was. She wasn't sure if it connected at the spillway with a bridge or if the entire route was just a U shape, in which case only Marion's house and the one next door were on that side of the lake.

It was peaceful, serene, beautiful, and perfect. Though the setting was different from her grandmother's cabin, being a lake home rather than a mountain cottage, the atmosphere felt identical, and even the scent was the same from the pine trees intermixed in the forest.

Everything was perfect except one thing… one thing that sent shivers down her spine… the thing she hated more than anything in that world to see, because it meant a new life wasn't beginning. It was a thing that shattered any semblance of a dream for her. It was a familiar red Camaro that entered the community from the lake entrance and stopped.

She knew it was Si. He was sitting, debating which way to

go and which house to look for. She wasn't sure, but she assumed the houses didn't have numbers and that mail was dropped outside the gate. He had to figure out which house she was in, and without any vehicles in the driveways, he would go one by one.

Si would drive around the lots looking for movement and signs of life. That meant she had to hide to protect Marion's home and herself. She wasn't a victim; she wasn't going to let him take that from her. It was the only opportunity for escape that had presented itself, and she'd rather die than give it back.

However, fighting Si was a losing battle, and she knew it before it even began. For all his faults, he wasn't weak by any means. Grabbing a knife from the butcher block, she started looking for a hiding place. He would search the house, and if he knew she was there, he would tear it apart in the process. But if he wasn't sure which house she was in, Lacey hoped the search might not be so vigorous.

She searched the house for any place to hide, but it was just a small cottage with nowhere to go. Marion's bedroom had a small walk-in closet with a gun safe on one side. The best she could do was to squeeze herself between the safe and the wall and keep herself as still and quiet as possible. If he stuck his face through, she would have one shot to hit him with the knife and run before he killed her.

Her breathing was heavy, and it took all her strength to control it and calm her exhausted mind. *Don't be afraid!* She commanded herself to stop the shivering that had uncontrollably taken over her body. She waited for him to show, with no sign or audible noise.

A part of her wanted to leave the safety of her hiding nook, but she kept thinking he would certainly find her if she did. It would be like a horror movie, with him waiting in the living room. She envisioned Si smiling to himself, sitting on

Marion's couch, and knowing she was there scared, tired, and alone and just enjoying the added turmoil it gave her. Thirty minutes passed when she decided to step out and see if he was still there.

As if on cue, she heard the door open and heavy footsteps moving around the home. Si's footsteps searched frantically; *he knows I'm here!* Her mind screamed. She heard her bedroom door open. The room's contents were being strewn about. He was trying to find her. Marion's door opened and then the closet door. *He's here!*

She readied her knife, holding it in front of her face to strike the moment she saw any part of him come into view. The rhythm of her heart pounded louder with each beat. He was close; she could hear him breathing. She knew her heartbeat would give her away; it was pulsing out of her chest. She focused on her breathing, trying to convince her heart not to explode. *He can't hear you… breathe softly, Lacey.*

"Lacey?"

She didn't move; the voice wasn't right; it wasn't Si. "Lacey, it's Mary."

Leaning her head out from behind the safe, she saw him there. In an instant, everything changed. Her heart calmed and raced at the same time, feeling like it might spring from her chest as the adrenaline ceased and soared. The beating in her ears silenced, and she let go of the knife.

"I thought you were someone else…"

"Who did you think I was? The guy in the red Camaro?"

"Yes… Si. He's my…" She intended to say pimp, but it seemed like such a vulgar word with a horrible connotation. She hadn't been that person that day. She wouldn't be that person again. She wasn't ever going back.

"Employer," Marion interrupted, sensing the word stagnate on her tongue. "It's okay," he said, holding out his hand for her to come out of the corner. "It's okay, Lacey."

She liked hearing him say her name. It was warm and caring. The serene nature of it calmed her beyond knowing that he was there. It was a crazy thought; she hadn't known him for more than a few hours, but he was safe, a good man, the type she hadn't known in her previous life.

Grabbing his hand as she stepped forward, she was led by Marion to the couch in the living room. "I'm going to light a fire… then we need to talk about what is going on."

"I don't mean to be rude… you've already done so much, and I'm sorry I didn't have a chance to clean your kitchen, but can I ask for something?" Her smile was flirtatious, showing fully bared teeth. She wasn't being needy or ungrateful, just playful like a small child wanting two toys instead of one. Marion didn't respond; he just smiled back.

"Can I take a shower?" she said, laughing. "I'm beginning to smell myself, and it's not cute!" Her laugh was infectious, filled with joy that would control any room she entered.

"Of course, you can. There are spare towels under the sink. I don't have anything other than bar soap and dollar-store shampoo, but you're welcome to it. I'll get you some clothes."

"That's fine, thank you." And she was thankful; she was truly grateful. The 'thank you' wasn't out of polite conversation or any need to meet social norms, but true gratitude.

"How's your shoulder?" His smile still lit up his face as he asked.

"Tender, but it will heal."

"Do you need any help in there?" He was playful, trying to skirt the boundary between playful banter and not treating her as if she were an item for him to lust after.

"No!" She clapped back, laughing. "I think I can handle it."

***

* * *

The fire was roaring, and steam escaped from under the bathroom door. She hummed in the shower, but the tune wasn't familiar to him. He could hear the water shut off and her movement as she dried and dressed. "Marion," she said, cracking the bathroom door.

"I actually might need some help." Her grin was infectious. But she opened the door wearing the jeans he bought that hugged her figure and hips as if they were attached to her skin. Her bra was on but not clasped in the back.

"I got the jeans on, but I can't get this strapped with my arm."

It wasn't an invitation for a sexual advance from him. It was a patient needing some help… help that didn't exactly bother him to give. He stood behind her and closed the clasp, sensing her embarrassment from her needing assistance. He was close to her, feeling the warmth of her skin from the hot shower. He could smell her. It wasn't the cheap shampoo that was intoxicating, but her scent and pheromones.

He grabbed the maroon-red sweater and white T-shirt from the counter and helped her get them on, being as gentle as he could with her arm. "Ouch," she winced as he moved it into the sweater.

"Sorry."

Turning to face him, the distance between them less than a few inches, she said, "It's ok…. Thank you, Marion, for everything. You don't know what you've done for me."

Marion couldn't release her gaze. He just nodded as she wrapped her hands around his neck and hugged him. "Thank you," she whispered in his ear. Her embrace lasted longer than she intended, but his body was cozy, like sitting beside a roaring fire on a cold winter day, the kind of warmth that made it difficult to remove yourself from, to go back outside.

They talked for a while after she finished dressing, Lacey telling him about her life with her grandmother and the way everything changed after her death. She didn't know her father, but she spoke about her friends, the other girls that belonged to Si. They talked until the evening about everything in their lives. Marion told her about being tailed, and she told him about seeing the Camaro there.

"Si drives the red Camaro?"

"Yes. He knows I'm here. I don't know how, but he knows."

"I think he followed me from your apartment and must have gotten my license plate number."

"My apartment! Did you get the box?" She barely let him finish the sentence as excitement poured out of her.

"Yes. It's on the counter." His language was always precise; 'Yes' instead of 'ya,'

Not waiting for an invitation, Lacey ran to the counter to grab it and bring it back to the couch. She curled her legs up underneath her and set the box on her lap, still favoring her non-injured arm.

"The code is 71925, my grandmother's birthday."

"What's in it? Why is it so important?"

"Everything. My life before this…"

She pulled the contents out one by one, setting them on the couch beside her. The box held pictures of her and her grandmother, trinkets from her childhood, a bracelet that belonged first to her grandmother and then to her mom, her passport, and what looked to be around $5,000 in cash.

Lacey didn't care about the money and tossed it to the side carelessly. She just stared at the items in it. It was several minutes before she realized no one had said anything, and Marion just watched her patiently.

"Thank you for doing this. I can't replace any of this. Nothing else there was important. I set the money back in case I was ever able to get away. It's yours," she said, placing the box to the side and handing over the cash.

"I don't want your money, Lacey."

"No, no, no, please take it. You've done so much; please take it." She was shaking slightly, trying to give it to him. Her voice quivered with the delicate, gravelly rasp that accompanied it. Paying him the money had more to do with cutting that portion of her life away. The cash was tainted by how she had come by it, and it was beginning to disgust her to hold it out.

Marion reached forward but didn't take the cash. Instead, he grabbed her hand. "Lacey, I don't need it, and I don't want it. Whatever you had to do to get this money, that isn't you."

With a nod, Lacey put the money back in the box, and Marion released her hand. "What do we do about Si?" she asked. "He knows where you live."

No one would blame her for being a survivor and thinking of herself, but she worried about him. There was little concern for herself in the way she spoke with him, almost as if she felt like an imposition in his life and was trying politely to put him first.

"There are only two options."

"Which are?"

"Either I kill him or convince him to leave you alone."

"Leave 'us' alone?" she emphasized. "Okay, assuming you're not open to killing someone in cold blood, how do we do that?"

"He's going to come back for you. Tonight, I imagine. We are going to let him come."

"So…" She paused, the realization striking her. "I'm the bait."

"No. I am. The house up the hill on the rocks?"

"Ya," she said quizzically, glancing over his shoulder at the house he referred to.

"I own it. You're going to go up there and spend the evening. I'll come get you after I deal with Si."

"No." She was emphatic. "This is not your problem. I won't just sit up there and let you deal with this. I get it; you're a man and you have to fix the woman's problem, but I won't sit in that house and let you do this." Her arms crossed over her chest. It was cute and determined; this was not going to be a discussion.

"Okay… Do you know how to use a gun?"

"I mean, I've handled them before, but not really."

"Si… can he handle himself? I mean physically?"

"Yes. He's aggressive, has a bad temper, and is violent. If I'm being honest, he won't take a warning."

"I gathered that from my conversation with him earlier. Want me just to shoot him then?" It was a crude joke, but there was a half-truth to it, and he could sense that she knew it.

"You mean like you did with Tommy?" Lacey stared blankly at Marion, not giving away her emotions on the subject. She already knew the answer to the question. It was rhetorical, but she needed him to answer it honestly. Any response other than an outright lie would be a confirmation. He sat staring, trying to come up with an excuse, something to lead her off the trail, some way he had gotten Tommy to go away without being dead, but nothing came to him.

"Don't look so surprised. I'm not stupid, Mary. You didn't get me out of there with him being alive." Marion was still at a loss for a response.

"Look, you don't have to acknowledge it. No one is going to be looking for Tommy, and certainly, no one is going to miss the fat son-of-a-bitch. But don't lie to me. I know when men are lying, and I don't deserve that. He's not the first person you've killed either… You'd have still been sick the next day, but you weren't… you were calm. As if you'd done it before. Maybe even a lot."

"Fair enough. I won't lie to you. Tommy's gone, and he won't be back. That's all that matters."

"So then… What's the plan for tonight?"

"If we kill him tonight, I'll have to answer for you and why you're here, which will lead to questions and a discussion about Tommy. Tonight is going to be a trap, but I can't kill Si, not without being able to make him disappear, which would be hard if he's killed in my house."

"I understand, Marion. I'm not asking you to kill anyone. But what are we going to do?"

"The only thing we can do… Send another warning. A hard one. One that he would either have to abide by or actively come after us."

"And if he comes after us?"

Marion paused for a moment. He wasn't sure how deeply he wanted to get involved, but at that point, it would be hard to turn back. Handing her over to Si wasn't an option. If nothing else, he had a huge moral objection to pimps and slavers. She would certainly be killed, and even if she weren't, he couldn't force that life on anyone. Marion stared at her before answering, as if asking her permission.

"Then I'll kill him."

6

"The ultimate choice for a man, in as much as he is given to transcend himself, is to create or destroy, to love or to hate."
–Erich Fromm

Si had been parked for a few minutes at the entry to the lake before traveling around the community. He watched the houses through his binoculars, searching one by one until he saw Lacey in the sunroom of a small cottage. She was eating breakfast without concern. He watched her chewing and sipping from a mug, eyeing the water and enjoying the peaceful moment. Her face turned toward him, and the change in her demeanor was apparent enough that Si knew she saw him.

The fear was obvious in her eyes, and the sheer panic that hit sent her running to another room out of view. He could only guess what she was doing then. *Run and hide, little girl.* It was time for him to leave. He hadn't planned on attacking the house in broad daylight, and he knew the man wouldn't be far behind. It would be easier to take them both that evening while they slept.

He had initially wanted to kill her before the man in the black truck returned, but there wasn't time. After wasting 15 minutes changing the tire, he only beat him there by a few minutes while he had paid the parking fee. Leaving the dead girl cut up in his house with an anonymous tip to the police would have been the sweetest deal his imagination could construe.

He wondered if they would leave or go into hiding. *It didn't matter if they did;* he could be patient. Waiting for them to return was a simple enough process, and it wouldn't cost him anything for them to leave and come back with their guard down. Even if he were able to hide the girl, Si could get the answer from him. He could make people talk.

Instead of leaving the subdivision, Si pulled his Camaro into the carports of one of the houses on the opposite side of the lake. It was hidden from view of Marion's house and would give him a place to wait and watch until nightfall. There was no one home, and he hadn't seen any cameras. A small break in the lattice gave him an over-watch position while remaining out of sight.

He watched Marion's truck pull in from the protection of the lattice hiding the Marlboro red car. *Marion… What a stupid name.* His sources at the police department had been able to return a name, an address, and a "fuck you" for asking. The cops resented him, but they took the money, nonetheless.

The picture windows overlooking the water had a reflective tint that didn't allow anyone to see in. Only the sunroom was visible with the blinds open. The tint made it impossible to determine what they were doing, but he assumed by then they were either panicking or fucking if the mystery man had any brains. They might try to leave and come back, maybe go on the run for a bit, or maybe they'd hunker down and hope he didn't come after them.

It didn't much matter. That wasn't the first guy Si would teach a lesson to, and as soon as Lacey was back, he'd sell her off to South America and be rid of her forever. Really, the only question he hadn't answered yet was whether he wanted to kill the guy. It would depend on the demeanor of the conversation that night.

If he didn't try to be a tough guy, maybe he'd live. It was generally cheaper and easier to keep people alive when possible. But if he wanted to be defiant, Si would bury his knife between Marion's ribs and burn the house down. Either way, the girl was coming back with him. He wasn't leaving without her. But if Marion showed him the proper respect and didn't try to be a hero, he would live with a few marks and scars to remind him not to mess with Si in the future.

Watching patiently from the opposite side of the lake, Si could see only shadows of movement behind the window tint. After several hours, the sun went down, and the lights came on, giving a better view through the windows, but obstructed just the same. *God, this is boring… How do cops do this shit?* The lights on the old lake house didn't go out until 10:30 PM, but it was finally dark and quiet outside. If they were watching for him, they would be looking for a car to come. Si intended on leaving the vehicle parked there and walking the mile loop around. He could travel back using the man's truck and leave it regardless of whether he killed him. *The man,* he thought to himself wondering who the guardian was.

Si waited another hour until it was well past 11:30 to ensure they were asleep and then started the long walk around the loop. He stayed in the shadows of the tree line, not wanting to alert anyone if by chance they happened to wake up, or if someone were home in another house. It was more out of habit than anything, and it provided a sense of comfort rather than being exposed. Completely alone for the next 15 minutes while he stalked toward the house, it appeared they were the only people in the community that night.

With the front of the house facing the water, the rear of the home was the front door. The wood siding looked black in the moonlight, and a small arctic entry led into the home, creating a separate entry area between the exterior weather and the kitchen. *Those are probably fake…* Si thought to himself when he noted the security cameras; most of them were. If they were real, it would be simple enough to take the hard drive with him when he left, and a fire would take care of anything forgotten.

He had practiced lock picking but never got proficient with it. But prying open the door with a crowbar would be quiet enough too. In his experience, people sleep soundly enough that the one crack wouldn't wake anyone without a dog. It didn't matter much to him, regardless. Marion didn't appear to be that tough, and he would need more than that little pocket knife to deal with Si tonight.

Removing the pry bar from his inner jacket pocket and inserting the flat end between the frame and the door, he pressed hard until the latch broke free and popped open with the typical crack he expected. A loud crack echoed through the home as he pushed softly on the door to create a gap only large enough for him to squeeze through.

Waiting a moment in the arctic entry to see if anyone heard him, he was satisfied after a minute or two that they were still asleep. He entered the main home door passing the threshold to the kitchen. Si crept slowly, not detecting any movement but not wanting to risk turning on lights until he had the drop on them and knew where they were. Tucking the breaching tool back in his jacket, Si drew his pistol. It was a nickel-plated Beretta 92F he got a few months back in trade for a few nights with his cash cows. He eyed the pistol, liking it more and more each time it was clasped in his hands. *I need to get some more girls… maybe, open shop in Atlanta.*

His eyes had adjusted to the lack of light on the walk over, and as he rounded the living room corner, the two bedroom doors were wide open and coming into view. A door between the two was closed and presumably was the central bathroom for the main room and the guests. Someone was sleeping in both beds. *Faggot… Should have at least fucked the girl while you had her here.*

Easing another two steps forward, he avoided making the floorboards creak by walking near the wall. One more step forward, and the walls lit up in a spray of light, silhouetting his shadow against the wall. He was illuminated from behind by someone, presumably with a flashlight. The sound of a shotgun chambering a round behind him was more evidence than he needed that it had been a trap. Lowering his gun in an admission of defeat, he didn't have time to react.

"Drop it," a man's voice said, from a few feet back. It must have been Marion, recognizing the gruff undertone from his confrontation with the man earlier. Si cursed himself for not grabbing a friend or two to help him, but this was supposed to be easy.

The pistol clattered to the floor. "Now what, Marion?"

"This is where I warn you never to come here again… but that won't work, will it."

"Listen, give me the bitch, and this will all be over for you. Your life can go back to the normal boring routine you had a day ago." He wasn't sure at first what it was, but a metallic snap came from behind him, and a moment later, a crashing pain hit his knee.

Marion had shattered his knee with a side blow from a steel police baton. His scream would have been heard across the lake if anyone had been home. "Don't call her that." His tone was calm… Lacey noticed that Marion was at peace with the moment. *This was his element,* she thought, watching his movements and the ease with which it all came to him. Marion was comfortable when he knew exactly what needed to be done, even if those things were hard.

Si couldn't walk; he collapsed to the ground and began crawling over to the couch. Facing Marion, he watched Lacey standing to his side and slightly behind, instinctively shielding herself behind him with him blocking her from the threat. He sat quietly, trying to catch his breath, salivating over his shirt from the excruciating pain throbbing through his knee. The drool fell from his open lips as he winced and writhed with each pulse of pain shooting through his entire leg.

"At your age, Si, the wound won't heal right. You'll walk with a limp for the rest of your life." While Marion spoke, Lacey took a few steps back and watched the doorway to ensure a second attacker didn't come through.

"Throw these on," Marion said, tossing handcuffs to him.

"Go ahead... call the cops. I'll be out in a week; you'll never know when I'm coming back for you and..." the last word trailing off.

"You don't get it, Si. You can crawl out of this place right now, or I can kill you and end this tonight. Right now, I'm trying to buy your life. The only reason you're not dead already is because of the hassle it would cause me to answer for Lacey and the reliance the other girls have on you. If you disappeared, as much as it pains me to say it, they'd be worse off getting picked up by the next piece of shit that came in to take your place. Better the devil you know for them."

Si made a questioning face at Marion before smiling once the realization hit him that he was being lied to. "Ahhh... I get it now. You can't call the cops, can you? Can't have them asking why I'm here and how you came across the girl. What happened? Tommy tried to sell you a piece, so you killed him instead of paying up? Or maybe you just couldn't get it up." He started laughing and motioning to his genitals. "Sometimes first-timers get so nervous they can't perform, and I'll toss them a blue miracle pill for an extra Benjamin. It might help get you hard." He leaned forward with his hands cuffed and resting on his knees. "Or maybe you just couldn't get it up with a worn-out…"

Before he could finish the last sentence, the muzzle of Marion's shotgun struck him in the lips, splitting his face just above the chin and knocking out two of his teeth. Si winced and groaned as the sharp pain shot through his jaw. He was holding his face with his cuffed hands, covering his mouth and nose. "Motherfucker!" he screamed at Marion. "I'll fucking kill you, motherfucker!"

Without responding, Marion set the shotgun aside and reached into Si's pockets to search for weapons and whatever else he could find. He found a Benchmade switchblade, his cell phone, a large roll of cash, and his wallet. Marion shoved the cash in his pocket and tossed the switchblade to Lacey. "Consider this an investment into your health plan, or to fix my door, whichever makes you happier." Marion flipped the phone open to check it but decided that there was nothing of use and placed it back in Si's pocket.

He sat down in the chair across from Si and stared at him in uncomfortable silence. Neither man said a word for several minutes until Marion reached a hand toward him and pulled on his collar, toppling Si forward as he caught his balance on the one good knee he had. Marion waited again; there was little that needed to be said, and the less he spoke, the more the message would be sent.

Telling a man like that he intended to kill him if they met again would serve only to fuel his determination and stoke his rage. Si would either not believe him or believe that he was capable of stopping it from happening. Marion needed that warning to work, and to give it the best chance meant controlling himself and playing psychological warfare games with his opponent.

He tightened his grip on Si's collar, twisting the fabric so it began to depress around his throat. Marion pulled his knife from his pocket, ensuring the stainless blade flickered in the dim light of the room as he had done earlier that day. He squeezed the knife as hard as his grip would allow, forcing his hand to tremble. Not in a way that could be construed as fear, but rather as if it required all of his self-control to not run him through in that moment. He had intended for it to be an act, but in the moment, he found himself losing control.

Pushing the knife into Si's neck, he began to see drips of blood oozing from the puncture. He hated the man sitting across from him. It was an existence he despised, like a schoolyard bully picking on a handicapped kid. Only this was worse; Si took advantage of desperate women at their weakest, and it enraged him to the point that his trembling hand and piercing gaze were not a lie, and Si could sense it too.

Marion recognized Si's mouth moving but felt his mind leaving his body in the moment. The words were falling around him as though they weren't meant for him. Si was a television with the mute button pressed. He stared into his eyes, feeling the knife getting deeper and deeper. It wasn't until the blood started soaking the collar of his T-shirt that Marion was able to pull himself back to the present and catch what Si was saying.

"...Stop! Stop! Stop!" His voice was filled with the fear needed to send an effective warning.

"If you come for the girl again..." his voice trailed off, knowing the point was set and nothing else needed to be said. He had him where he wanted and the message was clear. "Come for her again, and I'll skin you alive and bleed you." The moment was approaching for Marion to return him to the car when Lacey stepped forward and was standing six feet away, holding the pistol Marion had given her. The barrel was pointed at Si, with her finger resting on the trigger. "We have to do this… he'll come back for me! I won't go back to that!"

Shit. Marion had Si right where he needed him to get rid of him. Lacey stepping in was likely to upset the balance, and then he was forced to stop her, which would tell Si everything he needed to know, maybe not in the moment, but soon. Si's courage would be restored, or at least his drive to finish that and send the right message.

"Lacey…" His voice was calm as he stood and walked toward her, closing the gap between them. A gentle and experienced hand placed over the gun, and he guided it safely to the ground before taking it from her grasp. "We can't do this tonight." It was the only thing he could say to salvage his warning. Any ounce of tenderness from him toward her would be seen only as a weakness to be snuffed out.

Lacey had tears running down her face, filled with frustration, anger, hate, and hurt. She wanted him dead but didn't want to pull the trigger. Marion wanted to reach a hand to her face and hold her. It wasn't a romantic attraction so much as it was a protector's instinct, like a father would to his daughter or a brother to a sister. His hands remained firmly pressed against his side, holding both the knife and the shotgun. Lacey was shaking from the overwhelming emotions surging through her veins; the spectrum of her emotions swung from one extreme to the other in an instant.

Lacey sank into a ball on the floor and curled herself into the corner of the room, resting her back against the wall. She had entered the black stage of her emotions and was completely shutting down. Marion turned back to Si, who had sat watching the entire display unfold in front of him. Marion knew the moment he saw Si's face that the warning had failed. Si would come for him.

Maybe Lacey was right, and he should just kill the son-of-a-bitch, but it wasn't that simple. These things rarely were, and he didn't think his luck would hold out trying to make two bodies disappear in less than 24 hours.

"Get up!" Marion's voice remained in a slight monotone, stagnant without felt emotion. He was firm, and it was clear that Si should do as he was told. But he wasn't yelling or snapping; he was commanding. "We're leaving."

Attempting to stand out of habit, Si realized instantly he couldn't walk, needing to hop from one piece of furniture to the next. "Get in the back of the truck. I'll drop you at your car." It was comical watching him hop and bounce to the back of the truck. Each jolt of his landings sent a searing pain through his knee from the dangling appendage below. Finally, making it to the truck, he rested on the truck bed, unable to pull himself into it fully until Marion dropped the tailgate.

The drive to his Camaro took less than a minute or two until the headlights illuminated the taillights in the carport. Marion barely pulled to a stop before Si was hopping out of the truck and racing as fast as one leg could take him to the car. Thankful for an instant that the blow had only been to his right knee, pressing the clutch with a shattered kneecap would be agony. The chore of driving would be difficult enough to make an attempt at controlling the accelerator.

As soon as he climbed in, Marion reached through the broken window and held onto Si's hand for a moment, forcing it through the driver's side window. There was little for him to say in that awkward parting farewell. With one fluid motion, the baton extended from his other hand and crashed down on Si's left wrist with all the force he could muster. His wrist was pinned for an instant between the car door and the blunt instrument. The impact sent enough force through his hand to dent the frame of the door. The sound of the metal buckling inside the paneling was drowned out by another of Si's screams.

***

When he arrived back at the house, Lacey was still curled in a ball but had moved to the couch and turned the lights off. The moon cast enough light into the room that he could see her crying had subsided, but her eyes were red and still filled with tears. There wasn't anything he could say to help her. He was powerless in the moment to fix the situation, nor was Marion emotionally equipped to deal with a crying woman. That was a problem he didn't have the answer for, or the skill to adapt to.

Marion hesitated for a moment before committing himself to sit beside her on the couch and put his arm around her without saying a word. It was a strange sensation for a moment because they hadn't known each other for even a day yet. He wasn't by nature a warm person, and in another circumstance, he would have left to get someone more suited for counseling. But Lacey didn't have anyone else: no mother or friends to call, just s stranger sitting there in the dark beside her—a washed-up soldier with an aimless existence. She sank into his chest but not completely giving control to him. For what felt like hours, neither of them spoke. Marion passed the right of way to her; he rested his head on the back of the couch and closed his eyes.

He had not slept much the night before and and so far had not slept any tonight, his eyes were beginning to water from fatigue. He could feel his mind drifting quietly into a dreamlike state, but his body was unwilling to fully commit. He was edging on the point of exhaustion where he was almost too tired to sleep as his mind failed to turn off.

"I'm scared," she whispered to him in the dark, bringing

him back to reality.

"Of him coming back?" he said, rubbing her shoulder tenderly as he spoke with his eyes still closed.

"Yes and no… Not so much of him. This was the first time since I was a young girl that some other life seemed possible, where the light and happiness were creeping in. But when I saw him, everything left, like being hungry with the perfect meal sitting in front of you, but a cockroach is climbing on top of it. Do you understand?"

"I think so… Him being here is less about his actual existence but that he's a part of something you want to let go of. It shatters the picture of what you were moving toward?"

"Yes…" she said, settling down more into him.

Her eyes were heavy, and she could feel sleep overtaking her. Leaning against his chest, she could feel the rhythm of his heartbeat thumping against her ear. The hypnotic pounding soon matched hers as her breathing slowed. She was soon dreaming of her grandmother, of being a little girl in the mountains again. Everything was perfect there, peaceful and serene.

Marion held her, afraid to move and wake her up. He was exhausted, but his mind was still racing. He thought of Si and whether he would heed the warning or come back with more men. He thought of Lacey and her deserving a shot at a normal life. He thought of his father and his reaction in a situation like that.

An impossible situation… I can't kill him, I can't go to the police, and I can't leave her on her own. It would be a lie to think he wasn't attracted to her, a bigger one if he were unwilling to admit that there was some enjoyment in being her knight in shining armor. But there was no joy in what Lacey was going through.

As a young girl, she was left abandoned and alone. Her mother had passed, and a brother was somewhere in the ether. She had taken solace in a handsome stranger named Si, who preyed on every vulnerability and insecurity she had. *She deserved something better;* the thought rolled through his fading mind. *She got a nightmare.* Slowing further, his final thoughts were of the woman next to him and that once again, she was taking solace in the arms of a stranger.

The drive home was painful. His thoughts raged in mad frustration. Something about Marion sent chills down Si's spine. He couldn't place his finger on it, and it wasn't something he could state out loud, but Si knew that man was out of his league. Despite his grip and control over the whores, Si knew he was nothing more than a low-level thug. He would need help in dealing with him, and he was no longer in the physical condition to handle it himself. Even if he had been, he was certain it was beyond his skill to do so.

He would need money. Money to get by until he healed and money to pay for professional help. Racking his brain for any way to make the substantial investment into his future that was needed, he determined his only course of action was to sell off the girls. The Colombians would take them all off his hands, leaving him enough cash to deal with things for a few months and hopefully buy a few girls to start again when that was done.

Once in Cartagena, they would be sold to the highest bidder, some to drug cartels, maybe if they were pretty enough, but most to the rebels. They would be kept for a few years and then killed when they couldn't be sold anymore. Si would sell them wholesale as a package to the Colombians, and it would take him less than a week to get his cash.

After killing Marion, he would sell Lacey into the worst hole he could find and get the hell out of that town. Atlanta would be a prime spot to start up again, only that time with more girls. He could buy a few rather than courting them into service. Courting took time, and he was anxious to start again, but ultimately it was cheaper to flip some himself.

The girls were traded like cattle at a sale barn. The backgrounders, like him, fixed up individual lost causes to sell at a profit. But the real money was made in bulk dealing. Si had decided to spend all his remaining money to start buying girls at volume and then sell them off in lots. A small crew could kidnap a dozen throwaways, vagrants, and washouts in a night and net themselves 20 grand.

Si knew what needed to be done but hadn't yet figured out how to begin. The police on his payroll wouldn't be willing to help him, and certainly not for what he was willing to pay. The emotional trauma of the evening was eating at his psyche, and he was furious at himself for letting a guy named Mary get the drop on him. Si pounded his fist into the steering wheel, forgetting it was broken. His anger was then exploding from within him and pulsing through the broken hand. *Marion should be dead already!* Who could he hire? His local guys couldn't handle anything more than tweakers and hookers. The El Salvadorians had hit squads that would work in the US on occasion, and Marion would be turned inside out within a few days.

He wasn't sure how to contact them except through the cartels, and that would take a few weeks. Even if they came early, Si wasn't sure he had the cash to cover them, and they weren't people he wanted to owe money to. He couldn't simply contact them to ask the price of a hit like you would order a biscuit from a local coffee dive. He ran through his options multiple times, his effrontery getting the better of him at the moment, thinking he could still do it himself.

Si ran through every conceivable option available to him. The road noise from the broken window interrupted his thoughts as the air moved through the cab, cooling his skin. He was nearly back at the hotel when the realization struck him like a blacksmith's hammer on an anvil. There was only one option: a team that killed for enjoyment rather than money, a team that was capable of taking someone with a high degree of skill. A team that he wasn't even sure existed... *The Pigs!*

The thought hit him loudly and with such force that he nearly missed the turn into the parking lot. Si had never worked with them, and everything he had been told was only a rumor. He had never known someone directly who had worked with them, and it may have all been rumors to throw police off the trails of other hitters. If they were true, the murmurings in the shadows of society were of an old group of cops that occasionally took out the trash for some of the cartels in El Paso. They didn't have jurisdiction there, but it wouldn't matter. They weren't here to make arrests and charge Lacey with prostitution.

Sending The Pigs, as they were known, after the two of them would give him the best of both worlds. The notion was that the cops did it more out of enjoyment than cash. These were violent men who killed for money and for the pleasure of doing it. They charged, certainly, but he may be able to get them interested with what he had saved. Even before selling the girls, Si was sitting on a small war chest of cash. They would be the best hitters he could bring in, and they would be within his price range. *Bargain shopping for hitters.*

Before anything could be done, he had to get painkillers and the doctor over to cast his arm and knee. Wanting to go to the hospital was an option not often on the table in his profession. X-rays and doctor reports would lead to questions that he didn't need right then. Raising any suspicion before killing the PI and turning the girl out would make it difficult to sell off the other girls without bringing undercover ICE agents into the mix. Colombians would not buy them if they thought it would cause heat at the shipping yards. Any reports on a known pimp would do just that if a patrol officer came asking about it.

For the time being, he would have to be patient and track down The Pigs; he could get X-rays after they were taken care of. For the first time that evening, he smiled at the thought of them both squirming. Hopefully, they would be able to capture Marion. He intended to break his knees and wrists before killing him. *Or maybe he would let him live... Live with the knowledge that the girl had been sold off and was gone forever. That he would never walk again. His hands would be in pain for the rest of his life, and he'd be blind when Si burned his eyes out... I won't kill him; I'll let him live.*

Unable to drive and use his phone simultaneously, Si waited until he had parked safely in the hotel lot before dialing the number. It was a number not saved in his phone but one he had memorized. The call would connect to a burner phone with a gruff, older man on the other end. The line opened, but there was no answer—just silent breathing as the man listened.

"I hear you can find me a man to paint houses?" Si said into the open line. There was a short pause before anyone responded.

"Yes. And we do our own carpentry."

"So, old man..." He took a deep breath before asking. If The Pigs were merely a rumor, the call would be embarrassing. But if the rumors were true, the men he was about to ask for were akin to something out of a nightmare. "Do The Pigs still paint?"

There was a long pause before the man spoke again into the phone. "Are you sure that's what you want?"

"Yes."

Ewan awoke the next morning with a growing obsession to find the girl. The torment of wanting to kill his attacker became secondary to his desire to butcher the girl. He had no idea how to find her, but he knew she had to still be in the area. Figuring the man to be her pimp was his only lead on locating her.

He stood in front of his bathroom mirror and pulled the straight razor from his shelf, preparing to clean the scruff from his face. He often found himself identifying with the razor, hearing it speak to him as if it was more than an inanimate object but an accomplice in his life.

His recalcitrant nature protected him from the morals and values of modern society, proving to have little to no effect on his conscience. He simply cared little for the authority of anyone else or the opinions surrounding him. When the razor blade spoke, it gave him permission to indulge his volatile characteristics embedded deep within his alter ego.

Did you get the girl? Where is she? Cut her throat… Kill the bitch. Kill the bitch.

He could hear it as if the blade were standing next to him. Ewan knew the logic of it and understood that the blade hadn't said anything. He realized it was his mind that kept the image progressing forward, but still, he found comfort in the companionship of it. His sense of intimacy was dulled to the point of being fulfilled by a razor gleaming in the incandescent glow of the room.

Somehow, it justified his need for blood and his actions, as if he were meant to draw blood in the same manner as the cool steel edge of the blade was designed with one purpose… to cut. By design, neither of them intended to harm, but through an accident of their use, they did as they were capable. As if by the nature of being born, there would be blood in their future path.

Find her. Kill her. Cut her throat. Cover me in blood.

The emptiness he felt placing it back on the shelf when he had finished was akin to the feeling one gets after finishing a particular series of books, the feeling that your companion is done and put away to be enjoyed by another but never by you. A hole in his stomach formed a pit in his intestines. The day wouldn't wait forever, and Rebecca would be up soon, so he made his way to the kitchen to enjoy the remainder of his morning ritual in solitude.

The coffee burned his split lips from the punches to his jaw as he sipped it in irritation. Rebecca was still asleep upstairs in her room, and leaving soon, he could potentially avoid the dreadful interactions with her. Thoughts of the girl filled his obsessive mind, and he wasn't prepared to deal with Rebecca that morning.

The daydreams about the woman in red continued while he finished his coffee. Taking his last sip, he slipped out of the house as silently as he could to fulfill the object of his compulsion. Finding her was his first step, and admittedly an enjoyable part of the process. The gratification in the end would be worth the amount of work involved in locating her. Like exercise, it wasn't fun in the moment, but the overall process was certainly a part of his ritual.

He enjoyed stalking and watching more than finding them. It was a subtle difference, but tracking them didn't give him a look at them. Watching them daily for weeks before acting was like edging himself closer to climax before a grand release. He was a child on Christmas Eve, eating in anticipation for the presents to be opened the following day. Being forced to follow the pimp until sighting the girl was certainly a less desirable pretext for his ultimate goal. He panicked slightly at the thought of the pimp, wondering if Si had already killed her.

Objectively, Ewan was an intelligent man, but finding lost people was not something he was accustomed to, and he had developed no skill for the process. The problem in front of him was simple in its principles. He decided on applying

Occam's Razor, the simplest answer being the right one.

He would sit on the pimp and watch from a distance until an opening presented itself to him to intervene. His employment allowed him the ability to leave for a job site at a moment's notice to approve zoning issues. He hadn't really ever considered losing his job before, but that was certainly possible. It wasn't, however, anything he was concerned with. The job gave no more satisfaction than he would get working at a convenience store and could be easily replaced.

Find the pimp, find the girl… he told himself, needing to regain control to return to his normal life. The girl occupied more and more of his senses. He had to have her, needed her, obsessed over her, and finding her was the only way to clear his brain, to think right again. He could feel his life slipping away as the urge to kill her grew stronger with each passing moment. Everything to him was becoming superfluous when compared to the whore.

Losing control would get him caught, and getting caught would mean he could never do it again. The thought of prison frightened him, knowing his eternity would exist in a box, that his fantasies would never again be a reality, and that the consuming thoughts would never be purged from their cage inside his body… *Find the pimp, find the girl.*

Vincent Mahon walked calmly down the hall, his cowboy boots clicking as each step hit the hardwood floor. The broad rimmed Stetson hat cast a shadow over his face, darkening his expression. It was a somewhat conscious attempt to show outwardly who he was: the man in the shadows. His hat was black with a scarlet hatband, and he wore a thigh-length black duster with blue jeans and a white western button-down shirt.

Each pace was long in stride to match his 6-foot-4-inch frame. Thin by design, he was not a small man. Underneath the shirt, lean muscle threaded over his bones, with popping veins like a marathon runner. His boots were selected to match his hat, and every piece of the ensemble registered as high quality, intricately designed to complement one another and himself.

Tony Lama ostrich boots skimmed the floor while the Stetson hat rode proudly on his head. A lightly dusted beard trimmed closely to look like a 5 o'clock shadow wrapped up to sideburns, and an equally short-trimmed haircut covered his balding scalp. The hallway was dim and silhouetted his body the way a shadow would on a dark wall. Each apartment on the side passed with the sound of his heel clicking.

Mahon didn't run or walk; his pace always seemed to move in a stride of its own. He didn't hurry; there was no need. He was the one people waited on. Every room he entered was his, and every suspect he interrogated was owned upon his arrival. It was as if his movement was commanded by something beyond that world. The world today considered him an alpha male, but he was more than that, with a preternatural control over every aspect of his life.

On his belt, a Texas Ranger badge glistened in the flickering lights of the distressed scones on the wall. A 1911 pistol hugged his hip in a traditional leather holster, with a Glock 26 resting on the back of his left hip.

Stopping in front of apartment A3, he stood for a moment —not giving pause or thought to anyone inside, but because he wasn't ready to enter the room yet. There was no need to knock; the door wouldn't be locked. Everyone in the building knew who he was and what was in the room. The tenants were too afraid to make eye contact when any of The Pigs walked the halls.

As the door opened, he saw exactly what he expected to see: Miguel Gomez and Marshal Hathcock sitting at the kitchen table with a pistol in each of their hands, ensuring it was Vincent who entered. Miguel and Marshal both carried Glock 34 pistols, each as proficient as the other.

Gomez was a shorter half-Mexican officer with the El Paso Police Department. His height, just under 5 foot 6 inches, was nearly a foot shorter than Mahon. His stocky frame and muscular build made up for the size difference between the two. A black western shirt with white buttons, bright enough to match his bleached teeth, popped against his darker skin tone. Though he never wore hats and hated the feel of the felt around his forehead, his attire matched well with Mahon's dark country look.

The other man holstered his Glock underneath an ill-fitting T-shirt that hung over his jeans. He was an older man in his 60s with a few missing teeth and a white thinning ponytail, sitting casually sucking on a drag from his lit cigarette. Over the years, his retirement from the Texas State Troopers had added to the girth around his midsection, but he couldn't be confused as weak or fat. The tallest of the three, he stood over 6 and a half feet tall, with long legs and workman-style boots that made him appear taller.

Though Gomez and Mahon were clean-cut and looked professional in their attire, Marshal was the odd man out, appearing more like a roughneck coming straight out of the oil fields. His Caucasian skin was littered with sun damage and wrinkles from years of working in the Texas heat before and during his time as a police officer.

"We have a job," Vince said, taking a seat at the table.

"Thank God. I've been bored out of my fucking mind. Should never have retired," Marshal said.

"Where?" Gomez asked in a Texas accent. He had grown up in a bilingual house, with his father being a Texan and his mother from Juarez. Though he elected to take his mother's name, he spoke Spanish and English with native and fluent accents in each language.

"Some fucking Dick Tracy in Alabama. We need to drive in so we don't leave a trail getting there. Apparently, he's fucking around with some spic dope dealer's girlfriend, and he wants them gone." Gomez winced at the racial slur but ignored it, allowing Mahon to continue.

"He wants them dead?" Marshal asked, taking another drag on his cigarette.

"He wants them delivered. We can kill the guy if we have to, but the girl he needs alive so he can sell her off." Mahon stood, giving the others a moment to think through the ramifications. There was a subtlety to his standing over the two of them, presenting himself in a dominant position. None of the men questioned that he was in control of their team and would always lead.

"Cocky little fucker, isn't he? Making demands like that," Marshal said in annoyance.

"Maybe. But that's what he's offering."

"How much?"

"Shit, $70k."

"$70,000?" Gomez said, laughing. "We aren't the fucking March of Dimes."

"I don't give a shit if it's $70; I'll take it... I'm so fucking bored," Marshal said, crushing out his cigarette and immediately lighting another.

"We need to leave tomorrow morning. The PI thinks he scared off the dealer, so he should be at home."

"Do we get a go at the girl?" Marshal asked half-heartedly.

"If you want to, go ahead. She's a fucking whore; I'm not sticking my dick in that."

"Whose car?"

"It's like a 15-hour drive... we'll take my Escalade. I'm not making that drive in your truck or some shitty impound car," he said, motioning to Gomez. "We'll meet back here in an hour; get packed."

There were no 'goodbyes' around the table. No 'farewells' to bid a friend a nice night. The three men left, each with the order known to them from many past meetings identical to that. Mahon first. Twenty minutes later, Gomez followed through the door, closing it behind him.

Marshal sat alone in the dark with all the lights off. He smoked several cigarettes, thinking about his next job. The thrill of something to do with his retirement time and pension appealed to him. The money wasn't important; he wasn't a man of high-end taste and had more money than he would spend in his life.

For each of them, the power of killing a mark, studying their target, and executing a plan was the appeal. Their desire was to assert themselves as superior hunters over the person targeted. The man would beg, and so too would the girl. He'd seen it time and time again. First, they would offer more money. Then he'd offer everything he had. He'd finish by blubbering like a schoolgirl, begging them to let him go.

In the end, it would fall on deaf ears. It was nothing they hadn't heard before from any number of men, women, and in some rare cases, even kids when a message was required with the job. Marshal puffed out a pillar of smoke, contemplating other hits they had done throughout the years—a father babbling about not killing the kids because they weren't a part of that. The cartels didn't care, and neither did they. Marshal just shot them all and moved on. They weren't sadists and didn't revel in the pain of their victims. It was a job, nothing more and nothing less.

They were hunters, each experienced in their own ways at hunting people. A hunter doesn't get pleasure from the pain of his prized buck but enjoys the thrill of dominance and of the chase. He snubbed out his cigarette in the glass ashtray on the table and stared silently into the dark. *Hunters get their prey.*

Lacey and Marion woke the next morning on the couch, nestled into one another. They were both drowsy from a long night, and a slight hint of discomfort lingered in the air around them. Questions surrounded their thoughts that morning about embracing each other for the evening. The mutual attraction could be felt with every passing glance and in the aura around them, but nothing could be done about it… Not then, maybe not ever.

Lacey had her own issues and demons to deal with, and Marion was in no better shape emotionally to consider anything beyond helping her. There was a certain poetic satisfaction in being her savior. But the simple fact was he felt sorry for her. It was a position that was impossible for him to reconcile. Anything between them would have to start as equals rather than one indebted to the other.

Life had never thrown her a break, it seemed, and he wanted so badly to be the one to give that to her. Beyond being a fixer by nature, he saw through to her—her true demeanor, her nature, her heart. She was a good person surrounded by bad in a world that was ugly beyond belief. But she endured and was happy with her existence in it, as bleak as it was.

"So… uh, what are we doing today?" she asked with her usual grin.

"First, we're going to have some coffee… or at least I am. You're welcome to join me."

"Yes, coffee would be great… Got any cocaine?" Her face was serious for a moment before a smile broke. "Kidding!" He stared bewildered for a moment and then broke a smile. "Come on, Mary! That was funny!"

"No cocaine, but I have some sugar you can snort if that will help?"

"Probably just the coffee then. It's a weird feeling, you know? Wanting it and simultaneously not wanting to touch it. Wanting nothing more than to get control of my life while something constantly draws me back to it."

"I'm thankful it wasn't heroin or meth you were on… The withdrawals would have been far worse…" He paused, realizing his mistake. "I mean, I don't mean to make light of what you're going through."

She interrupted him. "It's ok. I know what you mean, and I agree. It's much better this way. But you didn't answer my question… What's the plan for today?"

"I'm still piecing that together."

"Care to elaborate, Mr. Holmes?" She bared her teeth as she dug at him a bit.

"Our warning to him last night… it didn't take. He won't listen to it."

"How do you know? He was scared, Mary; I could see it on his face—he was terrified."

Marion didn't go into detail. There was no need to tell her or blame her for the warning not working. For all he knew, it may not have worked regardless of her intervening, and it was an irrelevant guilt trip. "Trust me. He's coming back. I need to find out everything about him. What's his full name? Where does he live?"

"His name is Salvador; he just goes by Si. His last name is Alvarez."

"I got his license plate when I was at the hospital, but with everything that happened when I got home, I forgot it and never wrote it down."

"What do you need his license plate for?"

"That would limit out anyone else in my search and tell me where he actually lives, assuming he doesn't live at the hotel. I can look up DMV records and dig into him further. That was one of the bigger reasons I went to talk to him.

Breaking his window was just…"

"Prudent?" she said, interrupting him.

"Satisfying." He smiled back as she released a giggle behind closed teeth.

"I could have told you that."

"You know his license plate number? I don't even remember mine."

"Yours is TY747Q. His is J97QRF. I don't know where his actual apartment is because he doesn't truly live there. He lives at the hotel in a long-term rental." She was blushing when she gave him the second plate number.

He didn't answer her right away. It struck him as odd that she knew all the plates. Everything suddenly felt like a setup to trap him, but with an angle, he couldn't identify. Lacey recognized his suspicion in the gestures on his face and decided to give him the answer to the questions he wasn't asking.

"Guess, it's probably something I should have told you… I have an eidetic memory."

"Eidetic?" He paused to remember what the term meant. "That's like with reading and stuff, right?"

"Yes, it's like a photographic memory, but it only really works with things I read, or rather remember. I don't read most things at the time I'm looking at them. It's like my mind takes a picture of it, and I can recall it later."

"So you remember everything you've ever read?"

"No. But some people do. It's more short-term, like the RAM on your computer rather than the hard drive. I can commit things to long-term memory that I want to remember, like a reference book I may need later. I did it all through high school until I dropped out. I had straight A's because I would just look at the book and recall the information during the test. Shortly after, the image leaves, unless I make a point of trying to memorize it."

"How do you do that?"

"Same way you do; I just keep recalling it until it never goes away, like a poem my grandmother had on the wall of her cabin. I can recite the whole thing, but not because I've memorized it, but because I can pull up the picture in my mind and read it."

"I'm not sure what to say… That's just cool."

"See? I'm not just all tits and ass." She was smiling at him again.

"I never looked at you that way, Lacey." He held her eye contact for a moment. She was beautiful, but he saw so much more than just a pretty face and a nice figure.

"I know you don't… you've never seen me that way."

"Well, maybe not never," he teased, before telling her about the first time he saw her walking to her apartment.

The water on the lake was calm again that day and drew their attention from the void between them of what not to say. There were no storms in sight until the next evening, giving a serene aura to the morning. They sat on the couch in his office, watching the water and sipping coffee. For several hours, jokes rolled in one after another, and laughter filled the air. She made a point of picking on him when she found out he drank his with one cream and seven sugars. "That's like syrup!" she exclaimed.

"Uh, yeah… delicious syrup. You want some?"

"I'll stick to the black coffee, pussy."

He broke the pleasantry of the conversation and changed his tone to something with a more serious attitude about it.

"We need to get out of here for a while. I can watch the place with the security cameras. Let's head up north for a few days and rent a cabin. I'll run it through my business so he can't follow us."

"He can't trace the cards if he decides to come after us? We may let our guard down if we go somewhere else; here we have the advantage, don't we?" Her concerns were legitimate.

"That's true, but he would have to have an investigator reverse-search my company and then get a court order for the bank records to track the card payment. It's possible, but he would have to be seriously connected at the police department and have cops dedicated to him.

"Okay… When do we leave?"

"After breakfast, we can pack and head out."

7

"Remember that all through history there have been tyrants and murderers, and for a time, they seem invincible, but in the end, they always fall."

—Mahatma Gandhi

Si was strung out on various painkillers and a bottle of commercial moonshine. His wrist throbbed, and without X-rays, the doctor was only guessing but thought it would heal. However, he suspected the knee would need surgery, and in the meantime, he had to walk on crutches.

The crippled pimp may have been a classic inner-city style, but it was only used because they weren't crippled. Walking with crutches and opioid painkillers in his pocket made him live bait for competitors. Besides appearing weak to the girls, it was impossible to navigate crutches with a broken wrist. It was important to show strength while he healed until he was able to sell them off.

Making an example of the first one to mouth off would be easiest, but damaging his product wouldn't help in offloading them. He spoke with the Colombians that morning and found out they would be in the shipping yards at the end of the week to take delivery—11 girls in all, sold for about

$20,000 per girl. However, they wouldn't go easily if they knew where he was taking them. It would require him to be aggressive or clever. Clever was not his style nor his strong suit; scaring them into submission was the easiest option to get them loaded into a trailer.

The Pigs were supposed to be there late that evening. He had already provided them with the address for the PI's house. And would meet them there with a van to take possession at the gate and deliver payment. It should be easy with Lacey getting sold off to cover her debt and Marion begging him for forgiveness and mercy. He took some pleasure in the satisfaction it would bring to crush Lacey's spirit and even more so to destroy Marion. His only hope was that The Pigs wouldn't kill him.

He was surprised that the hitters had accepted his offer, especially with the stipulation that at least Lacey be brought back alive. It wasn't their usual type of job. Their acceptance of it simply added to the mysterious nature of the team and, truthfully, made him more nervous than before he had contacted them. Negotiating was normal for hitters unless it was high profile or an open contract. The fact that they didn't negotiate confirmed the rumors that they simply enjoyed the hunt and the kill more than the money. A hit like that would normally cost in the range of a quarter of a million dollars from professional-level hit squads.

Certain sicarios had a reputation for attacking the owners of the contract if things didn't go right on the job. If the contract owner provided bad intel, it would often breed resentment. Rather than tracking the mark, they would turn on their employer and collect as much of their fee as possible. The notion of having The Pigs tracking him if they decided to turn sent a shiver down his spine. Si wasn't easily scared, but he was frightened of them, and he was terrified of Marion.

The Pigs had no honor and certainly weren't above turning

on their employer. But to his knowledge, that had never happened. He inferred that it was because there was no enjoyment in killing a target that was easy and vulnerable. There was no hunt in that kind of kill for them. *Wolves hunt the deer; there's no hunt for the sheep.*

His mental gymnastics to hazard these conclusions didn't calm the uneasy feelings in his stomach. They were an intimidating group in principle. Cops had the ability to ruin your life or certainly make it miserable. Cops willing to kill in cold blood were even more menacing. Beyond that, these men operated as a group without conscience, without remorse, and without compassion. Just like a pack tracking its prey would have no remorse for its victim, neither would they.

They would track, stalk, and kill their prey. Precision and experience guided their movement and honing in on the animal in their path. There would be no renegotiating, no amount of money or intimidation that could buy them off their quest, hardened killers, each of them, with no ability to feel pity or empathy.

There's a certain magic behind the courage that encompasses men in factions. They develop a supernatural power to do great and wonderful things—things thought impossible before being a unit. The indefatigability of such men built skyscrapers, colosseums, and worlds. But men like that were capable of tremendously terrible things—atrocities that riddled the imagination and shook the foundation of hell.

Si lay on his bed, thinking again of the two of them and the extent to which it would torment them both to be separated, to have their efforts terminated in such stoic and indifferent fashion, and to have their lives ripped from them as they learned the value of their lesson: *you don't steal my property.*

The opioids were taking effect again, causing his eyes to

get heavy when his phone chimed, indicating a text had come through. His heart nearly leaped out of his chest when he saw on the screen who it was from… the unread message displayed a name he had never expected to see again, a name he assumed was dead, a name that couldn't be sending him messages. Across the unopened screen, the name TOMMY was highlighted.

It was mid-afternoon when they began the winding mountain road in North Alabama to a secluded cabin Marion had rented for two weeks. His thought was simply to stay away and watch things from a distance to ensure Si didn't renegotiate. At that point, he was in too deep to go to the police, but it was never really an option he had given much consideration to. The simple fact was police would only help after he or Lacey was dead and could do little on the front end. More than that, if they went to the police, it would be on record. If he were forced to kill Si, they would be the sole suspects.

He had no emotional or moral qualms about killing a worthless pimp. As far as he was concerned, they were somewhere between a rapist and a pedophile, and all deserved a bullet in the skull. Still, he was always somewhat surprised at the ease with which taking a human life came to him. He had come to understand he was one of the few in the 2%: 1% of the population being psychopaths with no remorse, and the other 1% made up of people like him—normal people who would shed a tear at the death of their dog but could easily pull the trigger on someone they morally objected to.

Marion had killed people in the war, and he had killed Tommy. Lacey knew it even though they hadn't yet spoken of it. There wasn't a romantic warrior attitude toward the silence of war, nor did he have a desire to remain mysterious. Soldiers kept quiet because no one else would understand.

He understood that there are war stories a soldier can share at a meal with friends, and there are war stories that can only be shared with other soldiers because only they can understand them… and then there are war stories that no one tells.

Killing someone in cold blood in the United States where a body would have to be disposed of was something Marion was hoping to avoid. It was something he was capable of and something he could emotionally handle. But there was a natural resistance to it that was difficult to describe. He felt like a wild lion being placed inside a cage—years of killing on the prairie replaced with meals at the ready and the softness that comes from no longer being a predator.

His thoughts were interrupted by the abrupt change as the road turned to gravel before the switchbacks started up the mountain. The landscape was beautiful, and the road had a minor drop on each side. Even though the locals called it a mountain, anyone from the Rocky Mountain area would have called it a hill. The drop off the roadside was not enough to kill anyone in an accident, and the switchbacks were overkill in the sheer number present when only a few were needed. It gave a pretense that the hill was steeper and higher than it was.

The cabin sat several miles inland of a national forest preserve and was one of the few private land ownerships grandfathered in. The top of the mountain had cell service, and it was an advertising point for the rental, but there was no service on the way there. The last mile to the cabin turned steeper up the rocky grade as the truck lurched forward with tires slipping on the gravel. The cabin was sitting atop the hill with a majestic view over the entire valley.

He shifted the truck meticulously, down-shifting to increase RPMs on the way up the steeper grades, rotating between 2nd and 3rd gears. Lacey rested her arm on the center console, her hand wrapped around Marion's forearm.

The connection between them was apparent to both of them, and they didn't hide it from one another. Neither of them was ready or willing to move forward with anything, and their platonic relationship ended with occasionally holding hands or Lacey grabbing his arm when it was convenient to do so. She felt comfort in his strength, and he felt a connection with her tenderness. It was a friendship that both of them needed, absent from their lives for so long.

The feeling of her hand on top of his arm sent warmth through his body that he had been afraid to admit out loud to her. She had removed the fake fingernails and opted for a more natural look devoid of her past. Deciding to refuse cosmetics as well and ridding her face of any semblance of makeup had left a natural beauty that was unmatched. Her hair wasn't long enough to put back in a ponytail and draped slightly in front of her eyes, carrying with it an almost unkempt look that Marion found exceedingly attractive. Her natural appearance fit better with her rough-around-the-edges personality and pronounced her exquisite beauty even more.

She loved the clothes he had picked out for her and teased him about having good taste for a straight man. In her life before, she had been accustomed to wearing miniskirts and risqué dresses. Now she found enjoyment in jeans that covered her legs, making her feel less exposed. Those became her first steps toward having respect for her own body and not allowing it to be an object to those who would choose to view her as such. The shoes he selected were a knock-off pair of low-rise Converse All Stars with white laces and black paneling. Lacey had told him that she'd never wear heels again in her life and always wore 'Chucks' in high school.

"I've been thinking…" Lacey said.

"About?"

"About being able to help you with your business and

being a little more prepared."

"With my business? Are you negotiating an employment contract?"

"No. I'm negotiating a partnership," she said matter-of-factly.

He laughed, looking at her while trying to keep his eyes on the road. "A partnership? I've been doing just fine. Besides, I think business partners typically come after knowing each other for more than a few days. What makes you think I need a partner?"

She ignored the fact that they hadn't known one another long. It didn't seem to matter for either of them and was only mentioned in jokes passing. "Because you have too much work, and I have ideas on how to improve your... our business." Her smirk at adding the last pressure point was evidently self-pleasing.

"So how do we purpose we do that?"

"Well, you need an administrator. You don't like handling the computer stuff, and I'm good at it. You can teach me how to start the investigations from that end, and you can focus on the fieldwork that you enjoy."

"Sounds like I have to hire you, train you, and share the profits with you. It also sounds like a good deal for you. What's in it for me?"

"A fucking awesome partnership and the pleasure of my company."

He laughed at her cursing. She had a foul mouth and crude language but could dial it back when necessary. He supposed it was due to her past, but it came off naturally when she spoke, as if she may have always been that way.

"So, a Chief Executive Officer with a sketchy past and a Chief Operating Officer with a coke addiction. Sounds like the makings of a Fortune 500 company to me. Where do we start?" He had meant it as a joke but immediately regretted the jab at her struggling addiction. Lacey seemed to ignore it, not taking offense, and smiled slightly.

"Well, first with your negotiating skills, because you'll bend to a girl with C-cup tits and a round ass!" She laughed as Marion grinned at her.

"I think we need to start with training. I need you to really show me how to use a gun. I've fired them before and have a general idea of how they work, but I want to be capable of actually helping you when it's needed, instead of having to hide behind you and hope you don't get shot."

He had been contemplating the idea of teaching her how to defend herself, during the quieter moments of their drive. It was encouraging to him that she actually wanted to learn and somewhat relieving that she broached the subject. "Okay, we can start this afternoon at the cabin."

They were both silent for a moment as the cabin and landscape came more into view, enjoying the sight of it approaching. The tires continued to slip under the freshly laid gravel road as the truck edged in front of it. Not unique in design, it looked like a package cabin from a kit that could be ordered, maybe 1,000 square feet in total, with cedar logs stained a dark, nearly black color and a green roof that contrasted well with the surrounding landscape.

There was no yard or area for any activity, with trees growing close enough that they were nearly growing into into the structure. The space immediately adjacent to it wasn't the defensible design he had hoped for, giving his attacker the advantage of sneaking up to the house. Regardless, it would be difficult for anyone to track them there, which was a reasonable trade-off in his mind.

Grabbing their duffel bags as they exited the vehicle, they ascended the stairs onto the covered front porch. The entry door was solid wood and heavy, with a rounded arch top and a brass knob. A lockbox was bolted to the wall with laminated paper posted to it, detailing the rules for the cabin and the procedure of checking out. After entering the combination he received when booking the unit, the box opened, exposing the keys to unlock the facility.

Lacey held his hand as the door swung open, and they entered a large great room. A stairwell on the right side of the room extended to the loft that covered nearly half of the ceiling. Large beams crisscrossed above them, with a wood stove in the corner to provide heat in the winter. A kitchenette extended to the right of the main door, featuring a small two-burner gas stove and a gas-powered refrigerator.

There was no existing power supply, and the entire cabin ran on solar panels and propane. At the back of the room, a double glass French door provided a nice view of the park surrounding them, with the cabin built on the edge of a hill and dropping off rapidly behind them. A short hallway with a coat closet and two doors to the left of the room opened to a jack-and-jill bathroom and the only actual bedroom. Ultimately, it was cozy, reminiscent of his lake house, and brought back memories for both of them, with the scent of the cedar logs reminding her of her grandmother's mountain cabin.

Lacey brought her bag into the bedroom and set it on the dresser, while Marion set his in the living room next to the couch. There wasn't enough power to run a TV, so the only entertainment provided was a large cabinet filled with books and board games.

"We might get a little bored here," Marion told her.

"It's okay. I like hiking and the fresh air. Plus, we can always just have sex when we don't have anything to do."

The comment caught him off guard, knowing she was only partially kidding. He let out a heartfelt laugh.

"So what do you want to do?" she asked him earnestly.

Marion didn't answer at first. He unzipped his duffle bag

and pulled a smaller pack out of it, setting it in front of her at the dining area table. Reaching inside, he pulled out a Sig Sauer 365X Macro pistol. He unloaded the pistol at the table in front of her and retrieved a small push dagger, setting it next to the firearm.

"You wanted to start your training. So let's get started."

The full moon had passed the night before, casting a deep darkness over the night, making it impossible for Marion to see out of the windows. The glass door on the wood stove illuminated the great room in a dull glow, highlighting the figures of the furniture and casting eerie shadows throughout the room. He enjoyed the warmth it provided, the heat penetrating him to his core like an inferno burning inside.

Lacey was asleep in the bedroom, but despite his exhaustion, sleep wouldn't come to him. His mind raced as he fidgeted with his pistol on the coffee table. Whether in anticipation of using it or due to anxious energy, he wasn't certain, but he found himself unable to stop. Silently he wished he had brought a bottle of whiskey with them to take the edge off. Even if it had been there, he knew he wouldn't allow it to touch his lips. Taking the edge off wasn't worth the risk to his senses when he was working in an operational capacity, even if he hadn't expected anyone to find them there.

Staring at the ceiling, he heard Lacey open the bedroom door and looked to see her standing there in a tight tank top and silk black panties. The glow of the fire made her skin seem darker than normal, but her green eyes shone brightly in the light.

She marveled slightly at him lying there. That was the first time Lacey had actually seen him without a shirt on. The tattoo on his shoulder that had piqued her curiosity earlier was finally revealed to be a lion roaring into his chest, with the mane turning to flames as it crept down his arm. His chest was built from years of hard work, and the shoulder muscles bulged like pythons crawling toward his sternum. It had several scars that appeared to be old bullet wounds, and one slashing scar slightly disfigured the face of the lion.

There was no invitation given or needed; she simply walked over and climbed on top of him, nestling herself into him. He brought his hand down from behind his head, letting his neck relax on the armrest, and held her. The scent of her intoxicated him again like a poison taking control of his body.

There was no sexual tension in the moment beyond what always seemed to be present between them. The romantic interest took second priority to her just needing him in that moment. Marion held her as he would a grieving widow, with no selfish desire masquerading beneath the surface. She latched onto him as a rock of comfort in an otherwise turbulent sea. Neither of them said a word, and Lacey was soon asleep, breathing softly with the warm air tickling his chest.

He lay awake with a wandering mind, still restless but slightly more comforted than before. At times, it felt as if his mind were a diesel engine that struggled to turn off without starving for fuel, continually processing the situation until the depth of night crept over him, making sleep impossible. The phone chimed, startling Marion and waking Lacey from her slumber.

"What is it?" Lacey asked, sitting up so that Marion could reach the phone. He stared at the phone, confused at first, then clarity struck him as he realized what was happening. "Do you recognize them?" he asked, showing Lacey the phone.

The screen displayed an image of three men standing in his living room. One wore a black Stetson hat, while the other two moved through his house with pistols drawn. They moved with experience, fluidly navigating through the home. They didn't need to talk to one another; each man instinctively knew what to do as they moved from the living room to each bedroom. Outside, the security camera captured a view of a gray Cadillac Escalade, with an image clear enough to pick up the license plate number.

"Any idea who they are?" When he looked at Lacey, she was frozen, staring at the screen, unable to respond.

"Lacey, who are they?" he asked again.

"I've never seen them... but there are rumors. Rumors of a gang of cops, supposedly three of them, who work as hitmen. If that's them... Mary, this is really bad." She turned to look at him.

Marion didn't say a word. He stared at her, then back at the screen, and looked at her again. The men on the screen began searching the home for any indication of where they had gone. He was certain they would take the hard drive for the security cameras before leaving.

"Cops?"

"Yes."

"Then they'll be able to find us here."

"We should have killed Si," she said, irritated.

He ignored her comment. They both knew why that wasn't an option, but in the end, it probably would have been better.

"It would have been worth it," she said, crossing her arms and leaning back on the couch.

"Have you ever killed anyone?" he asked rhetorically as she glared back at him, refusing to respond.

"Hand me the burner phone in that bag," Marion said as he motioned to the black duffle bag next to her on the floor.

Pulling up his computer, he accessed the DMV records to pull up the owner and phone number of the Escalade. *These guys are brazen, he thought,* pulling up the car. It wasn't a rental; it was registered to a Texas Ranger named Mahon.

"What are you going to do?"

Marion didn't answer but dialed the number on his burner phone and called Mahon. It rang several times before the man noticed the vibration. Watching him on the video feed, he could see Mahon in real time at a half-second delay.

"Mahon," the tall man in the cowboy hat said, answering.

"I don't suppose I can talk you out of this, can I?"

"No," he added, nothing else—no alternatives, just a simple no, cold and indifferent.

"Then I'll be here when you come."

"Where's that?"

"Do your job, and you'll find us."

"Then this will be over for you soon. Can I assume you already called the police?"

"Why? So you could suicide me in a jail cell? You think I'm fucking stupid? Don't forget to lock the door when you leave."

Mahon was silent for a moment, taken aback by the call. He'd never had a mark reach out to him while on the hunt. "Bring the girl to me now, and I'll kill you quickly."

"And the girl?" he asked, looking at Lacey.

"Her life was over a long time ago."

"Okay. I've heard your deal; now hear mine… Walk away now, tonight, go back to Texas, and never return to Alabama."

"Why would I do that?"

"Because if you don't… I'll cut your heart out." Without another word, Marion hung up the phone. Not hesitating, he removed the battery and SIM card before tossing the card and phone into the wood stove.

Lacey watched him carefully as he walked to the stove and back. He was wearing jeans with no shirt or shoes. He was fit but not a gym rat. There was no six-pack set of abs, but a hard stomach lay beneath. He was built like a boxer who was out of training, with muscular legs visible through his pants and a chest and shoulders to match. The lion on his chest wasn't his only tattoo; his back was completely covered from top to bottom with a Soldier's Cross.

"Marion… What are we going to do?"

He didn't answer her immediately, still configuring the plan in his head. The thought had occurred to him that Si would hire a sicario after the incident at the house, and he had planned accordingly. "It'll happen tomorrow," he said, taking his seat beside her. "When the banks open, they'll start tracing my credit cards and then the businesses. Tomorrow night, they'll be here. They'll wait until between 3 and 5 in the morning when we are in our deepest state of sleep. We'll know they are here when the cell signal dies."

Lacey couldn't help but be captivated by his eyes. He had pretty blue eyes that shimmered brightly in the firelight. But there was something more—a calming effect within them, a danger hidden behind them. "So that's it? We have until tomorrow… Marion, I can't go back to that life."

"You won't have to. Tomorrow morning, I'm going to drive you someplace to hide. It's a domestic violence shelter I've used over the years. They'll help you get a new identity and disappear. It won't be impossible to find you, but it will be extremely difficult. When I'm done, I'll find you."

"Like hell, you will!" The words came out hurt and furious together. "I'm not leaving you to deal with this!" She was standing in front of him by the time the second sentence left her mouth.

"I can handle this. And I can't do it if I'm worried about you."

"Fuck you! I'm not leaving!" Tears of frustration began welling in her eyes. Marion stood in front of her then.

"Don't you get it? I can't keep you safe if you're here! I can handle them, but not with you here." He had calmed a bit by the time he finished speaking.

"No! You don't get it! I haven't had anyone to care about or anyone to care about me in years! I know you feel about me the way I do about you. So give me a gun, give me a knife, give me a fucking fork… and I'll kill anyone who tries to hurt you or take that from me."

Every urge in his body wanted to grab her and kiss her, but it was certainly not the time or place. Standing up, he reached out to hold her face in his hand; she did the same with his. "Okay." There was nothing else to say. No words of wisdom to comfort either of them, and he knew he wouldn't convince her to go.

"What are you going to do?"

"I'm going to kill them all."

Si awoke from his opioid-induced sleep early the next morning. Falling asleep before deciphering the message, he found himself equally confused after resting. There was no text, just a coordinate. The message must have been sent with poor service because he couldn't get another message back to him. The progress bar stayed stagnant, showing the message was being sent but not received.

The phone stared back at him as blankly as his scowl tried to pierce the meaning of the message and the location. Si pondered different options, but the only conclusion he could reach was that it must be the location where Lacey was going to be buried. *What's there now?*

He forwarded the message to Steve at the police department with a list of instructions to go there and see what he could find out. Steve responded in capital letters: 'FUCK YOU,' prompting Si to send another message: '$1000.' It took several minutes for Steve to respond until Si received a thumbs-up text in return.

His phone hadn't been closed for more than a second when the door to his hotel crashed open. A large cowboy entered, followed by two other men, the largest of them closing the door behind him. It was an intimidating sight, even if he had not been bedridden and injured. The vulnerability of his current state made him anxious as he sat up in bed, trying to posture himself in a more masculine manner.

"He wasn't at the house," Mahon said.

Si didn't need an introduction. Having only spoken on the phone and not knowing what they looked like, he only knew the voice of The Pigs. That sentence and their demeanor were enough to tell him who his present company was.

"And… what now?"

"Now we wait. In the morning, we will track his cards and get the bank records for him. You said he was a PI on the phone?"

"Yes."

"Then he has a business we need to track, too." It was a general statement, but he turned to Gomez to ensure it was an order that would be followed. Gomez nodded in acknowledgment.

"So, why are you here?"

"What can you tell us about him? He wasn't shaken knowing we were coming after him. He knew what we were doing there. It was like he counted on it. There was no worry or anxiety in his voice, even with us in his house. It was odd. We've never been contacted by a mark, but he called while I was there. They always run when they know we are on their tracks, but he didn't. He was daring me to come after him. I want to know why."

"Well, how the fuck should I know? He's just some dumb shit PI that gets his rocks off with one of my girls."

"Fucking idiot. He's more than that."

"Who the fuck do you think you're talking to, puta!" He went to stand after being called an idiot when Mahon reached out and grabbed his wrist, twisting it beneath the cast and sending Si's body caving back into the bed. Si screamed in agony as the pain pulsed through his arm.

"WHO IS HE!"

"I DON'T KNOW!" Si screamed in agony as his wrist was contorted against its natural rotation.

Mahon released his grip and looked at the pack of hunters standing behind him.

"He is more than he appears."

Mobile, Alabama, was warmer than the Birmingham area, but the air was still cool, and they weren't used to the climate coming up from Columbia. The three of them stood at the shipping lot, waiting on a delivery of girls from various locations around the Southeast.

The women would be packed into a shipping container with buckets for toilets and food and water to survive the trip. The container would be sealed, and they wouldn't see the sun again until arriving in Panama two weeks later.

They would then be moved south in shipments until the weather warmed. The heat of the summer would roast the inside of the steel containers like a slow cooker, killing the products and forcing transportation through other methods. Coyotes would move them on ground transport from the ports in Panama through to Columbia. U.S. customs was traditionally more difficult because it was much less susceptible than third-world customs agents to bribery.

The three of them spoke exclusively in Spanish to one another.

"How many girls are coming tonight?"

"Twenty or thirty."

"What about Salvador? He was supposed to sell us 11. The boss would have been happy with a larger load coming in. The rebels are taking in a lot more."

"We get Si's in a few days. We won't push them through

the shipping yards. He's going to bring them down here, and we will take them to the coyotes at the Texas border. They're expecting his group in Juarez next week."

"They've already been sold?"

"Yes, we've already been paid."

"What if Si doesn't show?"

"He will; he always does."

"You're putting too much faith in him. If he doesn't show, the cartels will go to war with us. It was fucking stupid to put so much trust in him. You don't fuck with the cartels, and we represent Señor Vega. He won't be happy if this goes wrong."

"If he doesn't show, we can track him down and get the girls. He should be here in a few days. If we don't hear from him, we can find him and figure out what happened. Worst case, we find some girls off the street in Atlanta."

"You'd better be right about this. We will have the devil to pay if we don't get the cartels their girls."

"It'll be fine; the fucker can't run right now. Rumor has it he got his ass kicked by a private investigator and has a fucked-up leg."

"Who's the investigator?"

"Some nobody up north."

"Si going to kill him?"

"I imagine."

"After we get these girls loaded, we should head to his hotel."

"Why?"

"Because if he's injured, I don't want to risk one of the girls getting away. You know what they'll say if we promised 11 and show up with ten."

The first of the two rented vans could be seen pulling into the yard. It was a large box truck with placards on the side for the big box store that owned it. A system was in place, which allowed smooth transitions of the girls to the container. The truck made a three-point turn, backing up to the open doors of the shipping container without needing direction.

The incessant beeping of the backup klaxon always made Luis nervous, but it was an irrational phobia. The noise in the shipping yard, and the space between them and any of the security staff that hadn't been paid off, was so large that no one would hear a foghorn going off. Gunshots had been needed in the past to garner compliance from the occasional girl hell-bent on fighting, and even the muzzle blast didn't attract attention.

The passenger got out of the front seat and opened the roll-up door on the back to count the girls. Each exited with their heads down. Some were sobbing, others scared, and some, having accepted their lot in life, seemed at peace with the choices made for them. Each knew their fate was sealed, and they would never see home again.

The man from the truck was handed a cheap black duffle bag by one of the three South American men. There was no need to count the money in it. No honor existed among thieves, but it was known that traffickers were not to be shorted on the count. If the count was wrong, it would be taken out in flesh at a later date or made right with interest.

The truck came, delivered the product, and disappeared in under five minutes. It was a fluid operation that had happened many times and would continue to happen. Within ten minutes, another truck arrived and followed the same protocol to deliver the merchandise.

One man stood at each door of the shipping container, swinging them closed without a word to the captives. Nothing needed to be said; the girls inside knew the rules and understood what would happen if they didn't obey them. The doors were sealed like a jail cell in an 18th-century prison. It would be the last time any of them would see home. Most of them would be dead within a year, and all would be dead within five years.

"You're right," the leader of the group said to the others.

"Let's head to Birmingham. This is too risky. If we miss that deadline, we'll be lucky if the boss just kills us. The cartels will do far worse if he hands us over as penance."

"What about them?" one of the men said, motioning to the container with the girls inside.

"They'll be fine. No one will mess with them; the harbor master and the dock workers have been paid. No one will look in the container or answer a scream if they hear it. Besides, we should be back early tomorrow morning or tomorrow afternoon."

"You think Si may not come?"

"I'm thinking it's not worth the risk. If he doesn't show, we are fucked. Best-case scenario, he's not supposed to be here for a few days. It's better to go get them now and not risk losing them in transport here."

"Okay. When do you want to leave?"

"Right now. Go get the truck."

8

Si Vis Pacem, Para Bellum. - (If you want peace, prepare for war)

The morning light streamed through the bedroom window. Lacey was still curled under the covers, and Marion had fallen asleep on top, with a blanket pulled over his legs. He looked silly sleeping in jeans, but she knew he was doing it to protect her honor.

Honor—that was something she hadn't had in a long time, something that had been taken from her when she was young. She knew she'd never wear white at her wedding… a wedding—there's a thought. It seemed almost plausible then, something that had never crossed her mind before. It had never occurred to her that she might one day have kids or be married. A normal life seemed out of her grasp, but not today, anything seemed possible.

Watching the sunrise through the window was nearly the perfect morning. She couldn't remember the last time she felt so at peace. It struck her as odd to be at peace with everything stacked against them. She snuck out of bed to start coffee on the percolator, trying not to wake Marion. The sky was clear, but off in the distance, she could see a storm rolling in through the kitchen window.

As a girl, she used to love watching thunderstorms come barreling in while sitting on the porch at the cabin. This wouldn't be that kind of night. The Pigs would come for them. She might die, or Marion… she felt confident that the evening would not have a happy ending. *What a shame.*

The thought hit her about everything that could be but soon wouldn't. In another life, she and Marion could have been happy together, like a real family with kids and a dog; she could see it in her mind's eye. An old plantation-style white picket fence would never have been her dream. But a cabin in the woods like this one, or her grandmother's, something off the beaten path, was her ultimate dream.

Staring out the window, she thought of everything that should have been but would never come to pass. Rays of light shining through the window told her the day was sweltering, like her emotions: sunny and bright at the moment, with a storm cloud in the distance, slowly moving that way but moving, nonetheless. It was a paradise with a storm on the horizon… *a paradise lost.*

She was briefly startled when his arm closed around her neck, hugging her into him. She reached up and placed a hand on his biceps, settling into him. It was an overwhelming emotion for her—the feeling of his warmth, the knowledge of what was coming for them, but she was at peace with it. She'd rather die there with him than go back to the life she knew just a few days earlier.

Deep within her being was an anxious energy to get the night started, but something felt wrong about her feelings. Marion was calm when he was on the phone the previous night. Knowing instinctively what to say without thinking, he had turned the tables on them. They weren't the wolf pack that day going after a lamb in the field. They were the pack coming after a Great Pyrenees guarding its flock—one that had been tested and battled these waters before.

She turned and looked at him, resting her hands on the scars on his chest. She leaned her head forward, connecting their foreheads when she asked him, "Something isn't right, Mary… What did you do in the Army?"

"What do you mean something's not right?" he said, pulling away and pouring two cups of hot, steaming coffee.

"That right there. Whenever I ask you about it, you deflect. You said once you were in military intelligence. Don't get me wrong. It's cool as shit and probably why you're such a good investigator, but it doesn't answer these scars. It doesn't explain why you knew exactly what to do last night. It doesn't answer what you intend to do tonight?"

"How do you know I intend anything?"

"Because you're too calm not to have a plan. When people don't have a plan, they're scared, they panic. It doesn't matter what your experience is; life isn't like a movie. Having a plan makes people calm."

"You're calm. Do you have a plan?"

"Yes. To trust you and do what you tell me. But I'm still terrified. So tell me what your plan is. Tell me what you did. Tell me why I should be calm. Please, I need that right now. Tell me why I need to trust you."

"Okay." Marion handed her the cup as they walked to sit on the couch. The cabin didn't have sugar, and he was forced to drink it black—not something he was unaccustomed to, but it was not nearly as satisfying. Normally, she would have teased him about the coffee, but her nerves were stealing the joy from the moment, and she truly wanted an answer to her questions. She eyed him patiently, refusing to speak until he divulged the information.

"I was in military intelligence. It was a unique assignment. I wasn't special forces, infantry, cavalry scout, or anything of the more grunt-style variety. I tested well and eventually got sent to the Defense Language Institute to learn Russian. A while later, Putin invaded Crimea, and my testing and language aptitude allowed me to move into a special position, working in overt intelligence in Russia at the embassy. It wasn't long before I had made enough connections with the CIA to get picked up as a contractor still wearing a pickle suit…"

"A pickle suit?" she interrupted, smiling and curious.

"It's what soldiers refer to other Army guys in uniform. Since Army uniforms are traditionally green, it's called a pickle suit."

She let out a laugh. "So what did you do with the CIA?"

He paused, unsure of what he was allowed to tell her and what in that moment he had to share. The moment of silence took him back briefly to the days when he was in uniform. At times, he missed it, but then he remembered all the less glamorous parts of the Army.

"I hunted spies. We would track them and extract them out of Russia to face charges in the U.S.; when we were able to, anyway."

"And when you weren't able to?"

"We'd kill them. It was a counter-espionage detachment. We had one job: find spies and terminate them. I got tasked with the job because I had a good record as a counter-intelligence agent doing it overtly for years. In my early 20s, I was given a psych evaluation. I fell into a unique group of people. I'm not a sociopath; I don't have any symptoms of psychopathology, but it doesn't bother me to kill anyone. It's a small percentage of the population that fits that category without being severely mentally disturbed—less than 1%."

"But you wouldn't kill Si at your house?"

"We couldn't at the time… not out of any concern for him, but because it would have meant covering up another body, the chance of getting caught, and the easiest solution at the time was if he had just gone away and let you be free. I had hoped his self-preservation would be enough to deter him. Or at least the hassle of it."

"You've got a good heart, Mary. But you don't understand guys like him. He could never just let me go, or he'd risk losing control of the other girls. More than that, he can't just have a loose end out there to come back and bite him if I decide to testify."

"I understand guys like him, Lacey. I was just hoping this would go away. Now that it hasn't, we've run out of options."

She stared at him for a moment. At that time, no more information was needed, and none was offered; it seemed like he never enjoyed talking about it, but it was interesting to find that it wasn't because he was ashamed of anything he'd done, as she had often imagined from Vietnam vets. She couldn't put her finger on it, but there was another reason he held back that portion of his life from her. Everything else had been an open book while they talked. She knew about his childhood, friends, and family, but he glazed over that part of his life whenever they spoke.

"Ok." She wasn't scared anymore. "Can you get us out of this?"

"Yes."

"So what do we do?"

Marion closed the gap between them and grabbed her again. She thought for a moment he was going to finally kiss her, but he held his distance.

"First thing, and probably the most important thing…"

"Yes," she said, hopefully. She wanted him to grab her and kiss her more than anything at that moment. Her mind, her heart, and her body were begging for his lips to be on hers.

"You need to brush your teeth!"

She smiled for a moment and lightly slapped his face a few

playful times with an open hand. "You ass! I thought you were finally going to kiss me."

"Not yet," he said, smiling at her.

"I know. It's not right yet... But you should know that I want it."

"I do too," he said, hugging her as they both stood from the table while he kissed her forehead.

"I'm going to shower. Then we will spend the day getting ready. I didn't think he would be able to find us here and there's no time to go back and get the right equipment from my cottage. We will have to make do with what we get in town today. "

"Okay." She clung to him, not wanting to lose the moment. "Go shower. You stink, anyway."

Ewan watched the tall cowboy enter and leave the pimp's room. *Who in the hell is this?* he wondered. It was a question that may never receive an answer. He was losing his patience with Si; the anger and need to kill the pimp began boiling in him once again. But he needed the pimp to find the girl.

His hands trembled slightly as he aimed the binoculars at the pimp's room. He wasn't sure if it was frustration, anxious energy, or the fact that his body was then fueled by coffee and energy bars. A group of men left in a Cadillac that seemed out of place in that part of town. Perhaps it was the tinted windows or the general aura they exuded, but they felt like cops.

Ewan had been patient, waiting for the girl, but he was losing control. *Why were the cops there? Was he an informant?* He knew that killing an informant might draw unwanted attention, but he was running low on options. More importantly, he was running low on self-control. Reaching under his seat, he pulled out the dart gun and tucked it into his waistband.

He had acquired the dart gun from a veterinary office years before after stealing drugs to incapacitate his victims. Initially, he didn't know what he was looking for and experimented with various drugs. Some had little to no effect, while others, like ketamine, proved far more useful. Purchasing fentanyl allowed him to render victims unconscious and then treat them with naloxone to wake them up, but it posed the issue of stopping their breathing if not handled carefully with medical-grade products.

The dart gun had only one shot, and if he missed, his chances would be foiled. Ewan had spent hours practicing in his basement and was extremely accurate with his method of delivery. Being of average stature, it was uncomfortable getting close to his victims, but the dart gun allowed him to incapacitate them from a distance. When he had seen the dart gun in the vet clinic, it was the perfect option—too good to pass up.

He tucked the gun beneath his sweater as he crossed the street, pretending to be just another businessman meeting a secretary for lunch. Traversing the mezzanine, he scanned the area meticulously, looking for any activity or anyone who could place him there. That was a body that would be found, and he couldn't risk leaving a trail or a witness linking him to it. He wouldn't have the time, and more importantly, he wouldn't have the control to resist going after the girl once he had his answers.

Noting the locking mechanisms on the doors as he passed the rooms at the end of the hall, he saw that none were electronic auto-locking doors. The person inside would have to manually turn the deadbolt. His best option was a surprise attack, hoping to catch him sleeping and that the door wasn't locked.

Rounding the corner at the end of the building, Ewan pulled the pistol from his waistband and held it close to his body to avoid being seen. Fingering the door handle down slowly to open it, he could tell it wasn't locked by the feel of the mechanism. He rushed the door with his shoulder, and in an instant, the latch popped, flinging it open with a large crash against the doorstop.

Si had been asleep on the bed but bolted upright when he heard the noise of the door slamming against the wall for the second time in less than an hour. His sleep would soon be restored as he found himself staring down the barrel of an odd-looking pistol. Panic surged through him for a moment as he wondered if he had breathed his last, if his world would soon turn black, and if the pain of death would rip him from that earth.

A snap and a hiss, much less pronounced than gunfire, sent something stinging into his neck. Instinctively, he reached for it to remove the item. He was on his feet in the next moment, ready to charge his attacker. The pain in his knee sent him forcefully to the ground the instant he put pressure on it.

He held the stinging object in his hand, confusion flooding his mind as he tried to understand what it was until it occurred to him: the yellowfins at the tail end and the syringe-like needle—a *tranquilizer.* He fought momentarily as his consciousness began to fade, his thoughts slipping away forcefully at first, then peacefully.

Si clamored to his knees, only to succumb to the fast-acting sedative moments later. His mind remained conscious, but his eyes closed, unable to muster the strength to lift them. An extended hand twitched in one last attempt to fight his attacker before his world went black.

Renting a day-use office in downtown Birmingham, The Pigs were busy gathering information and calling in favors. They needed warrants to access the banking records for the business and the individual accounts. Flashing a badge never worked in those instances, but most banks would never question the warrant.

They had leverage from a blackmail case involving a Texas judge, and within the first hour of their rental, a forged warrant was issued for Marion Gamble's bank records. The judge could never admit he hadn't signed it, or information would be released that could cost him his seat on the bench. It wouldn't hold up in court, but that wouldn't matter; the bank likely wouldn't pay attention or ask too many questions about it.

Gomez and Mahon worked diligently at their computers while Marshal visited local banks, pulling paper copies of the records. It was late afternoon when he walked back through the door, his large frame filling the space from the floor to the top of the molding.

"I found him!" he said, excited as he shut the door behind him.

"Where is he?" Gomez asked.

"I focused on the business records; personal records could have been found by the pimp, and he'd have known that. The business records would be much harder to track. He uses a local bank in Birmingham for his business, and one record stood out. It was to a rental property company."

"So he's using a rental property he owns?" Gomez interrupted.

"No. The rental company handles both short- and long-term rentals. I called them up, explained that I was following a case involving a fugitive, and asked to see their recent short-term rental contracts. They emailed everything to me, and there it was: Gamble Inspection Services."

"Did you get the location?" Mahon was then interested in the conversation.

"I didn't want to give them any reason to be alarmed. I was worried they might try to involve local law enforcement, so when they sent the contracts, I asked for the addresses for all of them. They're staying at a remote cabin about three hours North of here."

Mahon didn't respond at first but pulled up his computer. "What's the address?"

Marshal handed him the paperwork with the addresses listed, pointing his sausage-sized finger at it. Working on his computer for a moment, Mahon was able to access the county tax records to look at a map of the building and surrounding area.

"It's in the middle of nowhere. There isn't even a ranger station within ten miles. Fucking idiot. We could use mortars on him out there and just kill them both if we didn't need them alive," Marshal said, staring at the screen over Mahon's shoulder.

"No one around for miles, but he has the high ground at the cabin," Mahon said cautiously.

"So what?" Gomez asked, frustrated. "He's a fucking dick. Seriously, you're not worried about this guy, are you?"

"I'm not worried, just alert. I like to know who we're dealing with, and we still don't know much about him. Don't you find it strange we can't find anything about his military record? It's like he was in but didn't do anything."

"Maybe, he didn't."

"No. You didn't hear him. He's not just a fucking nobody PI."

"So it's classified?"

"I think so."

"Okay, so he was an intelligence officer. What difference does that make? We've never bothered worrying about that in the past, and this isn't the first Soldier we've taken out."

"I told you already… He's wrong—everything is wrong. It feels like we're hunting someone who wants to be hunted."

"He's up there buried balls deep in the hooker right now.

He doesn't actually think we're going to find him. When we get there, he'll be laying on the couch buck naked with her." Marshal was getting frustrated.

"Fine. We'll leave this evening. We can park at the base and hike up the hill," Mahon agreed, unsure of what else to do. They had his location, and there was nothing more they could determine about Gamble that would benefit them. It was simply time to move forward with fulfilling the contract.

"Hike up the hill? Are you fucking kidding? I'm 65 years old. Let's just drive up there, turn off the lights, and go in the front door. He won't be ready for us."

"No!" Mahon was getting irritated. He wasn't used to being questioned that much and certainly didn't like his team arguing with him. "I agreed to go and get him without any more investigation. But we do this smart and right. We'll come up the hill one on each side. We can take surveillance from the trees and watch the house. Then when I say so, we'll go in and take them."

"Fine. You're the boss."

"Yes, I am." Mahon wasn't paying attention anymore. He was looking at the DoD photo on his computer of the man he was going to kill that night, staring coldly as if he were face-to-face with him right then. *Something was wrong, but* he couldn't place his finger on it beyond not knowing anything about him.

Who are you? he asked himself, as if willing the computer to answer back. A blank file of a man who seemed oddly comfortable in his present situation. When they were hunted, targets would run and hide; when they were found, they would try to buy their lives. The PI ran and hid, only to taunt them to come and get him. *What would he do when he was found?* Mahon wondered to himself without alerting the others to his concerns.

Run, hide, fight… he thought, remembering the FBI's

guidance for active shooter incidents. Run if you can get away. Hide if you can't run. Fight if you're found. Gamble ran not because he had to, but because he wanted to. To buy time to plan. He's hiding because he wants to. *Is it to set a trap? Or to buy more time? Time for what?* The questions gnawed at him, devouring his every thought in the moment. The one question that troubled him most was what would happen if Marion Gamble decided to fight.

Si awoke dazed and groggy. Looking around, he immediately recognized the facility, even through the haze of the drug's effects. It was the warehouse next door to the hotel. He was staring at Lacey's apartment, with the open paneling directly behind him. The sun was setting in the distance, and he was suspended from the steel rafter beam with a braided wire cable underneath his arms, cutting into his ribs.

All of his clothes had been removed, and his hands were secured behind his back in what felt like zip ties. The zip ties had been pulled so tight that his hands were starving for blood flow. The cable was just high enough off the ground to force him to support his weight on his tiptoes. Relaxing his feet into the cable caused it to cut into his skin more, forcing him to choose between pain in his feet or pain in his ribs. He couldn't tell what was beneath him, but it felt different—soft and slightly textile in character, not the concrete he had expected.

He knew the facility well, and there was little use in crying for help. The hotel was far enough away that the distance between the two would drown out any sound. Counting on that particular feature himself many times in the past, Si knew the benefits were all in his attacker's favor. It was an irrelevant point; even if someone happened by, no one would call the police to help in this neighborhood. His eyes were still cloudy as he regained consciousness, and the man in front of him was currently indistinguishable but spoke with a familiar voice.

"I see you're coming around," he said calmly, fidgeting with something in his hands.

"What am I doing here?" Si asked groggily, still trying to determine exactly what was going on.

"You're here to tell me about the girl."

"Marion?" he asked, still unclear on who his attacker was.

"Marion? Is that who has the girl?"

"Who are you?" His eyesight was beginning to return. "Wait, I know you… You're the guy that was here yesterday." Ewan didn't answer. There seemed little need to acknowledge the question.

"So what do you want?" Si was irritated, growing angrier as he recognized the weakling who had kidnapped him.

"I told you. I want the girl. The one who lived here."

"Lacey? She's a fucking whore. I've been looking for her as well."

"Really? You don't know where your whore is?"

"No! She fucking ran off with some guy… A PI named Marion Gamble. I've been trying to find her. I had to call in a crew from Texas to hunt her down…" Si paused for a moment, trying to determine how much information he wanted to provide. "Look… let me go now, and I'll give you the girl as soon as I get her. You can do whatever your freaky mind wants to."

"Oh." Ewan looked as if he were entertaining the notion. Suddenly, his quizzical expression changed to a demented half-smirk before he spoke again. "I'm afraid we're beyond that point."

"If you don't let me down now, I'm going to fucking kill you!" Si screamed. "And since you haven't killed me already, I'm guessing you don't have the stomach for it. So let's just say you got one over on me, after I got you, and we can be even. I'll sell you the girl for what I was getting from the Colombians, and you can do what you want with her."

"I'm afraid that won't work either." He was smiling then, sending a chill down Si's spine. It wasn't a happy smile, baring his teeth, but something forced. Si felt as if he truly enjoyed the moment but expressed it outwardly only for the benefit of his captive. "I'm just a government employee; I simply don't have the funds to buy her from you."

Si watched, horrified, as the object Ewan had been fiddling with came into focus. The man who had yet to introduce himself was sharpening a boning knife he had taken from Lacey's apartment.

"So what do you intend to do with me?" Si was nearly too petrified to move. Not the kind of fear he felt in dealing with police or even the cartels. He could control that, and ultimately they had rules, codes of conduct, and a type of honor that governed behavior among thieves. As long as he covered his tracks, the police were powerless, and if he didn't shortchange the cartels, they would leave him to run the girls. This was different—a darker fear resting deep within his soul. The amount of pain he imagined his body would feel momentarily had him frightened to the point of losing control of his bladder.

The man didn't answer; he seemed to take enjoyment in the outward appearance of Si's distress as he sat calmly sharpening his knife, even whistling occasionally and refusing to acknowledge his captive.

"What do you want?! What the fuck do you want from me?! I told you I don't know where the girl is! Let me go, you motherfucker!" Si screamed in desperation, his body shaking and convulsing in fear and despair to break free from his bonds. All his shouting and screaming fell on deaf ears, as if the mystery man couldn't hear him.

Ewan finished sharpening his knife and began stripping off

his clothes, carefully folding them and placing them on the bench in the corner. Standing awkwardly naked in the disgusting building, he was holding only the knife in his hand. Si realized for the first time that he was his toes were resting on sheets from Lacey's bed. They surrounded him and would serve only one purpose: to catch the blood.

"Now, typically I like to do this with women. It does little to nothing for me to have male clients. I'm not sure why," he said, staring inquisitively at Si for a moment as if pondering the question himself. "Please bear that in mind as we proceed, because this may not be as smooth as normal, and I don't want you judging my performance too harshly. Now, where would you like to begin?"

"Begin? What the fuck are you talking about, you crazy motherfucker! Let me go!" he screamed, but no one would hear him. Si pulled at the zip ties, desperately trying to free himself. Shaking his feet with each bounce, he dug the wire further into his skin with each tremor of his body.

"Excellent! I agree we will start with the ears and work our way down. We will have to take a brief intermission when I get to your penis because it can cause you to bleed out, so you'll want me to cauterize the wound."

"Fuck you! Help! Help! Help!" Si screamed at the top of his lungs, but it wouldn't be heard. His voice would echo inside these walls for an eternity. He would soon watch horrified as pieces of his body began to litter the floor in front of him, each portion placed delicately on the floor as if it were a sacred artifact.

Closing his eyes to avoid feeling his own horror, Si felt a tug on his ear and a sawing motion at the base where it met his skull. He screamed louder than he had ever heard himself scream, his own personal horror show that would last the rest of his life was now playing out in front of him.

"NO! NO! NO!" he yelled, until the empty walls of the

defiled building went silent.

The sun had set while Lacey and Marion anxiously watched their day pass them by. They spent most of the morning talking—talking about a life beyond that moment, each of them realizing what could have been had they met under different circumstances years ago.

That afternoon, they left to go into town. Marion hadn't told her the entire plan yet, but most of it. He needed some supplies from town, particularly from the hardware store, to make this work. *He had done this before,* she kept reminding herself, but everything seemed so insane. He told her how it would begin.

"…They would use a cell phone jammer to cut the signal from the base of the hill. Then they'll come up the mountainside, leaving the car at the bottom." Marion paused, as if envisioning the night's future events unfolding. Each moment passed before his eyes in real time. "They'll try to flank us, either breaking one person off to come around the back of the house or all three separating."

"Why won't they just drive up here with the lights off?"

"They might. But I'll be waiting in the woods. If they do that, I can put them down with a few shots, and it'll all be over. I don't think they're that dumb." He paused briefly to let her contemplate the situation.

"When they get to the house, they'll post one at the back door and two at the front. The two coming in will blow the door with a shotgun and toss in a flash bang. The one at the back door is only to keep us from running out that rear of the house. If you have to get out, use the window in the bedroom. When I leave you tonight, barricade yourself in the house as I showed you. Don't open the door for anyone but me."

The evening light faded as they enjoyed a quiet dinner

together. It was nearly perfect, with the roaring fire in the background providing light over their meal. Lacey thought about how nice it would have been had their minds not been preoccupied. When they finished eating, Marion broke the silence. "It's time to get ready."

She didn't say a word and only nodded her head. He grabbed the duffle bag and helped her with her clothes. She had never worn body armor or a pistol before and needed help with the straps and latches. Her arm still hurt forcing him to aid her in some of the more awkward positions. His assistance was given in an honest attempt to prepare her, but each motion was plagued by lingering touches, their fingers brushing against one another longer than necessary.

The house was cooling down without the fire roaring in the background, and the rain began to pelt the metal roof. Lacey wore the Sig Sauer 365X Macro he had helped her learn to use the day before, along with a soft armor vest he kept around for protective cases. Her jeans hugged tightly, carrying the pistol without sagging. She covered the vest with a red flannel shirt that was short enough to leave her pistol exposed.

Lacey tucked the push dagger he had given her into the left side of her waistband. It was a wicked-looking blade that was carried between the index and middle fingers. "If you have to use it, clutch it in your hand and start punching. Don't stop until they stop moving. Aim for soft tissue like the neck and abdomen," he had told her the day before.

Marion fashioned himself in similar attire, with a protective vest and his 1911 pistol on his belt, along with three spare magazines on the other side. He silently cursed himself for not bringing a rifle. It was a stupid decision he hadn't thought through when they left. Truthfully, he hadn't expected to need it, and in the rush to leave, the plan hadn't fully formed in his mind.

The local hunting store had given him a few options of rifle selection, but lacked anything of tactical value. They had no optics or laser that would be compatible with the night vision googles. The selection was slim with an array of lever and bolt action hunting rifles that would need a scope and the time to sight them in. Ultimately it was a failed venture to purchase a rifle fit for fighting. If he had known the fight was coming he could have brought one from the house and eliminated the threat from the safety of a fallen tree.

Focus Marion. It wasn't the time to live in regret of what could have been or should have been. He was forced to play the hand he was dealt and fight with only his pistol and his head. *Never have a favorite weapon.* He thought of Musashi's famed advice for tacticians and Soldiers, as the glistening steel caught his eye in the ambient light. Glancing at the table again he saw his final piece of equipment glistening in the ambient light from the oil lamp was his final piece of attire.

He never cared much for large knives and tended to stick to pocket knives and small fixed blades for their utility. What he found most useful was a hatchet he carried in a leather holster on the back of his belt, tucked underneath the black denim jacket. He had brought it to use for the fireplace, but after giving Lacey his defensive knife, he figured the tomahawk would work well, and he could wield it better than she could.

"Lacey," he said, looking at her in the lamplight. "It's time for me to go."

"I know." Her throat felt like it was closing around the words. She wanted to scream at him, *Don't go! Don't leave!* She wanted nothing more than for this to be over and to, maybe, have a life with him.

"You pull that trigger when you need to. Don't hesitate. Those men…"

"I know," she interrupted his pause and brought herself in

close to him.

"Marion… Thank you. For everything. For giving me a chance at a life."

He didn't respond; he just held her face in his hands for a moment, hers resting on top as she leaned in and kissed his palm.

"I'll be here when you come back."

"I know."

"Go, baby," she said to him as he turned to walk out the door. Marion grabbed his night vision goggles from the counter and fastened them to his head. He stored them in his truck for surveillance work and was thankful to at least have them. *A fucking rifle…* He thought again. It would have ended the fight in a matter of minutes leaving 3 dead hitmen with virtually no risk.

Watching from the window, Lacey saw him disappear into the wood line a moment later. His silhouette vanished, leaving her wondering whether that was the last time she'd see him… or the last time he'd see her. All she knew for certain was that she would die that night before going back to Si, before being sent back to that life to be used like a carton of eggs and then disposed of when they had had their fill. *No!* Either The Pigs died that night or both of them.

She used the boards he cut earlier along with a hammer and nails to place two cross pieces over the door, extending from one side of the door frame to the frame on the opposing end. He had told her it wouldn't hold for long, but it would slow them down enough. The back door had been sealed shut to the point where it would take a small explosive to breach it. They could still come through the windows, but Marion had told her the goal was to slow them down so she could shoot them, or he could come from behind them.

***.

* * *

Marion worked his way toward the bottom of the hill, moving slowly to ensure they hadn't arrived unexpectedly, periodically checking his phone to see if the signal had dropped suddenly. A downed tree about halfway down the mountain provided the perfect hiding spot. He had a distant view of the main road coming in and could quickly return to the cabin. The log was rotted enough that he could pull his body inside of it. Unless they were using thermal goggles they would walk right past him.

Thinking of Lacey consumed his mind during his walk down the hill. He forced himself to concentrate on the task at hand and the events of the night. Setting his mind and will on the notion that she would have a better life had become his focus. It became less important to him that he survived that, and more so that he could provide her with a life worth living.

Had he known they were preparing for a fight this mission would have been planned and coordinated. He would have protected her properly with a rifle and laser that would end this fight in a matter of minutes. But he hadn't known anyone was after them when they came, and there was no time to return to his house. His home was now compromised regardless and it wouldn't be safe to go back until this was over. Running would just mean more running and eventually facing them. *No.* It was better to fight them now. To end this rather than being surprised by them later. Even without a rifle Marion was dangerous.

He was the most dangerous man on the mountain tonight. A man with gunpowder for blood and bones built from lead and steel. He pushed the thoughts of Lacey dying out of his mind and focused on the task in front of him. They had the advantage of more men, all of them hardened killers. They had the advantage of bringing the equipment they desired to a fight and he was outgunned from the beginning. But they thought he was the sheep hiding in the corner. What they couldn't know at the time was that he wasn't the sheep… He was the wolf stalking the coyotes.

His thoughts were interrupted by the cold creeping in, forcing him back to reality. Waiting as the freezing rain began pouring on him, his clothes then soaked to the bone, he was suddenly jolted back to the world of chaos. His goggles picked up movement from the nighttime animals; the green illumination highlighted their figures until they were out of sight. He watched the road, waiting until the first movement caught his eye.

It was nearing one o'clock in the morning when he saw the Cadillac approaching on the main road. The lights were off to avoid signaling the two of them to their approach. He saw it pull into the base of the mountain and drop the first piglet off. The SUV continued forward a half mile, and the other two exited to begin their trek up the hill. He recalled something a commander had told him years before in planning successful missions… *Welcome to my home, said the spider to the fly.*

9

"No weapon against you shall prosper..."
–Isaiah 54:17

Gomez was dropped first at the base of the mountain, a half mile in front of the others. Mahon had sent him to take control of the back door in case they tried to escape out the rear of the cabin. The other two men would hike up together, assuming that with Gomez starting first and being younger, he would be in position when they arrived.

The mountain was steep and exhausting, requiring him to pull at trees and shrubs to gain a footing on his way up. It was a treacherous path, with stones and clay sliding from underneath his cowboy boots, making it impossible to gain traction.

They hadn't brought their tactical gear with them, thinking it would be a relatively easy job, and his designer clothing tore on the tree limbs. He had to continue turning on his flashlight to be able to see through the brambles but was intent on keeping the light low, using his hand to block the beam.

It became a vicious cycle of his eyes trying to adjust to the dark but not having time and then having to readjust when he pulled the flashlight out again to illuminate his path. Gomez hated that part of the job. Having served for a short duration on the SWAT team, he found it cumbersome wearing the gear and dealing with the extreme situations that were mostly training with only short durations of action.

It took nearly two hours for him to traverse the hillside and reach the top. He was winded and out of shape for hiking, his shirt drenched from perspiration and the intermittent rain. The coolness of the night chilled his body, making him shiver. A sense of relief washed over him seeing the cabin come into view. The lights were off, making the dark wood walls blend into the forest that surrounded it. Not overly surprising considering the time of night, but the lack of light struck him as out of place. He expected to see some light, maybe from a fire or lamp burning inside.

He rounded the back side of the cabin, skirting alongside the forest and positioning himself underneath the window next to the back door. Mahon had brought a shotgun for each of them, loaded with less lethal bean bag rounds to take Lacey and Marion down without killing them. Each of them carried their pistols, but Marshal's shotgun was loaded with buckshot for breaching the front door.

Checking his cell phone instinctively, he forgot they had blocked the cell signals for the area with a beacon in the car. His job was to sit and wait for the breaching team and watch the back door as Mahon and Marshal cleared the rooms and presumably came out with the two of them. So he stood his post, waiting patiently for something—anything—to happen.

Gomez stood unaware of the green optic lens that was watching him ascend the hillside. Each time the flashlight illuminated his path, Marion's night vision honed in on it like a distress beacon. Gomez came within ten feet of the log Marion was hidden in, with his pistol aimed at the green figure crossing through. *Not yet,* Marion thought needing to wait to pull the trigger. The gunshot would alert the others. So he sat patiently, holding his breath, praying Gomez wouldn't see or hear him. His heartbeat palpitated at a modest pace as he worried it would betray his position. One thought rolled constantly through his mind… *fucking amateur.*

Mahon and Marshal could see the cabin in view. With the cell phones off, there was no communication with Gomez, and they had to assume he was in place. At his age, it took Marshal longer than anticipated to climb the mountain, which should have given Gomez plenty of time to get in position. The lights in the cabin were off, and the darkness enveloped them like a blanket. It was impossible to see anything without the moonlight. Their eyes had adjusted to the lack of light as much as they could before Mahon signaled to move forward.

The cabin had a raised front porch, requiring them to step carefully so as not to wake the residents on their approach. Each one crept along the gravel driveway, the sound echoing in the stillness of the night. Mahon led the way, step by step, up the gravel road and past the black Tundra.

It had occurred to him to disable the vehicle, but ultimately it seemed unnecessary, and it would be hard to do it quietly. He cursed his cowboy boots the moment they clicked audibly on the hardwood front steps. They traversed the treads until both men were stacked at the door. Mahon whispered to Marshal.

"Let me check the door and see if it's locked before you blast it. We may be able to catch them sleeping."

There was no whispered return, just a nod from Marshal in understanding. Mahon took a step forward onto the grass-thatch welcome mat and immediately caved through the floor, letting out a scream when the bear trap below snapped close on his leg.

Laying limp on the wooden floor, he raised his leg out of the hole, yelling to Marshal. "Get this fucking thing off of me!" Marshal seemed to ignore him, opting instead to get inside the house by turning his shotgun at the latch.

Marion wasn't sure if he was trying to get Mahon inside the house to work on the trap or if he just didn't care about his acquaintance. It was an irrelevant question that he may not get the answer to but it forced Marion's hand. He had wanted to close the distance between the two of them with the night vision googles and then shine his flashlight over the sights at a closer distance to take them each down.

Instead the only thought crossing his mind was of Lacey. She would have her hands full inside the house if the other one decided to break through the window. Marshal coming through the door behind her was going to be beyond her skill level to handle.

With Mahon wailing in pain as Marshal raised his shotgun towards the door, gunfire erupted, engulfing their location with stray bullets. Each one buried itself into the thick cedar logs, the rounds whizzing over their heads and missing until one shot grazed Marshal's arm, forcing him to snap it back in reflex. "Motherfucker!" he yelled, still able to clutch his shotgun and whipping his hand in the air as if to cool the pain.

Marion lay in wait at the wood line, watching the spectacle through his night vision goggles. Unable to see the iron sights on his pistol, he had to fire blindly in the general direction. Point shooting at 30 yards was a difficult enough task in daylight, even for someone practiced. At night, through the optical distortion of his night vision, he felt lucky to have hit the building. Turning on his light to expose the sights would have sacrificed the advantage of the night vision and revealed his position. As it stood, they had no knowledge of where he was or what he intended to do next.

Marion had cut the floor boards of the deck out earlier that day and picked up a bear trap from the hunting store when they ran to town that afternoon. By keeping them from the front door, he was confident he could handle the two men. The bigger question was whether Lacey could handle the one around the back. *Stick to the plan,* he told himself in a half-hearted attempt to control his need to protect her.

Marion reloaded the 1911 while Marshal fired a volley of rounds from his pistol into the woods, seemingly trying to hit Marion or at least keep his head down while they removed the bear trap. Marion forced himself not to fire so the muzzle flash wouldn't reveal his location while Marshal was looking in his direction. With one of Marshal's feet placed on the spring, Mahon was able to push the other down and shake his leg free from the trap.

Moving to cover, the two men scrambled toward the side of the house, where the large logs would protect them from Gamble's bullets. Marion followed Mahon and Marshal around the side of the house, which was blocked from view by his truck and the plethora of trees encroaching on the home. "Get that motherfucker!" he heard Mahon yell, indicating that the trap had at least somewhat limited the man's mobility.

Mahon wasn't out of the fight, but he was slowed and in substantial pain. The cowboy boots had absorbed the full force of the trap, but teeth had penetrated his calf, causing a considerable limp as he tried to walk. Marshal disappeared into the woods, attempting to flank the position from which the shots had come.

Marion was maneuvering to get a better angle for his shots when he heard movement in the trees nearby. Marshal was in the woods with him. He listened and watched, unable to locate him with the night vision goggles. The trees were so thick that the night vision became more of a hindrance than a benefit, picking out every branch. A loud crack of thunder revealed their positions and temporarily blinded Marion's monocle. Shit, he thought, losing his advantage for a split second. Marion's eyes were still adjusting after the flash of light when his reticle went blind from another blinding flash.

This time, it was the light from the end of Marshal's shotgun, aimed directly at him. He could hear gunfire from inside the house, followed by silence. The shotgun erupted with a burst of fire from its barrel as the buckshot roared across the forest, striking him in the chest and sending him flying into the brush, rolling down the hill. He felt his ribs break the moment the round impacted; catching his breath became a struggle. Marion panicked for a moment, wondering if the round had pierced his vest and entered his chest cavity.

Lacey waited in the kitchen, hearing the click of the man's boots on the back porch. She knew he was there. Drawing her pistol, she aimed it at the window in anticipation. *Come on, you son-of-a-bitch, stick your head through.* The moment felt like an eternity as she focused her attention on the window, trying to ignore Marion out there alone.

Watching for the first sign of movement in the back window, she suddenly heard a man screaming at the front door behind her. It took every ounce of control not to look out the front window to check on Marion. She needed to know he was okay and not hurt. *Stick to the plan.* That's what he told her.

She waited and waited, the eternity of the man at the back porch not coming forward, stretching on. Finally, the moment she had been waiting for arrived. Like a hunter looking for deer, the man behind the porch smashed through the window with the front of the shotgun and began climbing through. She fired two shots into the window and heard a yelp. Knowing she had at least hit him, Lacey turned to run toward the bedroom.

The small room felt like a football field as she rounded the corner to the bedroom. A blast erupted from the shotgun behind her, sending a non-lethal round across the room and driving it into her spine. The dull pain felt like it shattered her back and ribs, sending her soaring across the room and slamming into the bench at the front entry.

Lacey lay on the ground with her eyes closed. The pain in her back was excruciating, taking all her will not to cry out in anguish. She wanted to grab at it, to remove the vest, to roll around on the ground in distress, but she couldn't. His footsteps were loud as he climbed through the window and crept across the open floor. Lacey listened as the footsteps approached, closing the gap between her and her attacker: one step closer, one step closer, one step closer. She could see the light of the flashlight shining off the floor.

He was aiming it directly at her. Closer and closer, the footsteps approached until his hand reached out and touched her back. Forceful fingers clawed at her shirt, and Lacey felt her body contort as he rolled her over. *Come closer, motherfucker!* Lacey opened her eyes wearily, looking the short Hispanic man in the face.

"Hello, beautiful," he said with a wicked smile.

"Hello," Lacey replied, smiling back and in one swift movement, she pulled the push dagger from her hip and thrust it into his neck. *Don't stop hitting until he doesn't move.* That's what Mary had told her: *keep stabbing.* She pulled the knife out and hit him again and again, over and over, stabbing the knife into his neck. *Soft tissue only.*

The feeling of the sinew ripping under the blade, along

with the arterial spurts, made her want to vomit. *Hold it together, Lacey. Don't stop hitting.* Punch after punch struck his throat, and she watched bubbles release from his trachea as air pushed through the blood. The artery was severed, and blood continued to pump from his body with each heartbeat.

Gomez was in shock at the realization of what had happened. His eyes began to glaze over as life slipped away. He saw the horror of his blood expelling from his body. Thoughts of death rolled through his mind as the warm liquid spurted from his carotid. Each beat of his heart shot warm fluid into the air like a geyser. In an instant, he felt cold, and his eyes grew heavy. He tried to fight her off, but his weakened limbs felt as if they weighed a ton.

His movements were slow and confused, failing to catch her hand or deflect the blows that struck him incidentally. He only managed to take the dagger to his hand several times while Lacey pulled it out again and stabbed repeatedly into his neck. As he looked into Lacey's eyes, she stared back as the last beat of his heart sent the life out of his body. Gomez's eyes closed, and his body collapsed lifeless onto the floor.

Keep moving! Lacey pushed him off of her and lifted herself off the ground. Kicking his body as it lay on the ground, she spit on it before departing. "Fuck you!" she yelled at the corpse. The blood soaking her shirt felt sticky on her skin. She didn't have time to deal with it; she had to hurry. Grabbing her pistol off the floor, she re-holstered it with shaking hands before securing the push dagger into her waistband again.

Stick to the plan. She bolted to the bedroom window, slid the sash open, and climbed through with the ease of a natural athlete. Marion had told her what to do, and there was no hesitation in her body as she sprinted into the woods to hide. He had instructed her to run to the truck and leave as soon as she killed the one at the back porch but to hide in the woods until the other two came after him. The keys were in the ignition, ready to go; all she needed to do was start it and drive.

The woods were cold, and the rain was pouring, mixing the warm blood with the cool water, leaving a tingling sensation over her body. The droplets struck her like tiny morsels of cold, expelling her heat and sapping her warmth. Lacey kept low to the ground, waiting for the other two to go after Marion.

It wasn't until that moment that she realized she had no idea what to look for. When was she supposed to go for the truck? She had no idea what Marion's signal would be or what would tell her the coast was clear for her to make a run for it. Should she wait or go? Were the other two chasing him into the woods? Should she try to help him? What if he was in trouble and needed her?

The thoughts rolled through her mind, unsure of when to act. She waited, debating with herself on the best time to act, when a blinding blow hit her in the back of the head. It was controlled but powerful, leaving her stinging with pain.

"Don't reach for it, darling," Mahon said from behind her as he pulled the pistol from her hip and tossed it aside. "Fuck you!" Lacey shouted back. *He didn't see the knife.*

"Get up. Walk toward the truck."

Lacey complied. *What do I do? Marion, what do I do? Stay calm, Lacey; you're smarter than him.* She subconsciously begged for him to talk to her and tell her what to do. Marion had told her, "Don't panic. Keep thinking; no matter what happens, be smarter."

"I got him," Marshal was walking out of the wood line. "The PI. He's dead in the woods."

"No!" Lacey screamed, turning to hit the cop behind her. She punched him on the right side of his face and kicked him in the groin, rage and sadness taking control of her body. Mahon clubbed her with the gun in his hand, sending her to the ground. "No!" Lacey sobbed on the as the dirt mixed with her blood soaked shirt.

"Go get him. We need the body. Where's Gomez?"

"How the fuck should I know? He was inside."

Lacey started laughing maniacally, lying on the ground. "He's dead, you fat fuck. I killed him!" Her laughter was a mix of emotions. She felt satisfied knowing she had bested one of them, sad that Marion had given his life for hers, and angry that it had been taken from her. "Go on, boy! Do what your daddy said," she taunted Marshal.

"Shut up, bitch!" Marshal shouted back before being interrupted.

"Go check on the body and get him from the woods! I'll get her down to the car. Get up and walk," he said, turning to Lacey.

She obeyed his commands in quiet submission. She wasn't trying to make it easy for him but to give herself time to think without being hit again. Walking toward the base of the mountain, they moved slowly with the pistol shoved in her back. Mahon was constantly irritated at her speed, controlling her pace with the force of the muzzle into her spine, indicating he was running thin on patience. The armor cushioned the blow from its full effect, but it was uncomfortable nonetheless.

Think, damnit! Think! Her mind roared between her ears, urging her to find a solution. *Marion, tell me what to do!* But he wouldn't answer her. He was dead. They had taken him from her. Si had taken everything from her: her youth, her innocence, her Marion… *Fuck you!*

They were nearly halfway down the hill when her nerves calmed enough for her to take her chance. In one swift movement, she turned and hit the gun from his hand, causing a round to discharge into the woods, and struck his thigh with the push dagger from her left hand, twisting it in the wound. Mahon let out a scream of pain when the dagger twisted, giving her time for another shot at him.

She struck him as fast as she could with her fist in the nose, breaking the cartilage and causing his eyes to water. She was too slow and took another heavy blow to the side of her jaw, staggering back and losing her grip on the dagger as it stayed buried in his leg.

It wasn't much, but it gave her the time she needed. She didn't wait to see if he was coming after her. Lacey ran as fast as she could into the woods again. The willows stung her skin as the cold made the surface tender to the touch. She didn't stop. Mary told her, "If *you have to run… run like the devil's chasing you. Don't stop, don't look behind you, just run.*

She could hear his voice in her mind. What had she done? She got him killed… her beautiful Marion. Did it even matter if she made it out of there without him? Three days before, she didn't know who he was; now she couldn't imagine her life without him.

Lacey found a large tree toward the top of the hill. She could see the truck from there. Her body was panting in exertion, and her blood felt like ice water pumping through her veins. *A little further,* she told herself before pushing off the tree and staggering forward. Thoughts of Marion plagued her mind. *If I can get help, he will be okay, she reassured herself.*

Crack! The pain hit her in the back, making her stumble into the tree. Another blow from Mahon's right hand struck her square in the jaw, dropping her to the ground. The blow spun her head fast enough to rattle her brain against her skull. Lacey kicked at his shin, but he was too strong. Mahon grabbed her by the hair and pulled her to her knees.

"Come with me, bitch!" he screamed, dragging her through the woods and back to the road. This time, he was unwilling to let go of her, determined to keep her from running. Shooting her would mean they wouldn't be paid, but at that point, it was almost worth it.

The walk down the road to the Cadillac was faster than she anticipated. She constantly looked for any opening to escape, but Mahon was strong and kept a death grip on her hair, pulling at her scalp until they reached the car. Her weapon was gone, and each chance of escape became less viable.

Mahon forced her into the trunk and handcuffed her hands in front of her, weaving them into the luggage strap to hold her in place. Without saying a word, he unzipped a bag and turned off the cell phone jammer before placing a call to Marshal. There was no answer.

He dialed the number again and again, trying to get through to Marshal, but there was no answer each time. "Shit!" Lacey's eyes widened for a moment as a glimmer of hope hit her that Marion wasn't dead. It was short-lived when Mahon's phone began ringing again.

"Marshal, where the hell are you?" he said angrily into the phone.

Marshal went back into the home to check on the Mexican. The door was barricaded shut and took five bullets from his gun to blow it apart enough for him to kick it open. Gomez was lying dead on the floor in a puddle of blood that looked like his entire body had been drained to the last drop.

"Stupid fucker," he muttered quietly to himself before turning to leave. The wood line where Marion had fallen was only 30 yards from the entry of the door. He started walking toward it, using the occasional lightning crack and his night vision as his guide.

There was a slight clearing in the brush, and he could see the spot where Marion fell. Marshal closed in on it, keeping his shotgun at the ready. *Where is he? The body should be right here!* There was no body. Nothing remained, and the rain had washed away any remaining blood residue, if it existed.

Marion's pistol lay hidden in the brush, thrown aside when the blast struck him.

Nothing remained except the body armor hanging from a tree limb. The holes from the buckshot peppered the front of it, but none had gone through. It would have hurt and dazed him, but it wasn't deadly. At most, a few ribs would be broken, but everything else was superficial. Marshal cursed under his breath, wishing he had not been so lazy as to walk over and shoot him again or at least carry him back unconscious.

Unable to track the movement, Marshal began walking cautiously back toward the house. He would traverse through the woods and down the roadside to meet up with Mahon. After securing the girl in the car, they could go hunting and try to find him. Taking Gamble alive was no longer an option.

Snap! He heard a branch break and stopped dead in his tracks. *That wasn't mine... That wasn't from me. He's here.* Marshal loved killing almost as much as he loved to hunt, and a smile grew across his wrinkled and scarred face as he flipped the light on his shotgun and began searching the wood line.

The light pierced the blackness with intense candela, creating a beam that penetrated through the dark of the night and deep into the trees. He couldn't see anything as he searched quickly in every direction, then slowly he scanned each sector. *Maybe that wasn't him, he thought,* wondering if the noise was just a broken limb or an opossum.

On turning the light off, his eyes had to readjust to the lack of light. *Shit. Should have kept an eye closed.* When he was a patrol officer, he always closed one eye when using a flashlight to save the night vision in the other. He had acted without thinking before turning on the bright light from his shotgun and was completely blind in the dark.

Snap! The noise came again, this time it was much closer. Turning his light on once more, Marshal couldn't see what made the noise. Gamble was a ghost in the darkness, moving like an animal through the jungle. He was daring Marshal to go after him. Each snap of a twig was intentional. He wanted him to lose the night vision, and Marshal realized it too late.

"You think I'm fucking stupid?!" Marshal shouted into the darkness, fear gripping his spine. "Come out and face me, motherfucker!" he screamed in a desperate plea to no longer be the hunted.

He was losing his senses. Fear and desperation gripped his very existence, and he could no longer see outside of his tunnel vision. The light began to move frantically around him in circles, searching for any sign of movement or life to fire a round into, but there was nothing. No movement, only the blackness of the forest and dense trees.

"Where are you, motherfucker?!" he shouted again, praying for an answer to know which direction his attacker was. The question was left unanswered, followed only by silence. Then the noise came from behind him, footsteps closing fast, followed by the whooshing sound of something spinning in the air. The dull thud of something striking the back of his head sent warm liquid immediately down his spine. The hatchet had been thrown with considerable force and buried deep in his brain.

His body moved autonomously, without his conscious mind to control it. He tried to fire a shot into the air, but the spasms removed any control over his hand. His eyes recognized the device in his hands, but they were no longer able to control it. He was sending the message, but there was no one to deliver it to his extremities. Marshal dropped to his knees, keeling forward as his body convulsed.

Marshal was dead before he even realized it. But from the woods to his left, a shadowy figure emerged, running at full speed across the clearing and closing the gap between them. He tried to raise the shotgun and fire, but the movement was still unresponsive, and the speed of his attacker was beyond his ability to counter. The hatchet viciously pulled from the back of his skull before another blow landed, striking him in the forehead and lodging itself into his frontal lobe before ripping free.

He stumbled onto all fours before trying to get to his feet. Unable to process the moment in its entirety, his legs seemed to think for themselves. The next hit came from behind him as he bent over, and the blade stuck into his back, severing the spinal column and opening a wound into his chest cavity. Instantly, he lost feeling in his legs and slumped to the ground, his body unable to support itself. He lay on his side, struggling to process what was happening to him.

Marshal's eyes were still open when the dark figure was illuminated by lightning, standing over him. The hatchet buried itself into his chest again and again, showering his attacker in blood. His eyes remained open, looking at his reaper delivering the final blow, and his body became a mangled ribbon of what it had once been.

Marion's shirtless skin was cold and drenched in rain, blood, and sweat. It dripped down his body, staining his pants as one word came to his mind… *Lacey.* He heard the gunshot come from down the hill when he grabbed Marshal's phone and took off.

"Where the hell are you?" He was frustrated and almost shouting into the phone.

"Let her go."

"Gamble?" It was a rhetorical question; he knew who it was. His eyes and face betrayed him as the emotions of a mark gripped his body. For the first time that evening, the chill of the mountain air sank in.

"Let her go, and I'll let you live."

"Fuck you! The girl's going back to the pimp, and then I'm going to put you in the ground. You think those two idiots are the only ones I can get? We will fucking hunt you down and gut you. The girl's going to be shipped off and traded to every rat's nest for the next five years until someone finally gets bored with her and cuts her throat." Mahon was furious but trying to control his anger. Marion didn't say another word and hung up the phone.

Mahon climbed into the driver's seat and started the engine to navigate the rest of the mountain. The rain poured, blocking his view behind the windshield and forcing a slow descent. Keeping a watchful eye on the rearview mirror, he looked for any sign of light, but it never came.

"I guess your boyfriend's not coming after all," he shouted back to Lacey.

"He's not my boyfriend," she replied coldly. The thought struck her that he sort of was her boyfriend. It was a unique relationship between two friends, both needing more but unwilling and unable to do so. "But he will come for me. And he will kill you."

***

Marion climbed into the truck and killed the lights from the override switch before turning over the ignition. The night vision goggles had taken a minute to find in the woods, and he would have to retrieve his pistol in the morning. Marshal's shotgun would at least give him something to fight with, though it was low on ammunition. When Marshal was covering their movement, he had fired all 17 rounds from his Glock 34 and the additional 17 from his spare magazine. The gun lay with its owner, empty and useless.

The night vision goggles illuminated the sky a dark green but showed the road brightly as the light reflected off the gravel. The engine cranked, and the windshield wipers immediately cleared the rain. The goggles provided better clarity than even using the vehicle lights, allowing him to close the distance between the two vehicles. Marion floored the truck down the gravel road, thankful the rain hadn't yet washed it out.

Bolting to the bottom of the long drive, the truck turned hard left, skidding into the Forest Service road. The mountain was behind them both, but the road was still winding, giving him time to catch up to Lacey. He could see the lights of the Cadillac in the distance, getting closer. It wasn't far ahead, and he was gaining on them.

With each switchback, he was able to floor the vehicle around and pick up some time, sending the rear tires spinning into position for the next stretch. The night vision goggles illuminated the entire area, and the Cadillac lights were bright as the distance between them shrank to under half a mile. The rain poured heavier, forcing Mahon to slow down as the lights reflected off the raindrops back into his eyes.

Marion remembered a switchback with a mild embankment a mile ahead. If he could gain on them before they got there, he would slam into the driver's side of the Cadillac and push it down the hill without risking it rolling. He would only get one shot at it, and missing would be catastrophic.

The Cadillac was close then, less than 200 yards in front of him. He was pushing as fast as he could, but Marion could go faster. The mud on the road caused his Texas street tires to slip and slide with little control. Marion's truck was built for the roads in Alabama, and the 4-wheel drive gave him added control. The kidnapper couldn't see the Tundra behind him; its dark black color and lack of light camouflaged it in the wilderness. The turn was just in front of Mahon, and the brake lights from the Cadillac illuminated as he tapped the pedal to slow down. That was the cue Marion needed to drop his truck into a lower gear and bring the vehicle under control. He couldn't slam into it but had to hit it at the right time to gently push it off the embankment.

The Cadillac continued to slow, and Marion was going below 35 miles per hour. He was coming straight on and not rotating into the turn. If he missed, his truck would barrel off the road, leaving her lost to Si for good. Shifting once more into second gear, he revved the engine high, giving it the most torque to push the heavier Cadillac off the road.

3, 2, 1… he counted in his head before turning the lights on. The beam shot through the Cadillac, illuminating the interior of the vehicle. The cowboy put his hands up instinctively over his eyes as the bright lights seared into his brain. *Bam!* The truck's front end connected with the driver's side of the vehicle in the center of the SUV, crumpling the side of the Cadillac as Marion's Tundra pushed, slipping in the mud.

Marion floored the gas hard, driving harder into the SUV as Mahon tried to gun the gas pedal and get out from in front of Marion's truck. The Cadillac tires spun on the slick roads, and without a 4-wheel drive, he couldn't gain any traction. Continuously, it was pushed further and further, gliding through the mud and muck. The push seemed slow, moving little by little until all at once, the vehicle leaped from the road sideways, tumbling down the embankment. Marion slammed on his brakes, bringing the truck to a stop at the edge of the road. The SUV continued to slide further down the decline until the undamaged side of the vehicle slammed into a large pine tree, crumpling around it.

The airbags in the truck deployed on impact, sending the night vision goggles slamming into his forehead and lacerating his face. When the truck finally came to a stop,

Marion was dazed and took a moment to regain full consciousness. His head was pounding, but he had to keep moving. *Get up, Marion. Get up!* He screamed to himself, forcing his body into action.

He could hear Mahon yelling at Lacey to get out of the vehicle. His mind still slightly dazed, he wasn't able to determine what was being said. Marion grabbed the night vision goggles before attempting to exit. *Shit!* They had stopped working from the impact of the airbags. His eyes hadn't yet fully adjusted to the night, and the headlights were broken from the impact. He could make out Mahon's figure in the darkness but everything beyond was dulled into a black haze. He extended the shotgun out of the window and fired a shot at the tall shadowy figure while beads of water bounced off the chamber of the gun from the recoil.

The pellets ricocheted off the Cadillac and soared into the sky over Mahon's head. Marion checked his chamber and loading tube before exiting the truck. *One round.* Mahon let off four rounds in rapid succession toward Marion, the bullets pouncing off the ground and the demolished guardrail. Mahon only knew the general direction, but his eyes hadn't adjusted to the low light yet either.

He watched as the kidnapper and captive headed into the woods to escape the open. Marion could see Mahon clearly and fired a shot into the forest, but the pattern was broken up by the branches, forcing all the pellets to disperse into the night air. *Shit,* he thought to himself before taking off at a dead sprint behind them.

Sprinting as fast as his legs would carry him, his veins pumped blood to his muscles as he chased after them, closing the distance. Lacey was slowing him down, and Marion could hear Mahon getting more and more frustrated with her. *Good girl.* He tossed the useless shotgun to the ground and reached again for his hatchet. The warm wood handle filled his hand, feeling like an extension of his arm rather than a foreign object.

The branches tore at his skin, but the adrenaline-fueled rampage blocked the pain for the moment. He ran as fast as he could toward the sound of Lacey fighting back. The boughs moved more furiously in one direction than any other as he bolted deeper into the wood line, tracking them. He heard her yelp in pain as a blow landed. She was close; he could feel them the way a hound could tell when a predator was watching.

Then he could hear Mahon's voice: "I'm going to kill you, bitch! I don't give a fuck about the money." Marion could see her figure in the dark, distinctively different from his. She was kneeling on the ground with Mahon over her. He ran faster than he imagined he could, his veins pumping oxygen as if his body were starving for it. *Crack!* Lightning snapped again behind him, illuminating them both. She was on her knees with a pistol to her head. Without a gun, Marion didn't have a shot, and his only hope was to close the distance between them with the hatchet.

Ten feet… five feet… Mahon was looking at Marion; he had heard the noise of him coming but still couldn't see enough for a clean shot. He turned the pistol toward Marion's direction as if it was happening in slow motion. Marion swung the hatchet as hard as he could into Mahon's head when the round went off, discharging into his stomach and sending the blow glancing off his skull. A gash appeared, but the hatchet hadn't broken bone.

Marion's shoulder buried into Mahon's chest, pushing the two of them over the ledge and sending them tumbling off a granite outcrop, landing painfully on the hard ground below. Each of their weapons was lost in the fall as they instinctively used their hands to cushion the impact. Both men were left dazed on the ground, but Mahon regained his senses first and let out a wild fist into Marion's stomach, accidentally striking the bullet wound and sending a shot of pain through his left hip.

Marion raised his arm and elbow, blocking the next blow to his head, and swung a hammer fist wide into Mahon's already broken nose with the blocking arm. Without waiting for a response from his attacker, he drove his left fist into Mahon's stomach as he simultaneously came to a knee. The motions were swift and fluid, with Marion moving like a machine, driving pistons into the steel backing of the engine head.

He pushed off his right leg, forcing his left knee forward into Mahon's face. The two of them were within inches of each other when Mahon noticed the wound on Marion's stomach, from the bullet. It wasn't lethal, since it had just grazed the edge of his love handle and blown the skin off the back side, leaving a superficial but painful opening. Mahon reached for it, grabbing and squeezing with his right hand, finally able to climb to his feet as Marion let out a scream of pain.

Marion struck the hand free, chopping down with his right fist and bringing an upward elbow into Mahon's face, sending him back another step and creating enough space between them. Mahon reached behind his back to pull the Glock 26 from his left side holster. Seeing the movement, Marion stepped in and closed the distance again, bringing both forearms up to block the gun from swinging into position. His left hand swung another hammer fist into Mahon's jaw before locking the pistol arm underneath his right armpit and lifting with all his strength to break the joint at the elbow.

Mahon howled as pain seared through his arm, and he lost his grip on the pistol. Marion didn't hesitate before raising his left foot and crashing it into the side of Mahon's knee, dropping him to the ground while Mahon sent his right arm swinging wide and ineffective into Marion's ribs.

Grabbing Mahon's forehead with his right hand, Marion pushed his neck backward against his knee, forcing Mahon to look up at him. "I told you to let her go." He didn't give Mahon a chance to respond before driving the same knee as hard as he could into the back of Mahon's neck, pushing with the hand on his forehead and striking the top of his own hand with the bottom of his other fist. The blow broke the spinal connection at the brain stem, dropping Mahon's body into a corpse instantly as the air left his lungs, unable to regulate his own breathing any longer.

Mahon was left suffocating, his body unable to control its autonomous functions. Marion stood over the body, breathing heavily from exhaustion. He turned to look at Lacey, who was trying to climb down the rocks to help him. His body covered in blood, the rain pounded it off like a garden hose, cleaning his body of the filth littering it.

Lacey ran toward him, her back and head throbbing. She rushed into his arms and he into hers as they dropped to their knees. She didn't say anything; she just held him, afraid to let go. *Thank God… he's okay,* she thought as she hugged him and kissed his cheek. "I thought you were dead," she spoke softly into his neck. "I fought Mary. I fought hard."

"I know you did, Lacey. You did good."

10

Wild animals never kill for sport. Man is the only one to whom the torture and death of his fellow creatures is amusing in itself.

–James Anthony Froude

The rain continued to pour as Lacey managed to get Marion inside the cabin. The wound in his stomach wouldn't stop bleeding, and the damage to his muscles was causing a slight limp. She set him down on the couch and hurried to the sink for hot water and a rag. Panic surged through her—*I can't lose him… not now.*

"Lacey," Marion said quietly.

"You'll be okay, Mary. I'm here…" The response was automatic.

"Lace!" he raised his voice to get her attention.

She turned to him, surprised; no one had called her that since she was a little girl. "I'm okay. I promise. The biggest risk is infection. Gut shots take a long time to kill when they're fatal, but this isn't fatal. The bullet came out the side; it didn't hit anything vital. It hurts and looks terrible, but it isn't fatal."

"Are sure? How can you be certain?" she asked, still panicking as she brought him the water and several rags.

The wound was displayed loudly in front of her. The open sore had removed a large chunk of skin in front of his love handle. It created an opening that looked like both entry and exit wounds combined in one large strip of flesh. The tender pink exposed flesh resembled something akin to chipped or ground beef in a slab about the size of her palm.

"Yes, I'm sure… this isn't my first time. Trust me." He smiled at her, and she couldn't help but smile back. His confidence was overwhelming at times. His skin was caked with mud and blood, a grotesque mixture as if he had rolled in a pigpen.

"Okay," she said, wiping him down.

"Lace… it's okay. I need a shower, not a sponge bath." She laughed again, holding back tears. Her emotions soared with relief that they had made it through the night.

As she stared at him, she noticed Gomez's body in the background. Her face dropped as the reality of what she had done hit her. She had never killed anyone before, and seeing him made it real. It was the first moment she had to process the information, and her emotions oscillated between disgust and satisfaction. Just hours before, she had been certain that she and Marion were dead. *You had no choice.* It was a strange feeling—guilty about killing someone but relieved that he was dead.

"It's okay. You didn't have a choice," he said, holding her face.

"Is it strange that it doesn't bother me?"

"No… not really. What you hear in the movies about it sticking with people isn't entirely true. Most people who finally bring themselves to do it—the ones who have to—don't feel as much as they think they should before it happens. In the end, it's harder to put down your dog than a person coming to kill you."

"He's dead… We're not. I'm okay with that… at least logically."

"I'll drag the body out. Leave the blood. We can explain this to the police in the morning."

"In the morning? If we're going to call the cops, shouldn't we do it now?"

"No. The roads are washed out. I checked the cell phone when we were driving back, and the service is down now because of the storm. As far as the police know, we didn't plan this. We were attacked by a group of cops hired to scare you back to…" He trailed off, unsure how to refer to Si. He wasn't her pimp… not anymore. That wasn't her life… that wasn't her.

"… My pimp," she interjected. "It's okay. That's what he was. It's not what he is."

He held her gaze and nodded. "We're going to spend the night here. We can leave at first light and give the police the address. They'll conduct their investigation, and it'll show that we were attacked and fought back. I'll throw the bear trap into the woods and tell them he must have stepped on one left by a hunter. Then I'll go to Si's hotel after I drop you at home."

When he said "home," it struck her… It was his home. Not hers, but God, she wanted it to be hers. She wanted that life with him. "If you haven't realized it by now… I'm not letting you go by yourself. What are you planning to do with Si?"

"Of course, you won't…" Marion smiled again at her. She was strong and wasn't going to be a victim anymore. "I'm going to shower, and then we can bandage this." He stood to drag the body outside, regaining some strength despite the pain radiating from his leg as he moved. Seeing him struggle, Lacey came without hesitation to help move the body.

When the body was safely on the front porch, they walked

slowly back inside; she supported him to ease the pressure on his leg and side. "What are we going to do about Si?" She knew the answer but wanted to hear him say it again. It was comforting to her that Marion was going to kill Si. She would finally be rid of the sociopath who had ruined her life.

"I'm going to end this, Lacey. Get your head right about it if you need to, but this ends tomorrow."

He didn't wait for a response and walked toward the bathroom and began removing his pants to undress for a shower. The warm water and soap poured over the wound on his side. The exit of the bullet had done considerable cosmetic damage to the tissue on his hip, exposing bits of fat and muscle beneath the surface.

He groaned in pain, hitting his fist against the shower wall as the water and soap cleaned the wound. Not wanting to scream and alert Lacey, his eyes watered as the stinging surged through his body, the lack of adrenaline and dopamine intensifying the pain. Every curse word he could think of escaped his lips as he endured the agony.

The mud and blood littered the floor of the shower as the plaster washed free of his body. Contorting himself to try and clean the wound, he struggled to fully see the rear exit portion of the wound and get it clean. He was allowing the water to flow over it again when the door opened, and Lacey stepped in, having heard his pain through the door.

She didn't say a word; instead, she pulled back the shower curtain and walked in with him. She had taken off her jeans but still wore the black panties and a white tank top from the night before. Grabbing the washcloth from his hand, she whispered lightly in his ear, "Don't move." Gently dabbing at the open pocket of flesh on his hip, Marion let out a soft groan as the pain surged. He found himself caught between two worlds—wanting to cry and scream but not wanting to appear weak in front of her. She dabbed at the wound tenderly, mixing soap with the blood that was continually pushing through.

The awkwardness of him being naked and her being somewhat dressed faded from his mind as she continued to clean the sore. It was a painful process. She had grabbed his trauma kit from the truck, where the iodine and bandages were stored. Reaching for the iodine on the bathroom counter, she moved around his naked body to turn off the water.

With no bullet inside of him to be concerned with there was no need to try and dig further into the opening. She poured the iodine over the large, disfigured area of flesh, letting the liquid cleanse it. Marion could smell the familiar scent of the antiseptic dissipating into the steam that enveloped them.

Handing him a towel, Lacey helped him wrap it around his waist before he turned his back to give her privacy to undress. In a moment, she was naked behind him, and it took all his willpower not to turn and look at her. *This wasn't the time, he thought,* before feeling her arms wrap around his chest, her breasts pressing into his back. She hugged him tightly, and he reached up to hold her hands.

She lingered in that position for a long moment. There was no sexual tension in the air beyond their mutual attraction; it was simpler, more primal. She wanted to hold him, and he wanted to hold her. Nothing less, and in that moment, nothing more. After a minute or two, she released her grip and climbed into the shower, letting the water cleanse her body.

They both dressed, preparing for bed. Marion was in his jeans without a shirt, awkwardly trying to bandage his wound, while Lacey was in a white tank top and a clean pair of silk black panties. She knelt on the floor in front of the couch placing her body between his legs, taking the bandages from his hand. The pain was slightly lessened by the presence of the beautiful woman tending to his injury.

She spoke in a low voice—not a whisper, but the soft tone a candle would make if it could speak. Sitting on her knees in front of him, she tried to be as delicate as possible with the tenderness of the damaged skin. "You're the first person to treat me with respect and not like an object... That's something I haven't had in a long time."

When she finished stuffing the wound with gauze and taping it in place, Lacey laid her head on his lap, hugging his waist while being careful not to hit his wound with her arms. Marion leaned back on the couch, resting his eyes but not fully committed to sleep. "Thank you, Marion." He didn't respond; there was nothing to say. He rested his hand on her head, caressing her hair.

The moment lasted for what felt like an eternity yet was entirely too short. Lacey stood up and took his hand in hers. "Come on, let's go to bed." Marion came to his feet without saying a word, the exhaustion of the evening weighing on him. They fell asleep holding each other, Lacey nestled softly into his chest, with his arms wrapped around her.

***

The next morning, Marion awoke before dawn, still holding Lacey. His mind raced with the day's agenda. He had to kill Si. *I have to end this.* Marion could hear his thoughts clearly as he watched Lacey's chest rise and fall with each breath. He would have given anything to stay in that moment forever, with her by his side.

"Lacey," he whispered, trying to nudge her awake.

"Hmm," she grunted, hugging him tighter.

"We have to go."

"Mmmm, let's just stay here." She smiled, still with her eyes closed.

Marion squirmed away, fearing that his will would give in to her. He slipped out of bed, still with his jeans on, and began to dress and pack his bag together.

"I'll get coffee," she said, rolling back over, face down into the pillow.

The morning passed slower than he wanted, but within an hour, they were out of the cabin and completely packed. As they walked to the truck, Lacey turned to take in the view one last time. The bullet holes were invisible from the truck, and the scene looked normal except for Gomez's body, being devoured by flies. It was a beautiful cabin, and with Marion by her side, it felt almost like a perfect vacation.

"Mary?" she said, stopping on her way to the truck. He turned to see her staring at the house. She wasn't sad so much as disappointed—disappointed that their time there hadn't been a vacation to spend together or a break from reality. Marion didn't respond but opted to set the bags down and put his arm around her, sensing her need for comfort.

"When this is over, I want to do this again."

"I would too."

"I want to come back to a cabin like this. With no one around. Just you and me."

"You're very confident in what you want, aren't you?"

"Yes," she stated matter-of-factly, settling into him. "I know my value. I knew my value three days ago, and I knew my value today. And I know you want to come back here with me, too."

"I do." He paused for a moment before continuing, "Your value wasn't less before all of this, Lacey. You just didn't know it."

"Thank you, Marion." She rested her head on his chest. "Let's go."

The storm had passed, leaving a substantial washout on the road. Marion had to put the truck in four-wheel drive to maintain control with Lacey transitioning her hand from his arm to the center console for stability. The front bumper had absorbed most of the crash, leaving the truck operational. He had cut away the airbags, but the vehicle was old enough that it still ran after they discharged, unlike modern cars.

The drive back to Birmingham remained uneventful, with Marion calling a detective friend to start the process for the crime scene. He explained who the people were and why they were after him. Lacey listened intently to ensure their stories aligned. Marion told the detective he would be in later that day to give a statement with his lawyer.

He debated silently about trying to get Lacey to stay at the house, but he knew she would never agree. She had been adamant about confronting Si with him. He explained that he saw no other option but to terminate Si. "Going to the police won't end this. He'll be out on bail, and there's no record other than a phone call from a burner phone that he even contacted The Pigs," he justified.

"I know. I'm not asking you to do anything different. This has to stop, or we will be running and hiding for the rest of our lives."

Marion liked the way she said it… "the rest of our lives," he replayed it in his head. It wasn't a separate venture for the two of them when this was over; she had lumped them together, both consciously and subconsciously. Her choice to stay with him gnawed at him. She could never freely choose to be with him if she couldn't freely choose to leave. Right then, she was tied to him, bound together by decisions he had made. His heart ached to have her with him, and he felt that hers did too, but it wasn't a choice for her right then.

Three hours after leaving the cabin, they rolled into the familiar area, the hotel in view and the warehouse off to the side. Marion noted the parking lot where he had first seen Lacey walking in. Six days before felt like a lifetime with everything that had happened.

Pulling the truck in, he tucked it behind a dumpster, leaving the front poised for a quick getaway. The driver's seat had a view of the entire side of the warehouse. "You can drive a stick shift, right?"

"Yes."

"Good. Check your pistol." Lacey did as he asked, checking the chamber and the magazine of the Sig Sauer 365x he had given her. The magazine was fully loaded, and the chamber held a round ready to fire. She re-holstered the firearm and pulled her sweater down over it.

"Stay here." It wasn't a question. Lacey knew by the tone of his voice that it wasn't up for negotiation. "If something happens, you need to drive off and call the police. Drive straight to the police station and tell them everything that happened."

"I'll go to the police station," she said. "But I won't tell them everything. I'm not going to do anything to hurt you, whether you're here or not."

They leaned in and hugged, exchanging a kiss on the cheek while the scruff of his face rubbed her smooth skin. Marion said nothing else; he just exited the truck as Lacey slid into the driver's seat. As he walked across the lot and the street, it took all his strength not to run and confront the issue. Rushing would only get him found.

Marion thumbed the Ed Brown Custom 1911 tucked in the front of his pants. He hated the thought of destroying the pistol after that, but he had no choice. Si's car was still in the parking lot... *he's here.* Lacey had told him which room was Si's and where to go. It was the last room on the second floor. "Walk down the mezzanine until you round the corner. It will be the only door on that side."

The mezzanine was rusted steel with an expanded metal floor to allow rain to drain through. It had the look of an industrial complex rather than a hotel. It may have once been a nice area, but the hotel was built as cheaply as possible in the late 80s and had not been maintained, targeting a specific clientele.

When he finally rounded the corner, Si's door was already open—just cracked. Not wanting to draw attention to himself, Marion didn't draw his pistol yet; he simply placed his hand on the handle, ready when needed. Peeking through the slit, he could see no one inside.

He slipped in quietly, drawing his pistol as the door slowly swung open. He checked the corners, under the bed, and in the bathroom—no *one was there.* Marion sat on the bed, waiting… Thinking. It wasn't immediately obvious where Si was. *Was he in one of the rooms with a girl?* The thought entered and left simultaneously. *He would make the girls come to him, not the other way around.*

The moment of silence was quickly interrupted when Marion realized Si had to be in the warehouse. He would be looking for Lacey, searching for any clues to her location, or maybe cleaning it out for another girl. Another fleeting thought crossed his mind: he would have made the new girl clean it up. But he had to be there looking for Lacey; it was the only reason he could think of for Si to leave the room with his car still here.

Exiting the room, Marion made sure to walk slowly, giving Lacey time to see that he was safe. The walk to the warehouse was quick, taking only a few minutes to cross the lot. The old building was just out of screaming distance from the hotel. Not that it mattered, the people there wouldn't lift a finger if the building were on fire.

He found the paneling at the back of the warehouse, which he had used previously. The rivets and screws had rusted out, making the panel easy to crawl through again by squatting down. The room opened up into the same warehouse that was empty except for construction debris and rafters.

Shock and horror took hold of him when he saw the body hanging in the center of the room. Blood and pieces of flesh littered the floor beneath it. The skin had been removed in patches, and the wounds were cauterized to prevent the victim from bleeding out. Marion carefully moved to the front of the body, scanning the area around him. The room was open, with no hiding places except the loft apartment.

The face was severely disfigured, with the ears, eyelids, and lips removed, but he knew instantly it was Si. A look of surprise was permanently affixed to his features, his teeth and eyes wide open. It resembled a skull with some skin remaining.

Maybe another dealer or trafficker was mad about a delivery… Maybe it was because he didn't have Lacey to sell? He wondered to himself, knowing his guess was off the mark; even the cartels didn't dissolve to that level of savagery. They'd cut off limbs, stick people in barrels alive, and toss them into the sea, but what had happened to Si went beyond that. His thoughts were interrupted when he noticed movement from the loft window above. Instinctively, he turned his pistol toward the window and began to back away slowly, keeping his gun fixed on the movement he had seen.

A weird hissing pop sounded, and he felt a sting in his upper chest. His left hand instinctively reached for it when he clasped his hand around what he instantly recognized as a dart. *Shit!* Marion had seen these before as a kid working on cattle ranches. His eyes began to close as panic set in. He couldn't let them get to Lacey.

Marion turned as fast as he could and ran toward the hole in the wall. The light shone through the opening as his vision started to fade to black. Dropping to his knees as his legs lost control, he began crawling toward the exit. No longer able to keep his eyes open, he could hear footsteps approaching him as the words left his mouth in a whisper that only he could hear: "Lacey… run!"

Ewan stood in front of Marion, having showered and dressed neatly in the clothes he had worn previously. Marion lay on the ground, struggling to open his eyes as if he had just awoken from a long-needed rest. His grogginess added to his confusion. Instinctively, he tried to move his hands, but they were bound behind his back, his feet and knees similarly restrained with zip ties, rendering him useless.

Marion strained with all his strength to break the zip ties, but the plastic was too thick to gain enough leverage with his hands behind his back. Prying his knees and feet apart, he groaned, unable to shift the bindings. They felt so tight he feared they would cut off his circulation.

"Don't fight it," a man said in the dark. Marion was still unable to keep his eyes open. "It'll be easier if you go along. The bindings work; I've used them a lot. You won't be able to work your way out of them."

"Why…" His sentence trailed off as he struggled to muster the strength to speak.

"Why are you here?" the man asked, with Marion only able to nod in response.

"You're here because I think you know the location of the whore that lived here. I want her."

"No." His voice was still too weak to form a full-sentence response, but his senses were beginning to return.

"Can I be frank with you?"

Marion nodded again as his eyes drifted from open to closed.

"The effects of what you're feeling will wear off in just moments, and then you'll feel everything. You must understand that when I carved up…" He pointed to Si's hanging corpse. "It really did nothing for me. Girls are my favorite, young girls mostly. I'm what psychoanalysts call a hebephile. That means I'm attracted to post-pubescent girls. But in this case, the woman who lived here was unbelievably arousing. I haven't been able to think about anyone else since." He paused again to give Marion time to process his words.

"I want the girl. I'm not interested in you… so if you tell me where she is, I'll cut your throat right now, and this will all be over." He made a swift gesture of slicing with the boning knife in his hand. "But if you don't, I'll do to you what I've done to the gentleman hanging from the rafters. Once I start, I won't stop until your heart stops beating. Understand?"

Shit. This is going to hurt. Marion knew he was about to experience pain beyond anything he could have imagined. He whispered under his breath, drawing his attacker closer. "I'm afraid I can't hear you." He didn't respond but simply whispered again.

He could feel the man closing in on him, the footsteps stopped, and he leaned over him, getting closer. "What did you say?" He could smell his attacker's breath as the man spoke. Marion's eyes opened to see his ear being held up to his mouth. "I said fuck you," Marion whispered before lunging his head forward and biting the man's ear.

Ewan screamed in pain as Marion held on, refusing to let go. He bit down harder, feeling the ear rip beneath his teeth. Ewan dropped the boning knife, trying violently to push Marion off him. The ear finally gave way and tore from the side of Ewan's face.

"Motherfucker!" Ewan screamed, standing up and moving away from his captive. The searing pain mixed with his inability to control his rage as he kicked Marion in the stomach with all his might. Marion rolled his body over the filet knife, trying to grasp it in his hands, and began cutting the restraints from behind his back.

"Give me that!" Ewan shouted, furious at what Marion had just done. He reached behind him to retrieve the knife when Marion bucked his hips, forcing Ewan to fall over him. Marion stabbed him in the hand with the knife. The blade pierced the skin, but with his hands tied, he wasn't able to get enough force. The knife broke free, leaving only a minor wound to his captor's hand below the base of the thumb.

Ewan yelped, but the wound wasn't deep enough, and he was able to retrieve the knife, twisting it out of Marion's grasp. His rage consumed him again as he stabbed Marion in the thigh. It happened quickly, but he felt the knife stop when it embedded itself in his bone. Marion let out a scream of pain as Ewan twisted the knife in the wound before pulling it out and backing away from his captive.

He panted in exasperation and pure rage, debating what to do next. For a moment, he worried that the knife had pierced the femoral artery but relaxed when he saw no spurting arterial blood. Ewan knelt back over him, pushing his knee into the dark, venous blood on the ground. He was calming himself and spoke in the disinterested voice from before. "That was a good try. But I'm afraid you've made this a lot worse on yourself. I'm going to make you watch while I kill the girl, and then I'm going to cut you up like I did her owner," he whispered the last sentence to Marion, grabbing a fistful of his hair and slamming his head hard into the concrete. The blow dazed him, but Marion continued to fight through it. *Stay conscious, and find a way out.*

Ewan placed the tip of the knife into Marion's shoulder just above the heart. "Do you know what a tension pneumothorax is?" He didn't wait for a response to the rhetorical question. "It's when there's an imbalance in the chest cavity's pressure... it has to be relieved by poking another hole in the cavity, or the victim will suffocate... It always sounded dreadfully painful to me." Then he smiled at Marion. "Let's find out."

Ewan slowly pushed the boning knife into the skin, not wanting the moment to end too quickly. Inch by inch, the knife buried itself in his chest, causing the wound to suck air in as each breath exhaled slowly collapsed his lung. Marion screamed again in pain before he noticed movement behind the warehouse wall.

Ewan must have seen him look at it because he turned and noticed the same shadow moving along the wall. "Ahh, is that our girl there? Coming to help you? That is ever so sweet. Now please be quiet; I wouldn't want you to ruin this." Standing up, he kicked Marion in the head, rendering him unconscious again for several minutes. His last thought was of Lacey… *Don't come… run, Lacey… run.*

Lacey watched from the car as Marion disappeared inside the bedroom. Her window was rolled down to listen to the surroundings. Hoping to hear a gunshot, she listened patiently, only able to make out the occasional passing car and a train in the distance. It was serene and almost peaceful, but she hated that place. The hotel made her physically nauseous, and the warehouse disgusted her. It wasn't her home anymore… It had never been a home, just a place to sleep until her nightmare was over.

She waited for ten minutes as he was inside the room. Her heart pounded with racing thoughts: *Is he okay? Did Si get the drop on him? Where are you? Baby, are you okay?* Her head was filled with images of him being hurt or killed.

She waited and waited, listening, straining her ears to discern what was happening inside. Her hand rested on the door handle, ready to go in after him. Having told him she would go to the police, she never intended to do that. She couldn't leave him; if he was hurt, she was coming in. If he was dead, she would shoot until they put her down.

Her heart calmed as she watched Marion emerge from the room. *Thank God.* Expecting him to casually walk back toward her, and assuming Si was dead, she was surprised when it didn't happen as it had in her mind. Walking down the mezzanine stairs, he turned and headed toward the warehouse. No, *no, no! Where are you going?*

He crossed the side street and the open parking lot to the warehouse. She couldn't see the alley behind it, but he had to have gone in through the hole in the back. Lacey listened again; there was no sound coming from the building. She wasn't sure if she could hear anything from that distance.

Lacey had been waiting with the window down for over an hour. *What is he doing?* Her mind was screaming at her. She couldn't leave without some indication he needed help. But what if Si was hurting him? What if he needed her help? The torment ravaged her mind from one extreme to the next.

Not watching the clock, she figured an hour had gone by. *What was that?* A faint noise sounded, but it was unclear if it was in her mind. *Was that a scream?* She wasn't sure if she heard something or imagined it. Lacey listened for a moment, waiting to hear the noise again. Unable to contain herself any longer, she exited the truck and walked closer to the building. Using the crumbling structures on the side of the parking lot as cover, she hugged the wall tightly to avoid being seen.

She was 40 feet from the truck when she heard it again… The screaming was coming from the warehouse. *It had to be Marion… he wouldn't be torturing Si. Not for no reason. He wouldn't do that. It had to be him screaming, didn't it? Or was she just hearing things out of fear that something had happened? There it was again…*

Marion was screaming, the sound drowned out by the distance and open air between them. It was faint, but she knew it was there. She couldn't wait anymore and took off at a dead sprint across the parking lot and through the street to the rear of the building. The open paneling was directly in front of her.

The photonic barrier from the dark interior and the sunlight outside blacked out her ability to see before she broke free of the light threshold. She was cautious, entering the building… *Slow down.* If something happened to her, she wouldn't be able to help him. She drew her pistol and held it out as Marion had taught her, before climbing through the open paneling at the back. Si was hanging naked and suspended from the rafters. His body was lifeless and covered in blood, disfigured almost beyond recognition.

On the ground next to him, Marion was lying bound with his hands behind his back and feet together with zip ties. There was no one else in the building, but she took her time traversing the space. *Go slow… someone is here.*

She approached Marion cautiously. He wasn't fully conscious, as if he were drugged and dozing in and out. She had seen this before, like when druggies get too much opium in their system or were spinning in a K hole from too much Ketamine. His face was bruised, and he had a busted lip, but around his mouth was substantially more blood than the lip warranted. She saw bits of flesh that had been chewed up and spit out on the floor next to him.

Marion lay in a pool of dark red blood, and he had wounds to his leg and chest. They didn't appear to be fatal… at least not immediately. Keeping her gun out, she knelt to check his pulse. *Please be okay.* *"Marion,"* she whispered, pulling the push dagger out of her waistband to try and cut his restraints.

"Lace…" Marion whispered weakly, without opening his eyes.

"I'm here, Marion. I'm gonna get you out of here."

"No, Lacey… run," he whispered, trying to open his eyes. "Run now."

She couldn't process what he was saying before she heard a pop and hiss, followed by a stinging in her shoulder. Immediately recognizing a dart in her arm, she knew the effects would be slower than if it had hit a more vascular area, but she understood it would render her unconscious in a moment. *Who shot her? Si was dead. It didn't make any sense.*

Where are you? She turned in the direction the dart had come from and saw the man—the one she had seen days before prowling the area. *Why was he here? What did he want with her?* It didn't matter; she wasn't going to be a victim… not today, and she wasn't going to let him hurt Marion.

Focus on the front sight, he had told her. *Come closer, you son-of-a-bitch.* The effects were coming on strong, but not as fast as she pretended. Her legs were failing beneath her, and she dropped to one knee to support herself. Lacey drew the pistol and aimed at the man, who moved cautiously toward her. He wasn't scared; he didn't even seem to acknowledge the gun pointing at him.

"Don't worry… this will all be over soon."

The world around her was going dark; she couldn't see the building anymore, just the silhouette of the man in front of her. *Focus on the front sight!* She squinted her left eye, using all her strength to keep the right eye open.

"Fuck you," she said quietly before firing. Not waiting to see if she hit him, she fired again and again. She wasn't sure how many rounds she let off before everything went black. But she knew she hit him when he screamed in pain.

Ewan bellowed as the bullet tore through his skin. The first round struck him square in the stomach, another hit his hip, shattering his pelvis, while a third missed before the final round struck his chest. The pelvic wound dropped him to the ground; he could no longer support any weight on his lower extremities, and even propping himself against the wall was excruciating.

"You bitch! You stupid fucking whore!" he screamed, filled with both anger and pain. He cursed himself for not moving when she pulled the gun. He hadn't thought she would be able to pull the trigger; he thought she had lost too much control over her body. The mistake proved nearly fatal. He was determined to make them both pay for that. He could crawl over and bind her before trying to get to the hospital. They would still be there in a few days when he returned, or they would be dead from lack of water. Either way, he didn't care. His desire for the girl was overshadowed by his will to remain alive.

Second-guessing himself, he realized these wounds would take weeks to heal, and having a witness present was the first step toward his departure to prison. He wanted the girl to be his prize, but ultimately, she would be wasted there. He had to kill her, knowing the man would succumb to his chest wound in a matter of hours.

Ewan crawled across the floor, pulling his body with his arms, while trying to keep his legs stationary to avoid additional pain. The grit from the floor lodged into the bullet wounds, stinging and burning with each painful movement across the concrete. *You fucking bitch!* The pain in his legs was more than he could tolerate. He wanted to pass out, to escape his anguish, but he had to stay awake. He had to kill the girl.

Lacey would only be unconscious for an hour at most. It seemed like a considerable amount of time until he began dragging himself, little by little, as slowly and painlessly as he could manage. He snatched the knife on his crawl toward her. It had been dropped when she shot him, and the movement required him to navigate over various pieces of debris.

He dreaded the thought of having to support his legs while crawling through the panel opening, but he would ultimately have no choice. It felt like an eternity before her body was within his grasp. He was sweating, and each movement sent pain through his wounds. *There she is, he* thought as her unconscious body came into view, less than two feet from him.

Her beautiful body resting peacefully on the floor. He hated to kill, hated to end this too early. But he was simply out of options. As much as he desired the girl it was overshadowed by his desire for freedom. He was lost in thought for a moment staring at her exquisite unconscious body when he was interrupted.

It took him a moment to realize what had happened as the pain reared through his face. A blow from an unknown foot landed squarely in the middle of his face, breaking his nose and sending him rolling away. Ewan instinctively clasped both hands over his nose and mouth which proved to be a mistake, and without his arms supporting his weight the pressure of the concrete surged through his shattered pelvis.

As quickly as the strike had occurred, two Hispanic men entered the warehouse, appearing not to speak English.

"Necessito medico," Ewan yelled to them. "Necessito medico!"

His cries for help went unanswered. The three men debated in Spanish, determining what needed to be done.

"That must be one of his girls, but who the hell are these two?"

"How the fuck should I know? That's Si hanging from the rafters. They fucked him up… What the hell is going on here?"

"Maybe Si was trying to sell her to this pussy out from under us?" one of them said, pointing at Ewan.

"Then who's the other guy, and is he still alive?"

One of the three walked over and kicked Marion's body. He had awakened to the men's return but remained as still as possible. His mind urged him to play dead and not move.

"No, he looks dead. He's not moving, and he was stabbed in the chest."

"What do you want to do?"

"Load the girl in the truck. Kill him. We can't have him calling the police before we get them loaded, and we still have several hours to drive," the leader of the three said again, pointing at Ewan.

Without hesitation, one man pulled out his pistol and aimed it at Ewan, firing three successive shots into his chest. His life was terminated in an unceremonious manner. There was hardly time for him to react or to even recognize the death blow. A moment of terror filled Ewan when the gun was aimed and an even brighter one came as he felt the bullets tear through his skin.

Ewan sat upright, gasping for breath as his lungs filled with blood and fluid. The pain was excruciating for the brief moment it lasted. As the world began to fade to black around him, he was afraid for the first time in his memory. Blood filled his mouth, but he didn't have enough breath to blow it out before the world collapsed around him. His last thoughts before fading into death were of the girl.

11

"I am not free while any woman is unfree, even when her shackles are different from my own."

—Audre Lorde

The scene was almost poetic; an old cowboy sat on the front porch with his feet propped on a handmade wooden table, the rocking chair remaining stationary, its owner unwilling to release it into its natural kinetic state. The black Stetson hat was pulled low over his brow, casting an eerie shadow across his face.

His sun-damaged skin was blackened from years of ranching and sun exposure, causing wrinkles that resembled worn leather more than the skin of an aging man. Edward was clearly in his mid-sixties, but to see him move, most would guess he was younger. He was a spry man of considerable strength, towering over most people and just an inch shorter than his only son.

The strength of his age came mostly from the labor involved in running the cattle ranch, but nature had provided him with a muscular structure reminiscent of a Viking from the Middle Ages. Lean sinew covered the bones beneath his worn-out western shirt, showcasing every movement of his body as he sat patiently, waiting for news of the day.

His jeans and boots matched the black button-down shirt he wore, adorning his body with the image of a hardened rancher. Though the rancher persona was not a facade, his clothes were of designer quality, and the worn gold bracelet around his left wrist told a story of something more than the rancher he pretended to be.

Edward sat with a skinning knife in his hand, a handmade Randall Made Knife of superior quality that never left his belt. In the rare moments when he found himself waiting on others, he would toy with the knife, carving on sticks to occupy his hands while his mind wandered.

At that moment, he was waiting for the Texas Rangers to deliver a message. Retiring nearly ten years before from the same organization had left him with a few friends remaining on the force. In the distance, he could see the dust rising as a vehicle approached. Edward followed it casually out of his peripheral vision, refusing to divert his eyes from the stick he continued to whittle.

A cloud of dust settled in front of the small ranch home as the car pulled into the park. Two men exited the vehicle, both wearing blue jeans and blazers with Texas Ranger badges shimmering in the bright sunlight.

Can't be good news, Edward thought to himself as they approached, ascending the few steps to the landing of the front porch. *Good news came with grins and smiles.* He wondered for a moment if someone had finally issued an arrest warrant to take him in. Years of his crimes were finally coming to a head, and he was paying for the sins he committed during his time holding a badge.

"Edward," one of them said, taking a seat across from the old man in an open rocking chair while the other leaned casually against the railing.

"What is it, Chris? Gotta be important to drive all the way

out here to tell me in person."

"It is, Ed." Chris waited patiently, hoping Edward would set the knife aside for a moment before continuing. Chris Carter was not a man that was easily intimidated. But Edward Mahon had the ability to do just that to most men in his path.

"Ed, I'm sorry. There's really no easy way to say that. It's about your son." Finally grabbing all of Edward's attention, he set the stick aside and sheathed the knife.

"What about him?" The worry in his voice was that of any father hoping against hope that his worst nightmare wasn't about to be realized. Only Edward's was different… It was feigned and came from a place of narcissism rather than love.

"He was killed last night, Ed."

"Killed?" Having delivered that information himself dozens of times, he knew the proper responses cops would want to hear, but it didn't matter to him. A frustrated and angry sadness brewed within him.

"How was he killed, Chris?"

"Local cops are still piecing it together. It looks like he picked up where you left off when you retired. He was killed trying to serve a contract in Birmingham."

"Birmingham? What the fuck was he doing there?"

"We don't have a lot of information yet, Ed. All we know is that Vincent was beaten to death by a PI working a protection detail for some hooker. Vince and the others were contracted by a local pimp according to the PI's statement, and he led them to the mountains and killed them."

"Them?"

"All of them, Ed. Vince worked in a group like you always did. He killed the three of them."

"One fucking PI killed three cops? How?"

"One was stabbed in the neck. The other was struck multiple times with a tomahawk. Vince was pushed off the road by another vehicle and beaten to death."

"Charges?"

"Local PD says it was a clear-cut case of self-defense. The PI claimed he got the hooker out of town for a few days to protect her from the pimp, and the three hitters tracked them there. The bottom line is the PI has a legitimate reason to be there, and your boy didn't. They don't have the girl's statement yet, but the detective said she is corroborating his story. The DA isn't touching it, and they know it was hitters after them, so the extreme violence of the deaths is less important."

"You're telling me a private investigator took on three men with guns, stabbed one, chopped another, and beat Vincent to death with his bare hands? And I'm expected to believe that?" Neither man interrupted as he paused, clearly unfinished. Edward continued, "He didn't fire a shot? He didn't have help?"

"Right now, I'm not sure if any shots were fired. They're still investigating the scene. The statement from the PI said the girl killed the one that was stabbed in the neck, and he killed the other two."

"Where's Vince's body?"

"At the morgue, I imagine. I'll get it sent back here as soon as I can so you can bury him."

"I don't give a shit about burying him. I want to see the body. I want to know how he was killed."

"I can't do that, Ed, but I'll get you the police files from the autopsy."

Up until then, the man leaning on the rail hadn't said a word. When he spoke, his voice came out gravely, like a younger version of the father he was addressing.

"What do you want to do about the PI, Mr. Mahon?"

Edward looked off into the distance, debating his options. He had little ability to love anyone beyond himself. His narcissistic traits created conditions for an extremely self-centered person intent on keeping his interests alive and growing. Vince hadn't spoken to him in years for no other reason than having nothing to say to one another. Regardless of the simple emotions he felt, Vince was his son, and he felt slighted by someone taking him.

It wasn't clear in that moment whether he hated more that Vincent was killed or that it was done without his acknowledgment. Edward was the man who killed people and gave permission for lives to continue living—permission he was then intent on revoking from the PI and his whore. *His whore…* He toyed with the notion for a moment before speaking again.

"Get everyone here. I'm going to hang him."

Lacey awoke, still groggy from the effects of the sedative. She was draped over someone's shoulder, unaware of who the man was carrying her. *Marion, she thought,* wondering if he had gotten her out of there. But it wasn't Marion; the clothes were different, and he smelled unkempt, as though it had been several days since his last shower. *Marion*—it was the only thought that passed through her mind, the only thing she could focus on in that moment. *Focus, Lacey.*

She forced her eyes open, her eidetic memory capturing everything. Like a disposable camera, it would fade with time, but for then, the images were burned into her mind. She focused on the writing everywhere she could see: the label on her attacker's pistol: GLOCK. The license plates in the parking lot burned into her memory. A large box van was in front of her; she knew they were heading there. License plate number: 0VR357.

The attackers were discussing something in Spanish. The dialect was fast but proper and easy to understand. They were Colombians; she was almost certain. It was easier

Spanish to follow than Si's Puerto Rican accent, which tends to break many grammatical rules. Port. Shipping. Girls. It was enough. They were going to the shipping port along with the other girls. It was Mobile; it had to be. There was no other port around.

Her eyes were heavy; it took all of her strength to force them open. *Focus, damnit.* There was nothing else, no other way to help herself. *You're not finished yet.* One of the men opened the door, and she could see ten other girls... all belonging to Si.

Quickly, she slipped her lifeless hand into the man's jacket pocket and squeezed the cellphone with two fingers as tightly as she could. He tossed her onto the floor of the truck, slamming her head into the wooden deck boards, her body still unable to react. The pain was dulled from the sedative, but a large contusion developed quickly underneath her scalp.

It didn't matter; the moment masked her pickpocket attempt, and she was able to roll her body slightly to hide the phone as they closed the door. Struggling with her eyes again, she recognized all the girls in the van... Kelly was there.

Kelly had come to Si years before Lacey had shown up. She was one of his first girls. The two had grown increasingly closer as times got hard, and they were each other's only haven in that chaotic world. Lacey's understanding of sisterly love came from Kelly. "Lacey!" Kelly screamed, running to her and resting Lacey's head in her lap. "Oh honey, we thought you were dead. Where have you been, sweet girl?" she said, staring at Lacey and stroking her hair.

"Missed you too," Lacey said weakly as Kelly brushed her hair back and placed a hand on her face. "Sedative," Lacey told her.

"It'll wear off soon. You're coming around."

"Where are they taking us?" A full sentence seemed to take

all her focus, though she was beginning to feel sensation returning to her feet and fingers.

"I don't know. The men that took us didn't speak English. I assume we got sold off. Si has been doing it for years to get new girls in."

"Si… He's dead," Lacey said, finally able to sit up on her own.

"Dead? How?"

"I'm not sure who… Just that he was skinned alive. They cut his dick off."

"Fucker deserved it, but this might get worse for us then."

"How?"

"Because without him here… and these guys taking us… I mean, I imagine we are getting shipped to South America. They'll fuck us 30 times a day until they get bored, and then we will be killed or traded again."

Kelly began to cry, recognizing the danger they were in. Si was bad, but nothing compared to the Columbians. Lacey was able to stand weakly, but the truck's motion made her legs feel unstable, forcing her back down. *How could this happen now?* She wanted to scream. She had finally escaped that life; she had found something worth holding on to. *Well, fuck them; they're not taking this from me.*

"We are getting out of here," she told Kelly and the other girls, reaching for the phone.

"How'd you get a phone?"

"I picked his pocket when he was carrying me."

Lacey typed out a message to Marion. BOX TRUCK. 0VR357. HEADING TO MOBILE. LACE. She had never had a reason to text him, and his number was a mystery to her. Closing her eyes Lacey's mind started scrolling through every image she had seen. All of the information she had taken without even knowing her mind had processed and cataloged it. *His number's in here keep searching.*

Scouring the memories in the vault in her head Lacey found it. A meaningless scrap of paper on the kitchen counter she had seen passing by it. It was an electric bill for his cottage. Lacey could read the entire bill without it being in front of her. She saw the numbered account, his name and address, and at the bottom of his personal information was the cell phone number for the account.

"Fuck," Lacey shouted in frustration. "The truck is blocking the signal. It's a steel box."

"It won't send?" one of the girls yelled at her.

"Yes, it will," Lacey said calmly. "Kelly, give me your shoe."

Kelly didn't question the order; she took off her stiletto heel and handed it over as commanded. Lacey knelt at the rear roll-up door. The rubber gasket was hardened and brittle from years of ultraviolet exposure. She slid the heel between the door lip and deck boards, kicking it as hard as she could. Slamming the spiked heel into the rubber until it broke through, and she could see light on the outside.

Lacey pulled the heel out and struck again an inch over until it broke through, widening the hole. She kicked again and again, each time creating a larger hole until the gap was big enough to slide a phone through. "Kelly… your bra, give it to me."

Kelly didn't hesitate; she unclipped her push-up bra, holding her smaller breasts in a position that made them appear larger than they were. Lacey removed the underwire and wrapped it around the phone as tightly as she could. The wire formed a basket around the phone, crisscrossing over all four sides. There were about six inches left, which she attached to another girl's wire to extend the length a bit. Slipping the phone through the gap, she pressed send just before it was out of reach for her fingers. The phone hung outside the truck, searching for a signal.

"What now?" Kelly asked her.

"Now, we wait."

"For what?"

"For Marion to come and kill them all."

Opening his eyes, Marion was fully aware and awake. He felt like a coward for not screaming as they took Lacey, but they would both be dead if he had. Before they came in, he had rolled his body to cover the push dagger he was using to saw at the zip ties behind his back.

It took several minutes, but soon he was free and was able to collect his pistol, press checking the chamber before tucking it back into his waistband. Grabbing Lacey's pistol to throw in the truck, he sprinted for his pickup as fast as his injured legs could carry him.

The knife wound hurt, and he could feel his breath tightening as the wound to his chest pushed forcefully on his lung. Moving to the vehicle proved exceptionally painful and exhausting. Each step sent considerable pain down his leg, with his chest screaming at him to stop breathing heavily. He had no support nearby to take the load off his leg, forcing him to hobble across the road, leaving a blood trail in his wake.

Damnit! His mind raced, feeling his chest tighten as each breath he exhaled sucked air through the open penetration just below the third intercostal space in his left pec. *Tension pneumothorax,* he remembered from his training. The air in the cavity would press on the lung until it could no longer expand and eventually press on his heart. He had to treat the chest wound before he could drive or risk passing out and dying before he could get to her.

Finally reaching his truck, Marion fumbled with the door latch with his blood-soaked hands. The trauma kit was in the back seat, and climbing over the console to reach it took considerably more energy than he anticipated. Grabbing a plastic chest seal and needle decompression, he knew it was only a temporary solution. He had to get to a hospital soon… *it could wait.*

Marion stuck the needle in his chest just under his clavicle and above the wound, making a popping noise and pushing a slew of fluids out of the needle. Removing his shirt, he placed the plastic chest seal over the knife wound to stop it from sucking in any more air. The relief from the needle decompression was instant. As the pressure was expelled through the hole, his breathing was restored.

Okay, Lacey, where are you? He thought about the men who took her asking himself questions about them. *Investigate them, damnit!* They were Hispanic; he recognized the accents—Colombian, maybe, definitely South American. He couldn't speak Spanish like Lacey, but he knew enough to recognize the accents and the proper textbook language common in Colombia. So where would they go? Heading to the border would leave them exposed longer than they would be comfortable with.

They would want to limit their exposure on main roads, so travel time would be a concern. Not the main concern; they would take a direct route to a shipping port but avoid the main interstate unless necessary. He pulled out his map and started tracing lines. Blood trickled down his arm, staining the map as he moved his finger along various routes. The interstate was too risky, and the nearest shipping port was Mobile. The most direct route on back highways was to take I-59 to Highway 5 and then to County Road 43 all the way to Mobile.

It may have been a long shot, but it was his only shot. He threw the map into the truck and spun the tires, peeling out of the parking lot. Pulling out his phone, he placed a call to the only person he knew who could help in that situation:

Detective Proctor.

"Hey, Mary."

"Matt. Listen to me; I've got an emergency. I'm sorry I don't have time to explain. There's a human trafficking truck in motion right now. I think it's on its way to Mobile, but I can't be sure. I'm heading down to Mobile now, taking Highway 5 to Thomasville."

"What's the vehicle?"

"I don't know. They took the girl. I'm not sure if there are more girls, but I imagine so."

"Why do you say that?"

"Because they didn't send three guys after just one girl; it doesn't make sense."

"You saw them?"

"Yes."

"Where?"

"At another crime scene where I was being tortured. I'll send you the details when this is done and I'm safely in the hospital."

"You're injured?"

"Yes. I was shot last night at the cabin before I called you, and stabbed in the chest and leg. I'm bleeding a lot, and my lung is going to collapse if I don't get help fast. I'm sorry, Matt; I don't have much time."

"I'll put the word out, but there isn't much to do… I can't issue a BOLO out for every truck that could carry an unspecified number of people."

"I know, damnit!" His phone chimed in his ear as the text came through. "Hang on."

Marion's heart leaped when he saw her text come through. "I've got it!"

"What?"

"The fucking license plate number! It's a box truck, license plate number 0VR357."

"Okay, I'll get the BOLO out to the Troopers. How'd you get a text?"

"Somehow, she got a phone."

"Who is she?"

"The girl from the cabin! You want your witness, don't you?"

"What's the number? We may be able to get a location or at least get close," he asked, as Marion gave him the number.

"Mary, you need to back off and let us handle this. It's an incident in progress, and you're not a cop."

"Matt, you can tell the troopers to shoot me if you want, but I'm finding her. She's my responsibility. She trusted me to protect her. And I won't be backing off!"

"Fine! But I can't help you if this goes tits up."

"I don't care—just call me back when you get something on the number. I need the location Matt."

"Ok."

They hung up the phone, and Marion spent the next 15 minutes flooring it to get to Thomasville. The pain was excruciating, and he wondered if he would pass out. His determination to catch Lacey proved to be a greater 'why' than his pain could destroy. He had to hurry but couldn't speed and risk getting pulled over. Covered in blood, he'd never get to her in time if a trooper saw him; they would have too many questions. Sticking to five miles per hour over the speed limit was agony, and he was forced to use his cruise control.

His frustration was eating him alive. "Fuck!" he screamed at his engine, slamming his hands into the wheel. Marion's leg was bleeding worse; he had lost a lot of blood, but he didn't have time to try and bandage it. The artery wasn't hit, and he knew he had more blood to give. He forced himself to ignore the tremendous amount of blackened liquid mixing with the clay on his floorboards. Marion pulled his shirt off over his head and wrapped it around his leg. *Only in Alabama could an idiot drive around without a shirt on, in an old truck, and not cause suspicion.* He almost laughed if the situation weren't so dire.

His phone finally rang; he didn't even look to see who it was. "Matt!"

"Your man's cell phone is heading on 5 just like you thought. We aren't the FBI; I don't have an exact location, but it pinged a tower close to Thomasville ten minutes ago. I've got patrols on the way."

"I'll be there first," he said, hanging up the phone and slamming the accelerator.

It took close to fifteen minutes for him to finally get the truck in view. But Marion could see it. The box truck… it had to be. He was still a few miles back, closing fast and dodging traffic as he floored the accelerator. Weaving in and out of traffic, he was certain some of the cars had called the cops on him by that point, honking as he passed on the shoulder and flooring the accelerator as he down-shifted to raise the RPMs.

The engine groaned under the stress, and the tires screeched as he wove into every visible gap. "Come on, girl, don't give up on me now. One more ride," he said, talking to his truck, willing it to move forward a little more. The license plate was in view: plate 0VR357. *I got you, Lacey.*

He didn't slow his speed as he approached the truck. He could see the rearview mirrors for a moment, then quickly closed the distance to the rear bumper, attempting to stay in the truck's blind spot. *Wait, Marion… just wait.* His mind told him to floor the vehicle and ram them, but he knew he had to wait for a curve in the road. It was on his GPS just a mile ahead, and he needed the box truck to be turning for him to spin a vehicle that large.

The turn was approaching fast. He needed to time the gear

change right so as not to blow the engine from over-revving the RPMs too long. Marion quickly down-shifted the vehicle to bring the RPMs up. 5000… 6000… 6500 he was in the redline. The engine roared as the block strained to receive more fuel. The box truck glided into the turn without warning, and Marion merged his truck quickly into the oncoming lane.

Turning his wheels, Marion slammed into the back tire fender, sending a jolt through his entire truck and shooting pain through each of his wounds. The RPMs screamed faster and faster as he pushed the pedal to the floor. The truck began to skid sideways toward the guardrail.

It wasn't like the movies, where vehicles slammed and bounced back. Turning the truck at that speed could hurt the girls inside, but he wasn't going to risk losing her… not then. Not after everything they had been through and survived. The truck began to turn sideways as he pushed his engine harder and harder.

The speed began to slow with the Tundra perpendicular to the box truck pushing into the side fender. He down-shifted again, keeping the RPMs high and pushing the box truck off the road. Marion kept the accelerator on the floor as if he were trying to put his foot on the asphalt. His leg was aching from shifting and driving, but he had to push through. 30 MPH, he slammed the box truck off the embankment, tipping it on its side.

The slaver's truck flipped as the Tundra nosed into the bottom, pushing further down the embankment. He slammed the brakes reflexively, trying to stall his momentum and keep the truck from hurting the passengers in the back. Both vehicles finally came to a stop, with the Tundra bending in the frame of the truck as the two machines became one monstrous organism. The captors vehicle was resting on its side as Marion's Tundra was driven nose down into the undercarriage.

Don't stop. Marion grabbed his pistol from his waistband, readying it for Lacey's kidnappers. Moving slowly and holding his leg, Marion crept from the vehicle, supporting his body weight on the cab of the truck. The first of the attackers emerged from the driver's window with a pistol in his hand as he climbed free, from what was now the top of the vehicle. There was no option to wait and see if the attacker surrendered; knowing there were two more in the cab.

Marion took aim, silhouetting the body in the front sight of the 1911, and pulled the trigger twice in rapid succession. Both rounds struck the chest, tumbling him backward off the side of the truck and landing on the rocks below. Diving headfirst into the rocks, a large gray stone concaved the man's head, killing him on impact.

The other two men must have come through the windshield and started firing from around the side of the truck, striking Marion in the same leg with the knife wound, and dropping him to the ground. Screaming in pain, he fired the seven bullets remaining in his gun. Each round struck through the thin metal base of the vehicle, some getting lost in the engine compartment while others penetrated. Blindly firing with the intent of stopping the attack, he was grateful for a moment that his pistol carried .45 caliber bullets to penetrate the steel.

Pulling a magazine from his waist and reloading his pistol, he kept it aimed at the same spot. *Come on, you son-of-a-bitch.* He couldn't walk anymore. Looking down, the bullet wound had entered the side of his calf, breaking his fibula. The pain from each wound forced him to crawl toward the front of the truck. Each movement sent pain through his leg, with his chest screaming at him to stop breathing heavily. He expected to take fire again at any moment, but the bullets never came.

Crawling closer and closer, he started to smell the burning

of the electrical components as the engine compartment caught fire. He pushed himself harder and with more tenacity than he thought he could muster to try and get around the front of the truck, the pain clawed at his leg with each movement as he supported himself on the bumper and engine compartment.

Rounding the corner he could see two of the bodies: one with its head caved in on the rocks below and another still alive but dying. With the seven shots fired, one went clean through, striking the attacker in the neck. He was bleeding out and holding his throat in a feeble attempt to stop blood from squirting from the artery and restore his breathing. His death would follow in minutes. Marion was out of time to waste looking for the third man.

He pulled himself along the side of the truck, using the hood and broken windshield as handles to support his weight. With the truck to stabilize himself and relieve the weight off of his bad leg, he was able to move around toward the back of the truck. The heat from the engine compartment could be felt now on his back as the fire raged exponentially with each passing second, as if it had a life of its own. It was smoldering, and the truck would be a burning inferno in a few minutes.

"Lacey!" he shouted, trying not to cough in the smoke.

"Marion! We're in here!" His heart was relieved and more scared than ever when he heard her voice. The fear gripped him again as the vehicle's rear latch came into view. The locking mechanism on the door had broken free, but it was stuck on the rollers and couldn't be opened. "Lacey!" he shouted again. The girls were pounding on the door.

He couldn't budge the door open. "Lacey! Stand back!" The pounding stopped, and he heard her yell, "Okay!"

Drawing his pistol again, he shot the exposed rollers on the door frame. Each one received a bullet to blow it off its hinges. Marion reached his hand underneath the rollers and braced himself against the bumper. The pain in his leg soared through his body as he pushed with everything he had. His leg was so painful against the force of his body lifting on the door that he was afraid he might lose consciousness before getting it open. Without warning, it came free, making a gap too small to fit through.

Marion readjusted his body. *One more push.* He could hear the girls screaming inside the compartment as it filled with smoke. His veins bulged in his arms and neck as he heaved against the door. The metal-on-metal contact scraped as it slid further and further up. *Crack!* The door made a loud boom as the metal from one of the destroyed rollers broke free and widened the gap. It wasn't much, but enough for each of the girls to pass through. Marion collapsed on the spot, unable to support himself anymore.

Every last bit of energy was exerted trying to free the door, and he had nothing left to support himself. Marion could feel his eyes getting heavy as the heat from the fire warmed his body. It was a pleasant feeling in the moment, and the darkness was overpowering his ability to keep his eyes open. He wanted to stay in the warmth of the blaze, but something was trying to pull him out of it.

He could feel his body shaking as Lacey grabbed him by the waist. "Baby, come on!" she yelled, trying to lift him to his feet. Marion's eyes opened, and he made a feeble attempt to stand, relying on her body for support. The inferno consuming the truck was so intense that the heat was painful, singeing the hairs on his arm.

Supporting most of his weight on her shoulders, Lacey heaved and struggled to get him up the embankment. The top of the slope was beginning to crest, revealing the guardrails that his truck had smashed through only moments ago. The distant sound of fire engine sirens was now evident as his mind faded to black. They grew louder and louder, closing in on his location.

Finally, the pavement of the road was safely under his feet, requiring all his remaining energy to keep his eyes open and his feet moving forward. When they stopped, Marion collapsed into the soft earth of the median. The sirens were close enough to hurt his ears now. The last thing he heard before the world went black was Lacey holding his face, assuring him she wouldn't leave.

Epilogue

"If you love something, let it go."
–Sting

Officer Jacobson sat quietly in Detective Pierce's office, a small room with glass windows and an old wooden door. Pierce sat across from him, a cheap particle board desk separating them. The room was cluttered with files and cabinets overflowing with more files.

Detective Pierce, a 25-year veteran of the police department, bore the marks of age in his gray beard and balding head. He was slightly overweight, sporting a quintessential old-man belly protruding from his waistline. He stared inquisitively at the younger officer through his glasses, projecting a false sense of intelligence that was far less significant than he alluded to.

"You don't think Si killed this guy?"

"No, he wouldn't have asked me to look at the location. It was well hidden; I would never have found it if I hadn't had a dog trained to find cadavers. He kept signaling at the car. I searched, thinking it was drugs, until I realized a body must be buried underneath."

"And you buried it back?"

"For the time being, yes. Anyone smart enough to do this

would have disposed of the pistol, and we didn't want it going to the medical examiner, did we?"

"No, that was probably the best decision." The detective was intrigued but not overly interested. "Did you find anything else?"

"Nothing that made sense without involving forensics. I did pull a .38 special round out of his leg with a multi-tool. It looks like he just bled out; I didn't see anything else wrong with him."

"Is there anything that could tie this back to us?" The detective asked, his concern evident.

"No. I was always paid in cash. I assume you were too?" Officer Jacobson asked, his tone tinged with worry.

"Yes. Same for me."

"So, what should we do? I don't want to draw attention to us, but he paid well, and my wife is going to miss that money coming in."

"I imagine my alimony payments will get a little tighter now without the spare spending cash as well."

"You're the detective... How do we handle this?"

"Leave the body. Let it rot. It won't help us at all, anyway. Dig into Si's life, see if you can find any of the girls, and start asking questions. I'll get the phone records for Si and see what we can trace from that end. With his body showing up in that warehouse, we should have something to go on. Do you know who the body was?"

"Judging by his size, I think it's a lowlife drug trafficker named Tommy Johnson. What about the PI and his story of the kidnapping? Seems odd to me that a random zoning official was found murdered by traffickers, who he claims cut up the pimp."

"Supposedly, his basement was filled with weird tools and set up to dispose of evidence."

"Jesus, man, he could have been interested in

blacksmithing for all you know. How many serial killers have we had in Birmingham? This shit doesn't happen here—this isn't LA. I'm telling you he had something going on with the pimp, and this zoning guy Ewan got in the way. We need to look into that further."

The detective remained silent, watching the younger man, trying to discern what was on his mind by seeing through him. The constant gaze was uncomfortable, causing Jacobson to look away.

"You may be right. But the official verdict is that he was killed by traffickers when the PI tried to rescue the girl from the pimp. That's as far as the investigation is going. We can put some pressure on him, but we have nothing legally, and if he barks to his friends in homicide, we will have to back off. So we can't press him too hard. The DA doesn't want to pursue anything against the hooker, since he ran his campaign on aiding prostitutes back into society with those non-profits he supports."

"Fine, but he knows more than he is telling."

"I agree. Let it settle for a bit, and in a few months, we can get with the PI about the disappearance of Tommy Johnson. He may give up something if we can make him think there's a link between them."

"What do you want to do if he does?"

"We will lean on him. He will need to start repaying some of what we have lost in this messed-up situation. I'd rather get rich than get even."

"Fair enough."

"Either way, the first step is finding the people who killed him. Which means we need to let it settle and then talk with the PI." The detective finished his last sentence, wondering if he was better off letting that go. None of it sat right with either of them. A suspected serial killer and a skinned pimp were found in an abandoned warehouse. A PI breaking up a human trafficking ring had been stabbed and tortured by a random killer. Not to mention the three corrupt cops killed the evening before. *Somehow, this is all connected, and he was at the center*. The answer would rest on finding out who killed Tommy Johnson; he was certain of it.

Luis Delgado was finally back in Cartagena, Colombia. He sat in a small cottage on a 1,500-acre plantation. Though not exactly a prisoner, he certainly wasn't free to leave at will. He wasn't easily scared, but he had failed abysmally in his last mission. Failing to return with the 11 girls had cost his employer a substantial amount of money. Now his employer had to pay the cartels double what he had taken in advance.

The steep price could have been settled by handing him over to the cartels with the original payment. A double payment was sent to purchase his life. The cartels would have thrown him in an oil drum and tossed it into the ocean for him to cook inside for several days until he finally succumbed to dehydration. As terrible as that death sounded, his employer would do worse. He had personally sat in that same shack, watching as men and women were dismembered for failing to meet their obligations.

The room was small, barely more than a mud hut that peasants lived in. Stone walls surrounded a shake-shingle roof with hand-carved rafters overhead. A single chair was placed in the middle of the room, where detainees were either seated or suspended from the rafter directly above. In that instance, a clean chair was temporarily brought in, sitting immediately across from him.

Blood was never cleaned, and only bodies and parts would be removed after a session with the prisoners. The constant smell of death and decay drove fear into anyone who entered the room; rats devouring the leftover blood only added to the ambiance of the butchering floor. The aura of death lingered in the air as it did in a slaughterhouse. Each occupant knowing what was in store for them in the moments to come.

Luis trembled in fear as he waited alone. Being alone and voluntarily staying was worse than being captive. A captive had no choice but to be held. For Luis, staying was a matter of facing two competing issues. What was worse? Leaving and getting caught, or staying and finding out what the punishment was.

He contemplated the idea of running as fast and as far as he could when a large Colombian man entered the room with three guards who always traveled with him. Each man was dressed like a rebel from the Vietnam War, carrying guns, machetes, and army camouflage to complete the ensemble.

The man in the middle wore a custom-tailored black polo shirt and white slacks. He didn't bother to remove his aviator sunglasses, even though the room was dark and had no windows. One of the guards placed a collapsible cushioned chair directly in front of Luis, inviting the man to sit. Taking his seat casually across from the soldier, he spoke in well-educated and proper Spanish.

"Do you know who did this?"

"No, sir, but I can find him… I know what he looks like. I can bring him back here and double the…" He stopped mid-sentence as the nicely dressed Colombian held up a hand to silence him.

"I'm going to send you back with a team to help. If you expect to live to see your son's birthday, you will come back with his head and the girl."

"Yes, sir."

"If you don't return, I'll take payment with your wife Angelica and your daughter Aurelia, and your son will take your spot in this room. Angelica and Aurelia will be sold to the rebels to pay your debt."

The statement didn't require a response, and he

awkwardly placed the names in the sentence to ensure Luis understood the gravity of his situation. The conditions were clearly understood by everyone in the room. The mysterious man known locally as Señor Vega simply rose from the chair and walked out, leaving an aura of desperation in his wake. Out of earshot of his prisoner, he turned to one of the guards.

"Once you identify who did this..." nudging his head toward the prisoner, "kill him. Bring me the head of the man responsible and replace the girls."

"Yes, sir."

The guard walked back inside and pulled a skinning knife from his hip. Luis knew what it meant, and there was little use in fighting. Bringing his fingers together under his tongue, he whistled loudly for two other men to join him. Each man grabbed an arm, pinning Luis to the chair. They were strong and prohibited his body from moving, but the natural response would oblige anyone to resist and not submit to the pain.

Placing his left hand on Luis' head, he held the skinning knife to the eyebrow over his right eye, forcing the edge into his skull and slicing down in a single stroke. Luis screamed in pain and horror as his vision instantly went black, knowing his eye had been cut open.

The warm liquid trickled down his face, coating his bare chest with blood and clear fluid he could only guess came from the open eyeball. He instinctively held his hand to it, as if his mind were attempting to piece everything back together. That was the mark of his employer—a mark of shame meant to instill fear into everyone. Those who bore it were forbidden from concealing the wound with an eyepatch and were forced to wear it as a mark of betrayal.

"Put your clothes on. Where are we going?"

"We have to go back to Birmingham?" The words left his mouth in a silent scream of anguish as his hand continued to fill with blood. "We can travel through Mobile with the shipping containers."

"You travel in the containers. I will meet you there when you get off. You better be able to find him."

Rebecca Maddox had been informed by the police about the incident involving her husband's death. She spent the following weeks with a behavioral analyst from the FBI, who told her it was likely not the first or only killing Ewan had been involved in.

Instead of feeling sickened and disdainful upon learning that information, Rebecca was finally relieved. For years, she had been told that she was the problem, that there was nothing wrong with him, and how worthless and irritating she was to him. She had become a constant annoyance in his existence. It was always "she, she," "her, she, her, her"—never him; it was always her.

She had suspected for many years that there was something much darker about Ewan than she could ever pinpoint. She had tried to determine the relationships with Ewan's dark side, but nothing ever seemed to fit or make sense, until the FBI informed her of their suspicions regarding past crimes.

For the remainder of her life, she regularly attended Mass and lit a candle to remember and pray for the missing and unknown deaths he had caused. It became an annual ritual she would never miss, never make exceptions for, and never forget.

Over time, she began to wonder if she were the problem; wonderment turned into belief, and belief into acceptance. After a short stint with the FBI trying to improve their serial killer database, she was advised to attend regular counseling.

The suicidality of her emotional swings was curbed through several months of treatment, during which she began to realize that it was not her fault for the misgivings in their relationship. No longer afraid of saying or doing the wrong thing, she finally felt free and able to enjoy her life.

By plugging herself into social networks, from which she had been deprived for many years, she soon became comfortable and less awkward in making friends and meeting people. As a natural extrovert, being detained as a prisoner in her home had taken a significant toll on her mental health, which she was over-correcting.

Along with Ewan's pension, social security, and life insurance, she was well taken care of financially. Electing to sell her home and move back to New York, where she had some remaining family, she legally changed her name to usher in a new era of her existence, and the home was occupied by a young family with two boys, filling it with joy and love, unaware of the dark man who once resided there.

She began to explore hobbies and developed a particular affection for musical theater, becoming exceptional at her craft. Local theaters began to fill to capacity when her name appeared on the advertisements. Several years later, she would find herself married again to a musical director who loved to travel. The two were beyond excited when they discovered a baby would be joining their lives in nine months.

Kelly Slecha and the other girls belonging to Si were initially taken into custody and then referred to the care of a halfway house funded both privately and by the state. Housing was provided for a short-term stay while they worked and saved to begin anew.

Many of the girls found fulfilling employment, while some of the more addicted users struggled with their obsessions and required additional resources from rehabilitation centers. Over time, most of the women found happiness in their new lives. Some moved on to other cities, others were accepted to college, and some found their way into happy relationships and marriages.

Kelly moved to Denver after a year at the halfway home, opting for a completely new life. She was accepted into the University of Colorado, Denver, where she began a new career focused on helping people. A degree in biology, marked with a graduate with an honors certificate, led her to apply and be accepted into medical school.

Her husband entered her life during her senior year of college. He was a gentleman of strong character and a well-respected dentist in the area. The two enjoyed a quiet life in the mountains of Colorado, with Pikes Peak in the foreground of their mountain home.

Unable to have children due to years of physical trauma, they began adopting children from the system who had long been forgotten. Initially intent on growing a family, Kelly began adopting the most troubled children who needed their help the most. She dedicated her life to fostering kids that no one wanted and adopting the lost causes that were too far gone. Ultimately, they ended up with eight adopted children to shower with love and affection.

Edward sat in the barn on the back side of his property. Three other chairs were filled with members of the original Pigs—the ones who had started the operation years before, providing a service to the drug lords and gangs of the area: murder for hire, with the cartels in Juarez being some of their largest clients.

Each man in the circle was void of any electronics. Empty horse stables with cribbing marks on the doors remained, and the hay underfoot was several years in the decay process, having not completely deteriorated with no exposure to the elements inside the barn. The barn still smelled of the horses and manure that once occupied and filled its existence with purpose.

The Texas sun had beaten the color out of the exterior of the building, leaving only grayed board and batten siding that creaked and groaned as if begging for a drink of water. The tin roof was solid and waterproof, regardless of the rust covering the entirety of the building.

Structurally sound and pragmatic in its current state, Edward realized that he was the barn for all intents and purposes. The building could be used the next day for horses, cattle, or hay, as had been its intent. Its age and current aesthetic appeal had little to do with its ability to provide a service its owner desired. Edward could enter back into the game he had retired from with no need for a paint job or restoration of any sort.

The three men with him were similar in age to Edward, only a few years apart from the youngest to the oldest. Each wore a cowboy hat—one brown and two white, adorned with bands and belts to complete their traditional Western look. The grit of the men was unquestionable, but the man in the brown hat was noticeably portly compared to the others, having let retirement take a toll on his health.

The meeting would start when Edward decided to make a statement. For a moment, he allowed them to settle in and take their seats. None of them spoke, each having heard the news of Vincent's passing. Edward's knife was present, as it always was on his hip, but he opted for a Colt Python on his right hip, choosing a traditional revolver over more modern semiautomatic weapons.

It was a beautiful weapon with a six-inch barrel chambered in .357 magnum, its custom machining still evident on the cylinder. For 30 years, Edward had carried it as a Texas Ranger, enjoying the feel and finish of handmade craftsmanship. The firearm was meticulously cared for, but the wooden handle bore a worn finish from the thousands of rounds expelled from its barrel.

"By now, y'all know what happened with Vince." Though it came across as a statement, Edward waited for a response to confirm they had indeed heard the news. Each man nodded in unison without uttering a word on the subject.

"We have a job." He paused, letting the news of work sink in for men who hadn't had a 'job' in over a decade. "We are going to kill those responsible."

Not surprised by the request, one of the men in the white hat decided to address the issue. "No disrespect, Edward. I know Vince was your son and all... but we are retired. Shit, even if we weren't, we never took jobs for free. This was a business, plain and simple. I appreciate that you're emotional about this..."

Holding his hand up, Edward cut him off, not allowing the sentence to finish. "Each of you will be paid. I'm offering $100,000 to each of you and another $100,000 to the one who brings him in alive."

"Brings him in?" The man in the white hat spoke again, questioning, "You're not coming with us?"

"I'll be coming. But I want him alive. There's an incentive to bring him and the girl back alive."

"Two of them, Ed? For $100K? Come on, man. We'd have charged half a million for one of them 15 years ago."

"That's my offer. It won't go up. That pot will not be sweetened. Take it or leave it."

"I'm in, Ed." Speaking for the first time, the man in the brown hat said, "If nothing else, it gets me out of the fucking house. But I'll do this for Vince."

"Tom?" Edward said, turning to the second man in the white hat.

"I'm in, Ed. I'll be honest; it's not how I was hoping to spend the next few weeks, but I'm in."

"Few months, Tom. The next few months."

"Few months? Why the fuck are we spending months on this?" The first man in white protested.

"I'm not ready to kill him yet. I want to know why my son was there. I want to know who this man is and what he cares about. Then I want to cut it out of his life piece by piece."

"Well, gentlemen, I'm out. Sorry, Ed, I hate that Vince was killed, but I have a retirement to enjoy, money to spend, and casinos to visit. I don't want anything to do with this shit. Good luck to you, but fuck off, yeah?"

Standing to leave, he hadn't made two steps toward the door when Edward called after him. "Carter!"

"What, Ed? I told you I'm not interested. I've made my money. We had a business relationship, but I really don't give a shit about Vince…"

"I was just going to say I'm sorry to see you go out like this."

Carter reached for the pistol on his hip in a desperate attempt to draw it, realizing what Edward meant with his last sentence. Edward wasn't sure if he was as fast as he had been in the past or if Carter was slower; Carter's hand hadn't even grasped the handle before two bullet holes exited his back, exposing his spine through the wound and dropping him to the ground.

"Take care of whatever you need to at home." Turning to the men in brown hats, Edward spoke again, "James, I want you to go to Birmingham and find him. Don't do anything yet, just watch him. Find out where he lives, where he vacations, and who he sleeps with on the weekends. I want to know his favorite flavor of fucking ice cream."

"How long do you want me to stay down there?"

"As long as it takes. It'll take you at least a month to do it. You need to be invisible. He may just be a PI, but PIs know surveillance. He will pick up a tail quickly. Change cars every day or two with a rental agency and switch hotels often so he can't trace you back. No matter what happens, don't let him see you."

"Okay. I'll leave in the morning."

Edward tossed him an envelope. "There's $10,000 in it for your expenses. That should cover everything you need until you get back."

"What are we going to do?" Tom asked.

"We are going to wait and watch. We are going to be patient. When everything is right, when the conditions are set… then I'll rip his world from him and break his body until he stops breathing."

Lacey sat patiently in Marion's new truck. He no longer had to shift gears with the automatic transmission of the newer Tundra, and he held her hand on the center console. They passed through the mountains of Tennessee, winding through curves and the granite stonework along the road.

His leg hadn't healed completely, but after a week in the hospital, he was sent home and maintained some ability to walk. Running was certainly beyond his capability, but with the help of a boot on the lower half of his leg, he was able to get around. Most of the damage was to soft tissue; however, part of his leg had been broken, requiring several more weeks to heal. The biggest risk to him was an infection from not tending to the wounds.

"Why won't you tell me where we are going?"

"Because it's a surprise! I told you we would be up here for the weekend, and then we can head back."

"Fine, but when we get there, can we *please* get something to eat? I'm starving!" She laughed, showing all her teeth as her head cocked back.

He smiled back at her. "Yes, we can get some food. Don't worry; I have plans for dinner."

They had been driving for nearly five hours when he finally turned off the main asphalt road. The gravel path was old and steep, and Lacey began to feel a sense of familiarity. She recognized the trees; even the road looked the same—everything had a hint of nostalgia. Lacey rolled down her window to inhale the scent of the scenery, which brought her back to her childhood.

She breathed deeply, taking in the aroma of pine needles and cool mountain air with each passing second. The trees moved by slowly, creating the illusion of a green haze as she tried to look off into the distance. The sound of the tires slipping on the gravel reminded her of her grandmother's Land Cruiser. She couldn't help but wish for the song by Ashton Shepherd to come on the radio.

Cause there ain't nothing like the sound of a cooler slushing
On the bed of your truck
And ain't nothing like the sound of real country music
C'mon, turn it up

In that moment, she was dying for the song to play and decided it was worth asking Marion if he had it on his phone. Marion didn't respond but played the music as she had requested. The song had not been written when she was a child, but when she first heard it, it nearly brought tears to her eyes, reminding her of her grandmother. It wasn't until her twenties that she realized the song was a love story.

"Marion… How did you find this? How'd you find her cabin?" Her emotions were caught somewhere between shock and euphoric joy.

"This is what I do," he replied, without offering any further explanation. In truth, it had been a more difficult task than he had anticipated. Modern tax records were electronic in most counties in the state, but older records from her childhood were not yet digitized. Searching required manually pulling the records and sifting through them at the courthouses. In his injured state he had been forced to pay another investigator to do it for him.

The cabin came into view as they approached. It overlooked a large forest built on the steep side of the mountain, resting permanently in a soft meadow. The grass encroached on the cabin as if trying to tickle its belly with the blowing wind. The surrounding forest was dark, with thickets filling the spaces between the trees. Rain clouds had rolled in, and the drizzle began as the cabin drew closer, prompting Lacey to roll the window back up.

Marion pulled in front of the home. The hand-hewn cedar logs were square in design and stained a deep brown. The front door was glass with a wooden bottom, and the home had a simple roof with one peak extending from front to back. The windows on the front porch made the interior bright, even from the driveway, and the picture windows reached all the way to the peak of the eaves.

The storm was intensifying, with rain pouring down. "Should we wait for it to stop raining?" Marion asked, interrupted by the door of his truck flying open as Lacey sprinted to the front porch. "Come on!" she yelled, not looking over her shoulder.

He couldn't have cared less about the rain beating down on him like a shower faucet. Getting wet was hardly a problem, and giving her that gift brought him as much joy as it did her. Marion caught her just before she reached the step, grabbing her hand to ascend the stairs together.

Both of their bodies were soaked when they reached the front entry. The rain fell heavier with each moment, accompanied by the roar of thunder in the background. The metal roof echoed the sound of each droplet striking it and dissipating upon impact. Taped to the door was an envelope with her name on it.

She looked at Marion inquisitively. "Open it." He didn't offer any further explanation. The first paper was a deed to the property, with one name at the top: LACEY MEYERS. Holding the paper, she looked at him, trying to catch his eye while reading each line. "Marion, what is this?"

Marion took her hand before speaking. "Right now you feel beholden to me… Being with me puts you in a hard place because there's no alternative. Without having a place to go if you wanted to, you could never have the choice to leave. To choose to stay with me means you have to have the choice to leave." He paused briefly to let her process the information before continuing.

Her eyes filled with tears as he spoke, until they began to run down her face and drip onto the paper. "I bought you this property so that you can be free. It's yours. My name's not on the deed, and whatever happens to it is entirely up to you. For this to ever be anything real, you had to have the choice to be with me…"

Lacey dropped the packet of paper on the floor and grabbed Marion mid-sentence. Her hand slid behind his neck, holding his head as she leaned in and kissed him. Her lips pressed against his, thoughts of being with him swirling through her mind. Marion held her head with one hand and hugged her waist with the other.

It was a moment she didn't want to miss and one she never wanted to let go of, wishing she could feel that way forever. "Thank you for this," she said, her eyes brimming with tears as she pulled back from his face. She leaned her head forward, touching her forehead to his and holding his cheek in her hand. His beard was always rough, like a five o'clock shadow that was never trimmed. The gray hairs of a man nearing his mid-thirties peppered his skin, shining brightly in the dull glow of the storm.

"I choose you... I don't care about the house or anything else. I will always choose you, Marion." He smiled at her and leaned in to kiss her again, locking their lips together for several minutes on the front porch of her house.

Lacey nestled her face into his chest, hugging him tightly, not wanting to let go. "I just want you."

"That's good because if you'd have said 'no,' I was going to rip up the title paperwork," he said, laughing with her.

"That's fine; I can't leave until you buy me a car, anyway." She giggled, playfully hitting him in the stomach. "Besides, as the newly appointed CEO of Gamble Investigations, I'd have hated to fire you."

"So you're the CEO now?"

"Naturally! The competition was fierce, but in the end, I won the board over with a unanimous vote."

"I suppose that makes sense; you can be very persuasive."

"Had to strip down to my panties to get the promotion, but it was worth it."

"You always like to get the last word, don't you?"

"Yes... I'm the CEO," she said, pulling back and smiling at him again. "Thank you for doing this. No one has ever done something like this for me." Marion didn't respond; there was nothing he could say. She was grateful for the gift, and he was happy that she could choose him of her own free will.

"Will we be safe? Will someone else come?"

"I don't know, Lace... It's hard to imagine that there won't be something clawing its way back into your life... or even mine for that matter."

"What do we do?"

"The only thing we can do... handle them together."

Lacey nodded with a smile. That was the first time she had felt genuine happiness for as long as she could remember. She was falling in love with the man standing in front of her. Everything she ever wanted, everything she ever dreamed of, her wildest desires—all of it was coming true.

"Are you ready to go inside?" he asked her.

"Yes," she said, before leaning in to kiss him one more time. "You bet your hot ass, I am."

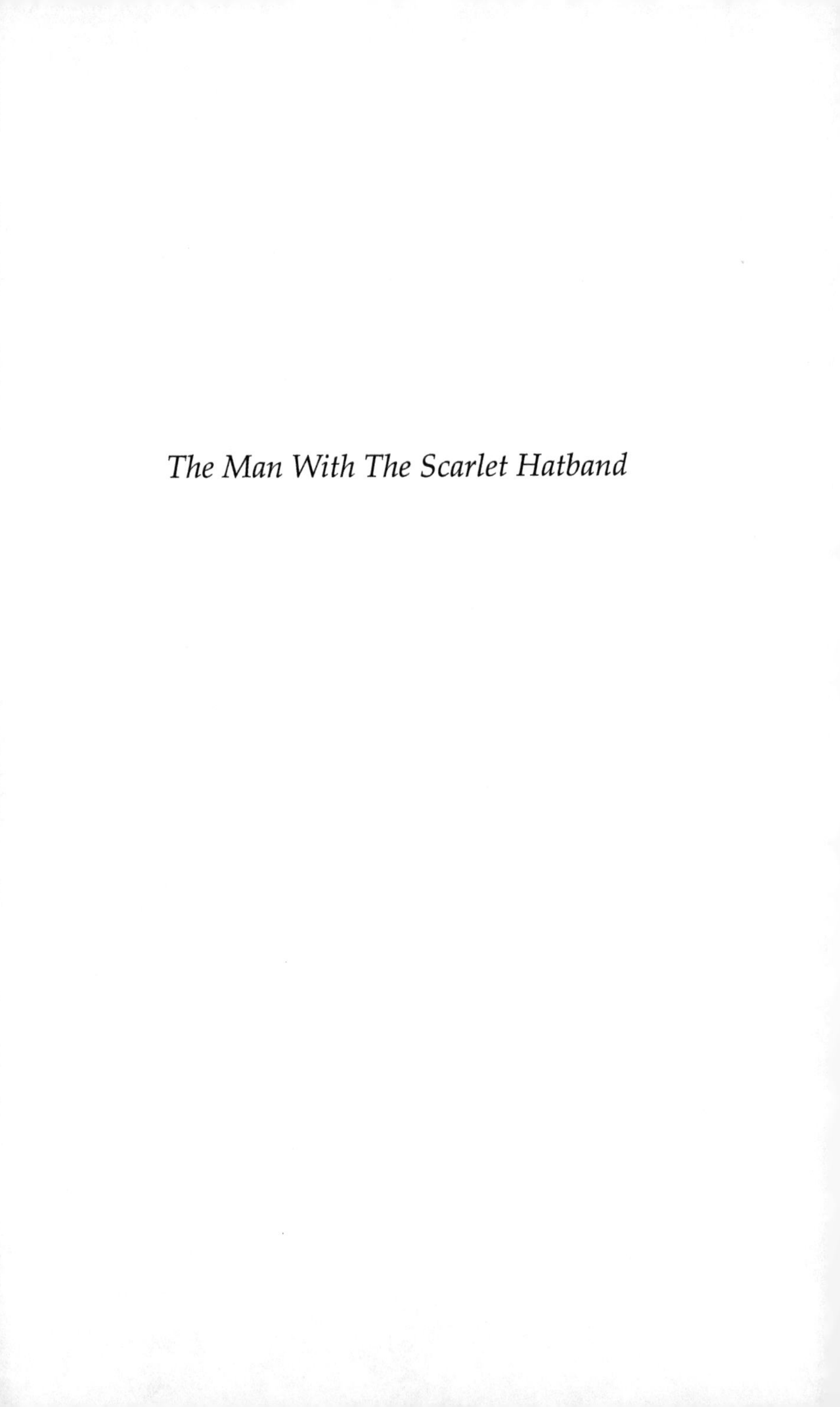

The Man With The Scarlet Hatband

Prologue

The arid Texas heat would have been driving the sweat from his brow any other time of year. But it was still January, and Southern Texas felt warm and unsatisfying, though not hot. No one outside of a native-born Texan would call it winter, but the cool air chilled him nonetheless. Today seemed to be an exception, with the sun beating down on him more than usual, while gusts of wind dried the sweat and cooled him. It was an impossible environment to dress for: hot in the sun and cold when the wind blew. A small sage bush sat next to him, casting a shadow that taunted him, though he knew it would be colder in the shade. The bush was small enough that its shade would never reach him, teasing him out of the corner of his eye.

Everything still "felt" hot to Mathew. Even at 55 degrees, the image of heat seemed to never leave this part of the world. Staring at the bush next to him, he imagined it might explode from the dry heat, only to be satiated by the gusts of cool wind. The spontaneous combustion would set the prairie ablaze. *Why the fuck did I come out here today?* he asked himself. Texas had a peculiar ability to make you feel as if you had fallen into an icy lake while simultaneously being set on fire.

The fact of the matter was that there were limited options

for a pastime such as this, and he needed the solitude to focus on the task at hand. *Focus.* He relaxed his body on top of a canvas mat to protect his elbows from the sand beneath him and keep the grit out of his equipment.

Through the glass lens, he scanned the wasteland in front of him for signs of possible threats or unassuming bystanders. He didn't expect to see anyone, certainly not way out here in the middle of nowhere. But he practiced the habits and procedures regardless. The principles are always the same… only the threat level changes.

He squinted his eye peeking again through the spotting glass, ranging targets in the distance. The first target stood at almost 1,000 yards—a small playing card held in a makeshift piece of steel set exactly 36 inches off the ground. His next target was slightly larger: an old bowling pin resting directly on the ground. At just under a mile, it stood tall on a small dirt mogul, nearly 1,500 yards from him. His final target for the day was sitting atop a large hill just in front of the Franklin Mountain backstop, exactly 1,896 yards from his location.

With no substantial meaning, the final target was a real estate sign featuring the smiling face of a local agent. She was attractive, with a hint of natural beauty behind layers of makeup and artificial intelligence filters. *Glamour shots,* he thought, doubting he would recognize her in person. Checking his ranges again, the scope traversed effortlessly between the targets as he backpedaled to the playing card once more.

It was a hell of a distance for an average shooter, though not out of the ordinary for highly competitive long-distance shooters. Few shooters were capable of hitting targets of this size at these ranges. Even fewer firearms were available on the market that had the necessary tolerances required for accuracy at extreme distances.

The average hunting rifle sold at a big box store would have a tolerance of around one minute of angle (MOA) at 100 yards, meaning it could be off by up to an inch at that distance and 2 inches at 200 yards. Moving out to extreme distances, the looser tolerances amplified the discrepancy, causing the round to miss the target wildly. For shots at 2,000 yards, he couldn't afford to be 20 inches off; he required a firearm capable of shooting sub-minute of angle shots.

Lying next to him on the canvas pad was a .408 caliber CheyTac (CT) rifle equipped with four spare magazines, glimmering with a dull sheen in the sun. The rifle had several layers of paint from camouflaging different environments it had operated in. The handle and cheek rest were worn through to the original black pattern, while the rest of the rifle was coated in a spray can Army green, showing wear marks from use. The meticulous maintenance was invisible to anyone but the rifle's master, who spent hours tuning, refining, and cleaning the weapon.

Mathew rolled his body fastidiously behind the rifle and adjusted the scope for the windage and elevation. Adjusting the knobs was a trigonometry equation that accounted for distance, wind, humidity, and even the Coriolis Effect at longer ranges. The ballistic tables were unpacked and available to him, but experience and time had taught him to memorize the majority of them for this rifle.

The .408CT was a round he shot often—in competition, as a contractor, and for years as a soldier. He was intimately familiar with its capabilities and flight pattern, knowing exactly what the bullet would do for each yard it traveled down its intended path. He aimed the crosshairs on the playing card and leveled the rifle, pulling it tight into his shoulder. *Steady.*

Mathew locked the rifle tighter into his shoulder and loaded the bipod on the front by pressing the rifle into it to stabilize his position. Squeezing his hand around the grip, his finger touched the trigger without applying any force. Placing his cheek delicately but securely on the stock, he welded the plastic to his skin as the crosshairs came into view.

Aim. He matched the rhythm of his breathing with the beat of his heart. The substantial range of these targets meant that firing out of alignment with his heartbeat and breathing would throw the shot off. A half-inch movement at 100 yards would translate to nearly 10 inches at the final target. Counting silently in his head, Mathew monitored himself, seeing only the target in his crosshairs as his left eye closed.

Fire. Without hesitation, he gently eased the trigger back towards the receiver until the figurative glass broke and the round released from the end of the barrel. The chamber exploded with 63,000 pounds per square inch of propulsion, pushing the bullet through the rifling, with the round and gases exiting the barrel nearly simultaneously.

The 370-grain projectile rammed its way through the air, creating a wake of hot compressed oxygen in its flight path. Traveling at 3,500 feet per second, the bullet struck the center of the playing card in less than a second, driving 8000 foot pounds of energy through the center of the card. Quickly, he rammed the bolt to the rear, removing the obturated cartridge from the chamber while sliding the next round into the firing position.

Without waiting for confirmation, the rifle transitioned to the second target in an effortless, mechanical manner. Without taking time to dial in the scope for the second shot, he adjusted his reticle on the target, increasing the notches in relation to the distance of his second target. Another round deflagrated in the chamber and traveled through the air, striking the bowling pin just beyond a second after firing. The pin lifted into the air and tumbled helplessly to the ground.

Adjusting once more, the rifle moved to the final target, almost mimicking a robot's maneuvering. Mathew aimed the rifle again at the smiling face of the real estate agent. He adjusted the scope from memory without removing his cheek weld and placed the crosshairs directly over her smiling nose. Letting the final shot escape the chamber, the rifle recoiled with a massive jolt to the rear, the movement absorbed into his bones and muscles.

Mathew opened the chamber, allowing the bore to cool as he rolled and positioned himself behind the spotting scope again. The spotting glass had a substantially magnified zoom lens beyond what the rifle was capable of, allowing him to see the playing card and the crisp hole that had pushed through the center of the seven of spades. Adjusting the scope out and then zooming back in again, he could see the real estate agent with a grotesque smile and a missing nose.

He wasn't given time to revel in his victory or even smile at his skill when his phone rang. It was a name he hadn't seen in years but one he instantly recognized—a name he wasn't sure he wanted to see again, but it was certainly one he couldn't ignore.

Watching the news for the past several months, he had expected the call. He was somewhat surprised it hadn't come sooner, but he knew he was one of the few men up for the task. The phone kept ringing, irritating him as he contemplated whether he should answer it.

He ultimately understood it was a call he had to answer. He hesitated again, looking at the number flashing across his screen before pressing the green button in the bottom corner. A familiar voice sounded on the other end of the phone, still standing in his distant memory after not having heard it for years.

He ultimately understood it was a call he had to answer. Mathew understood his skills would be required, that his past was coming back for another job. He knew he would be asked to pull the trigger, and answering the call meant he agreed to it. Mathew realized he was going to be asked to kill again. He hesitated again, looking at the number flashing across his screen before pressing the green button in the bottom corner.

The only name that seemed to matter in that moment crossed his mind before the familiar voice came through… Marion Gamble.

Chapter 1

"There is a kind of secret strength. It lives in you and no one, not even you, knows it's there. It lives inside you, waiting for the day it's needed, waiting for the darkest hour of the darkest night. And then, when you are defeated, when your heart is so broken you don't know if it can ever be put back together again, it whispers, 'Hello. You don't know me. But I am here.'"

–Lain S. Thomas

The cool morning air of the mountains filled his lungs as his diaphragm expanded to capacity, attempting to inhale as much oxygen as possible. Marion's leg throbbed where the knife and bullet had wounded him previously, but ultimately the scar tissue was now fresh and pink, without lasting effects.

His pace was somewhat slowed; he was unsure if it was due to his aging body, the injury, or the high elevation, but he couldn't maintain the speed of his younger self. Each step through the mountain trail pulsed with dull pain in his hip and thigh as the muscles and soft tissue restored themselves to their condition four months earlier.

Marion could see the cabin come into view as he crested the hill overlooking the open meadow. The trail he was on passed just to the north of the clearing and had an easement through the furthest edge of Lacey's property. A light dusting of snow left the scenery akin to something out of a Stephen Lyman print. The hill he stood on overlooked the cabin and public land, with Lacey's cabin sitting on 10 acres. The adjacent lots were privately owned cabins, each sitting on 10 to 20 acres, surrounded by National Park land.

The community was shaped like a horseshoe, with each lot privately owned on the ring and the public land extending into the center of the shoe. It was a serene setting, and Marion loved taking in the view as he cooled his body and walked down the slope to the cabin. Lacey would be up by now, but she had been fast asleep when he left the cabin 4 miles ago.

She couldn't stand to work out and had a natural figure that didn't require it, though he reminded her that being in shape is a part of working in this industry. Her response was fitting and somewhat predictable: "Running is fucking stupid; the only thing I'm running towards is a taco." At his insistence, she had found something that brought enjoyment to her life while providing her a workout simultaneously: boxing.

Over the past few months, she had taken some lessons from a local instructor in town, and Marion had worked with her during his own recovery. Ultimately, Lacey seemed to have a natural athletic talent and was less interested in learning how to fight in the ring and more intrigued by how to throw punches and defend herself. Combined with a few Muay Thai lessons, she was now throwing kicks and punches in solid combinations.

Marion eased the front door open in case Lacey was still sleeping, but he could hear the blows and pounding that her punching bag was taking the moment his hand hit the knob. As the door swung inward, the flat surface of the hand-milled logs filled his vision. With the interior walls made of solid wood as well as the exterior walls, the field of raw lumber would be almost overwhelming if it weren't for the large cathedral ceiling. A small loft blocked the view of part of the vaulted space, with a staircase descending on he side made out of old oak boughs.

The cabin had been nearly empty when he purchased it a few months ago, and Lacey resisted the idea of filling it with furniture for the sake of "filling it," as she had described it. A couch, wood stove, and roaring fire sat by the old casement window on the far side of the room. A small TV rested on an entertainment center slightly to the side of the stove. Beyond that, a bookcase and dry bar were built into one of the walls on the opposing side of the room.

Lacey had purchased wrestling mats that filled the center of the room, with her punching bag hanging from the beam that supported the loft. She hadn't noticed him yet and continued to throw combinations at the bag, focusing her energy into each stroke. Left jab, left hook, left hook, cross… each blow struck the bag with all her force, sending it skirting away from her before swinging back to be hit again.

It was more than physical conditioning; it was emotional and mental strengthening as well. Part of the reason Marion had been so insistent on exercise was to give her an outlet to work through some of her trauma. He had never told her that detail and used the pragmatism of their industry as the underlying factor. Never wanting her to feel broken—certainly not with him—it was an attempt to be supportive and allow her the space to work through it on her own terms. Ultimately, he was never certain if it was the right answer, but it seemed to be working.

A timer on her phone rang, indicating the end of her round. She finished the combination with a front kick, pushing the bag away as the impact of her sole struck the canvas. When she finally noticed Marion taking his shoes off at the front door, she started ripping her gloves off with her teeth.

"How was your run?" Her smile was infectious, all her teeth bared—a face that was genuinely happy to see him. There was nothing forced about her emotions.

"It was fine."

"Any pain?"

"No."

"Liar. How bad did it hurt?"

"It was fine, Lace. Just a little tender, that's all," he said, slightly irritated.

Lacey rolled her eyes at him in mock annoyance but didn't hesitate to cross the room and kiss him. She loved these little moments with him. The feeling of his return each time still made her heart jump, leaving her with a deep sense of happiness. Marion never spoke much about his emotions; he never spoke much at all. But he made sure to always show her how much she meant to him.

They had been living together mostly in the sense that Marion simply hadn't gone home, and Lacey had asked him to stay with her. The cabin only had two bedrooms, and she had taken over her grandmother's old room when she moved in. Marion had offered to sleep in the other room and honestly intended to, but somehow that had yet to happen. They shared her room together every night, seemingly fighting their primal desires for one another. They had been together for over four months at this point, and sex was off the table for both of them. Lacey needed more time to heal both physically and emotionally from the trauma in her past and had asked that they wait.

Marion couldn't deny his desire for her, but being Catholic meant that sex outside of wedlock was scorned by the church. Waiting seemed prudent for both of them, and he was in no hurry to soil that moment for her. It seemed obvious to both of them that they had each found their person, and neither was willing to jeopardize that by turning their relationship into a casual sexual encounter.

"Mary." Her voice was monotonous as she spoke, lacking the typical playful tone that filled her usual conversations. "We need to find some work to do. I don't care if it pays anything. It's not good for a man to have idle hands, and I don't like mooching off your money. I want to make my own. You haven't had any clients since your injury… I think it's time to get back to work."

He smiled at her, a glint in his eye indicating he already had plans for employment. "You think I just sit here all day?"

"No, of course not!" she said, laughing, half-heartedly afraid that she had hurt his feelings.

"It's okay, Lace. I agree. I've already applied for a Tennessee license and received the acceptance letter a few weeks ago. I've had a few lawyers reach out to me for some surveillance jobs, and we can start them anytime."

"What kind of surveillance?"

"Mostly workers' comp claims, but honestly, it'll get our name out there a bit and give us something to do."

"Okay, but before we dive into that, you need to shower," she grinned with her arms wrapped around his neck.

"Sure." He smiled back before squeezing her into him.

"STOP! YOU'RE GROSS AND SWEATY!" She laughed as he held her lightly.

Giggling uncontrollably, Lacey kissed Marion, teasing his lips with the tip of her tongue. The moment was filled with passion, their desire evident in their actions. Willing their bodies to take control of the moment, she locked into him for several minutes, unwilling and unable to break the physical bond between them. It felt to her like a giant magnet was pulling them together, an impossible force to break free from.

Without releasing her lips, she picked herself up by his

shoulders while Marion coaxed her body upwards, supporting her buttocks with his hands. Her legs wrapped around him as he placed her firmly on the countertop, her back against the hickory cabinets.

Neither of them spoke, allowing their lips and bodies to communicate. Lacey pulled Marion's shirt off over his head, revealing his muscular chest. She wore spandex gym shorts with a sports bra, providing little clothing for him to remove. Each piece slid off one by one, falling to the floor like a crumpled stack of dominoes.

Their hips aligned, both completely naked, the moment they had been resisting and waiting for finally arriving. *Oh God, I want him,* she thought to herself and unsure if the words had left her lips or not. Every fiber of her body was telling her to pull him into her, and there was even less Marion could do to stop himself. Lacey pulled him closer, reaching her hands under his arms and squeezing his back as she kissed his neck and moved her lips delicately up to his ear.

With a soft, pleasurable moan, she spoke gently into his ear. "Wait, Mary…" She wasn't sure where the words came from. She watched it happen as if her mind hovered outside her body. She wanted to scream at him to take her now. She didn't want him to stop. Why was she telling him to wait? It felt like her hips and body were disconnected from her brain. One part whispered gently to stop while the other wanted to scream *take me now!* "Marion. I'm so sorry… I'm not ready for this." Her words were met only with a smile and nod from Marion as he kissed her forehead. "Please don't be mad at me… You know I want this. God, I want this so bad."

"I'm not mad at you, Lace." He was honest, his words filled with tenderness and understanding. Marion wasn't frustrated as he held his hand to her cheek while she pushed her face into it.

"It's just… This is special. You know? What we have. It's pure, beautiful, and really special to me. Sex is something I've had to give my entire adult life… in a way that it became meaningless. I don't want this to ever be meaningless. I don't want this to ever feel like it has in the past… I don't know, maybe I need more time, but I just want this to always feel different and unique. I'm so sorry… I know you're ready to get in there and rummage about."

He couldn't help but laugh at her crass language. She had a knack for speaking eloquently one moment only to turn around and speak with a degree of vulgarity not common outside the military.

"I'm okay, Lace. I want you to be able to give yourself to me. I don't want it if it feels to you like I'm taking it. You only get to give yourself to me the first time once. Make it perfect when you do… I'll wait for that."

"Thank you," she said, pulling him in and squeezing tight against him. "You're supposed to be Catholic anyway… Doesn't that mean you have to wait and marry me first?"

"Shit, you're right…" He hums, "Should we just get married this weekend?"

"NO! You mook! You're damn sure not going to ask me like that." She pulled herself off him, slapping the back of his head as she did. "Besides, we're a ways off from that… you haven't told me you love me, and that comes first."

"Does it now? Well, Lacey, I…" He stopped speaking even before she interrupted.

"Marion, stop!" She couldn't stop laughing at his dry humor. Her heart was dying to hear what she already knew. "Not here. And certainly not like this with my sweaty ass on the kitchen counter."

"I do, you know…"

"I know, my love. Now please go shower; I'm not sure I can resist this twice."

Marion nodded, grabbing her nape and kissing her once again before departing naked across the living room to the bathroom. Lacey sat silently for a moment, contemplating the events that had transpired. Lusting after him as he walked away, she marveled at his figure in the shadows cast by the wood stove in the corner.

Her feelings aligned with what her body wanted, which was the first time she could remember that ever happening. It had certainly been a lifetime since she felt like anything more than a spot for a man to place his dissatisfaction. *No... I certainly couldn't have stopped that twice.*

"Damnit, Ed, they've been holed up in the mountains of Tennessee! What do you expect us to do?"

"I expect you to do what I've paid you to do! What you have been tasked with. I don't give a shit if you need to dust off your hunting gear; get in those woods and watch them. I want to know everything they are doing. Follow them to town, watch them get coffee, put thermals on, and watch them fuck inside the home."

James sat motionless on the phone, his mental faculties playing gymnastics as he attempted to find an alternative to sitting in the woods watching a cabin in the middle of winter. Freezing and shivering was certainly not what he had imagined when Edward had initially tasked him with surveilling Marion and Lacey.

For a few weeks, he watched as Marion stayed at the cabin. He wasn't bedridden, but it was obvious it pained him to walk, and with limited ability to get around, he elected to stay put. Lacey left on short trips for groceries and supplies only to return and care for him. By the end of the first month, James returned to Texas with nothing to show for his efforts. Convincing Edward that the man needed time to heal before any action could be taken, apart from killing him outright.

The logical solution was always to storm the cabin while Marion was recovering, but Edward hadn't been ready for it to end that quickly. His desires were peculiar and dark, seated deep within an anger arising after the death of his son. There was little love lost between the two when Vincent had been killed, but Edward felt more disrespected than emotionally damaged. Edward wanted pain.

He was insulted by the gall of someone believing it was acceptable to murder his son. Edward was a strategist by nature and decided the best course of action to inflict the most pain on Marion was to stalk him. Taking the girl and selling her across the border was an easy solution, but ruining his business, bankrupting him, and leaving him stranded in prison—knowing that his love, his business, his life had been stripped from him piece by piece—was the satisfaction Edward was looking for.

James had claimed first right to Lacey. Rape had been an intriguing topic for him personally. In the beginning, he hadn't considered himself a rapist or sexual sadist by any means. When he was a young officer working with the original "Pigs," they had killed a few contracts when a target's wife was found hiding in the kitchen cabinet. Her figure was exquisite, and James had been left to clean the scene. There were no witnesses to it, and she was going to have to be killed regardless, so it seemed like harmless fun. He was somewhat sickened with himself the first time it happened, but she was simply too good to pass up.

After finishing with the woman, he was forced to shoot her in the back of the head and dispose of the corpse. A new spark had ignited in his body, creating a litany of urges that became hard to tame. The power and control he felt over her in that moment of release was a level of ecstasy he was unable to reach again. Over time, his condition worsened to the point that he could no longer climax without unwilling partners. Forced to pay prostitutes to pretend to be unwilling, he was successful in gaining an erection for a while. But it was only a matter of time before his needs overtook him and an opportunity arose again.

Watching Lacey move around the grocery store was thrilling at first but eventually left him feeling empty and unsatisfied. For several weeks, he watched in silent anticipation but returned to Texas empty-handed and deprived . He had been home for two months when Edward sent him again to Tennessee to continue stalking until they had gathered enough information to plan their course of action, and the excitement returned as he closed in on the couple once more.

Marion was mobile now but still rarely came to town, electing to spend most of his time at the cabin. It made sense but ultimately gave James no opportunity for surveillance unless he wanted to spend hours lying on the frozen ground shivering while they sat in a warm cabin. It seemed irrelevant anyway since he couldn't see through the walls, and it wasn't likely to garner any new insight.

"Fine, Ed. But remember, you promised me the girl. Whatever plan you come up with, you promised me the girl."

"Fool! Is that all you're capable of thinking about? If you fuck this up because you can't think with anything more than your tiny dick, I'll bury it in the hills. The girl's yours; you can take her as many times as you want, but she's getting carted to the border when this is done, so don't kill her." Edward took a deep breath, giving himself a moment to control his irritation. "What have you found out?"

"Very little of use…" He paused, wondering if the information he was about to share was beneficial or would risk infuriating Edward more. "But there's a group of Colombians looking for them. They're trying to piece together the details of what happened in Birmingham. So far, it doesn't seem like they've put it together, but they will sooner or later. They don't have any cops on the payroll, which is partially why it's taking them so long, but the dealer's here are saying they're losing patience and ready to act. If they're found, they'll both be killed, and you won't get to do anything with them. It's some drug runner named Vega."

Edward didn't speak for several minutes. At first, James thought he was angry but realized after a moment he was contemplating options rather than writhing in fury.

"Get me in contact with them. I want to speak to whoever is in charge." His voice was calm but stern, leaving no room for argument.

"It'll take me a few days. I'll need to find an informant willing to deliver a burner phone to them. I don't have many connections in Birmingham, and I'm stuck in Tennessee for the time being. But I'll get them to reach out."

"Go to the police station in Birmingham first. Find someone you can work with and get them to deliver the message. I have a contact in the FBI office in Huntsville; he'll know who's on the take. His name is Max Teddy. Go to the office there first and ask to speak with him. I'll let him know you're coming tomorrow. If we can get an active police officer from that area on our side, it'll help with getting Gamble thrown in prison. I don't care how long we get him locked up for. Three months or 30 years, it doesn't matter. I just want him to watch his life destroyed while he's helpless behind bars."

"I can leave now; let him know I'll be there this afternoon." The spark in James' voice had returned, thinking he had dodged the bullet of sitting in the woods all night.

"No. You have a job to do there tonight."

"What?" His question was earnest, but in truth, he knew the answer even before Edward said it.

"Watch the fucking house," Ed said with a tone of finality before the line went dead.

Fuck!

***

"Why'd you have him do that?" Tom asked, his feet propped on the table as he listened to the conversation Edward was having.

"Because that fat piece of shit pisses me off. All he does now is bitch about everything. He was always soft, but since retiring, he's become a doughboy. When this is over, I'm putting him in the ground."

Tom nodded his head in understanding. The movement was exaggerated by the large brim of the Stetson hat on his head.

"How do you figure on doing that?" Tom wasn't worried for himself. They had all been irritated with James at one point or another. But he was useful—raping the women involved with the cases had always given them someone to pin the murders on if a contract was ever blown. He left DNA evidence everywhere he went, and it would have been simple enough to shut him up if the feds ever got wise to their actions.

They had never had to use it, but James was the built-in patsy for their team during the years they were operational. He would take the fall for anything, and Edward would pay off a prisoner or a guard to have him commit suicide in his cell. It was a simple chess move that James was unaware of. *Queen's Gambit*.

"I'm still putting the entire plan together. I need to get in contact with the Colombians before we do anything. But in the end, James is going to be killed serving papers to that fucking PI."

"You're going to have the PI kill him?"

"Yes. He's going to get tipped off so he can take him out

for us."

"How does that help? And what papers?"

"It's how I'm going to send him to prison… He's going for murder."

"And the papers?" Tom inquired. "What papers are you going to have him serve? He'll need a reason for being in Tennessee to avoid drawing suspicion."

"Tom…" Edward drew a dark smile across his face. It was unnatural to see the grin; his leather-like skin pulled back tightly to display a set of well-cared-for but yellow teeth.

Since his son's death, Edward had begun wearing the scarlet hatband around his own Stetson, which Vince had been so fond of. The red ribbon glimmered in the light and looked slightly out of place on the dusty cowboy hat, making Tom think of a crystal chandelier hanging in a dusty horse barn. Both items—the smile and the hatband—were out of place on Edward Mahon's face.

"I'm going to ask a friend to serve papers for my lawsuit. It's a very hard time for a father whose son was murdered. It's not unreasonable to ask a close family friend like James to serve papers."

"You're suing him? For what?"

"Gamble is going to get served a lawsuit for wrongful death. I'm gonna squeeze him dry on attorney fees, criminal defense attorneys, and anything else I can find. Ultimately, he will lose the criminal case, and then when he's in prison and out of my way, he'll get a letter from my attorney seizing all his assets."

"It's going to take a year to pull this off. Besides, you'll never get the wrongful death suit to stick in Alabama."

"It won't matter; he'll start feeling the pain of it in a matter of days. Sitting in jail waiting is worse on some accounts than being in prison."

"And the girl?"

"She's going to leave him while he's in jail. It's very hard for some women to accept that their man is a murderer. I'm going to deliver him an autographed picture of the whore getting screwed by a team of spics in Juarez."

"Jesus, Ed. How do you figure the Colombians fit in?"

"I'm still working that out. But once Gamble is in prison, they can have their network make him feel right at home."

Edward lit a cigarette, staring off into the abyss. He wasn't thinking of his son or even of Marion or Lacey. His mind was clear, focused on an indifferent task before him—something to handle that involved little emotion. Very little in this world affected him emotionally, and this was no exception. The darkness of his soul had crept into his life, leaving him with a mind occupied only by tasks rather than feelings, capable of executing the specifications of his purpose and unable to process anything so irrational.

The shipping container smelled of rot and decay. Several bodies of young women littered the floor; to an outsider, the scene would have appeared draconian, as if pulled from a textbook on genocide. The trip normally took 10 days to two weeks, but the shipping strike at the eastern ports had slowed their progress.

Luis had lost all track of time inside the confines of the cell. With his satellite phone's battery dead, he had no way of knowing when the strike would end. In total, there were 15 girls and himself alone in the container, with enough food and water to last the trip. Inevitably, one or two would usually die from various types of exposure-related illnesses. Even in winter, the containers cooked in the afternoon sun, feeling like a pressure cooker by midday. Their water was depleting fast, and two of the girls had already succumbed to the heat.

Luis' eye was becoming more infected by the minute,

where Aponte had sliced it open a few weeks before. Or maybe a month... or two, he thought, not knowing how long they had been there. Each morning, he checked his reflection in the knife blade. The curvature of the blade distorted his face, making it look like a grotesque figure sent from the pits of hell. He knew it was as bad as it appeared in the blade, judging by the girls' sideways glances and disgusted faces every time they looked at him.

Beyond their upturned noses, he could smell the distinct almond-like odor of the infection and see milky white liquid oozing from the hole in the center of his eyeball. He figured a fever had set in, but the heat of the container made that hard to determine, and he lacked a thermometer or medical supplies to address it. Reaching port soon was his only viable option for survival; in a few more days, he would join the dead women on the ground.

He looked at their bloated bodies and realized they had all become somewhat tone-deaf to the stench their gases must be emitting. The flies were atrocious, continually buzzing around the bodies and his eye, even with the bandana tied around it. He was surprised to see them in the middle of the ocean, but they arrived within minutes of the first body dropping to the ground. The rats came next, constantly feasting on the exposed skin as they slipped through the cracks in the floorboards.

Delgado hadn't spent any time at sea but had heard stories from old sailors; rats were the source of various diseases and issues aboard a boat. "A ship without rats is unnatural," they had told him as he watched the rodents nibble and scratch underneath the clothing. Their bodies moved like giant earthworms pulsing through the rags that remained as they feasted.

Watching the bay doors of the container, Luis hoped and prayed they would magically open, providing them all a sense of freedom as the sunlight hit their pale faces. The stench of decaying flesh and fecal matter piling in buckets would flow out the doors, bringing in the cool, fresh ocean air. His aching eye drew him out of the daydream as he cleaned the bandana in a bucket of water and wrapped it tightly around the sore again.

He was stronger than the women in the container and had a knife to defend himself. But he was a slaver, and they knew it and hated him for it. Even with the dead ones, the dozen or so remaining girls could overpower him and kill him if they wanted to. Showing a moment of weakness would only hasten their desperation in an attempt to escape.

The container he was in was buried within piles of containers, and his screams for help would be lost to the steel walls. Even if someone heard him, it would take hours of searching to find his container. It was a strategy they relied on for moving a girl who decided to yell and bang against the walls for help.

A sudden sigh of relief hit them all simultaneously as the large terminal tractor locked onto the eye bolt holes on top of the container and lifted them off the stack. For a moment, they could feel themselves floating through the air as the tractor jostled them around. It took only a minute or two for them to be placed on solid ground again, and the violent movement of the ocean's surface was replaced with the terrestrial feel of the asphalt underneath.

The container hadn't been sitting for more than a minute when the distinct sound of a tool cutting the band lock and the scraping metal of the latch being lifted was made audible to their ears. For Luis, the moment was as bittersweet as it was for the women. For them, they were escaping one prison for another, trading the violation of the thrashing ocean for the violation of men with cash in their pockets. For him, he was trading this prison for the life of his family.

Vega had promised that his family would be kept safe if Luis fulfilled his obligation. For all of his shortcomings, Señor Vega would keep his promise. One promise was to sell his wife and daughter, leaving his son to face the blades; the other was to keep them safely at his compound, never wanting for anything. All of his soldiers knew Vega would honor either deal when it came to them personally. It was his method of instilling loyalty.

Luis was under no false pretenses or wallowing in a fantasy. If he did what was asked, his family would never want for anything again. They would be unharmed and raised with affection. If he fulfilled his obligation, his own death would be quick and painless—a bullet to the back of the head when he wasn't looking or a garrote around his throat cutting off the blood flow to his brain. If he didn't, Pedro would cut him to pieces, dangling his own limbs in front of him as he watched his girls be brutalized. For Luis, this was the end; it was his final mission. The pain in his eye would soon be gone, and his family would live on in healthy harmony.

The doors opened, allowing beams of golden sunlight to enter and begin sanitizing the container as the girls were escorted out and placed into box trucks for transport. Pedro Aponte had opened the doors of the container, flanked by two other men. The putrid odor struck their nasal cavities, causing nausea to boil in their stomachs as each man swallowed hard to control himself. Pedro didn't wince, didn't move; he didn't even acknowledge the overwhelming odor. Everything about him suggested a man with virtually no moral compass or emotion. Without a semblance of remorse for the damaged product lying on the container floor, he asked Luis one question.

"Where are we going?" His demeanor was calculated, as if he were holding a machete against a rebel or ready to bleed a sow. His clothing was appropriate for the area a camouflage of sorts, with dark pants, a black jacket, and a white T-shirt. He blended in everywhere except affluent upper-class venues.

"We need to go to Birmingham. From there, we should head to the police station and get the reports from the incidents. That will tell us what we need to know to get started."

"Do you have any police that we can hire to look into this?"

"No. But I have a few dealers I can contact. They will know who can get us the information we are looking for. This is going to take a bit of time…"

"You don't have time. Contact the dealers you know and find out who at the police department is for sale. I want to know what happened with Si, who killed him and why, and what happened to the girls that were released." His voice didn't slow, and he didn't give Luis time to acknowledge the demands. "Señor Vega has informed me that your family is already in custody, and we are behind schedule. Contact the dealers and get me the information I need."

Luis wanted to scream; he wanted to kill Pedro right there. Every instinct in his body told him to pull his knife and bury it in Pedro's chest. But he had to remain in control. He figured Pedro was lying about having his family in custody, but it didn't matter. The men at the plantation could mobilize and pick his family up within an hour. He intended to do his job regardless and was well aware of the outcome for himself.

Pedro handed Luis a phone, and he began making calls as the men climbed into the truck. Pedro didn't respond to anything he had heard. His face was an expressionless mausoleum where feelings had long since departed. His purpose derived solely from his responsibility to Señor Vega. Dutiful and loyal to his chosen master, he would never betray him, never be bought or tortured into submission; he was a recalcitrant man with one obligation to authority.

Luis was able to see himself for the first time in two months in the rearview mirror. He desperately needed a shave and a haircut, but things had become considerably worse for him. The open wound in his eye was severely infected. It was worse than it had appeared in the distorted reflection of the knife.

The blade incision from Pedro slicing down his face had left two jagged marks on the top and bottom of the eye. Each incision was spreading black lightning bolts under the skin around the wound. He would need to see a doctor fast. He wasn't sure when the infection had set in, but it must have been from the disease and the rats in the container towards the end of the trip, or he'd already be dead. Luis looked at himself again in the mirror, seeing the pitiful image in front of him. He needed a doctor.

"I need a doctor," he said to Pedro, who didn't respond. "If you want me to stay alive long enough to help, the infection needs to be treated."

Pedro grunted, annoyed, but knew that Luis was right. Without responding to Luis, he told the driver of the van to take them to a doctor as soon as they arrived in Birmingham. Pedro's compassion was certainly not the driving force, but he was a dutiful soldier and wouldn't jeopardize Vega's operation to avoid helping someone.

Luis leaned his head back and thought silently to himself. There was only one thing for him to do. He didn't have a moral issue against it. This wasn't the first or even the hundredth group of girls he'd locked in the container. Ultimately, he needed to stay alive long enough to help them find the man who ran their truck off the road—the man whose name he didn't know was Marion Gamble.

Join Our Mailing List By Scanning The QR Code!
Become the first to be notified of new releases or current sales.

www.ingramcontent.com/pod-product-compliance
Lightning Source LLC
Chambersburg PA
CBHW070607310726
48982CB00001B/9
* 9 7 9 8 9 9 8 7 7 1 7 1 2 *